power play

Boston Grizzlies Hockey Club
Book Four

allie lasky

boston grizzlies hockey club

Reading Order

Here is the recommended reading order for this series:

Tending Her Heart (Seb and Audrey)

Puck Me Twice (Sven and Vanessa)

Home for the Holidays (Jake and Rachel)

Body Check (Jason and Amelia)

Defenseless (Ryan and Hailey)

Power Play (Al and Riley)

Game Misconduct (Nick and Bex)

Instigator (Aidan and Ceci)

One Timer (Adam and Avery)

Delay of Game (Parker and Ivy)

one

. . .

Al

THERE'S a baby on my doorstep.

Did I take a puck to the head at practice? Or is this some kind of weird-ass fever dream?

A horn honks down the street, startling me, the baby, and the woman holding it, and a solitary cry rips through the air before the squirming pink bundle settles again.

Nope. Definitely not a dream. The squawk was as real as it gets.

"I'm so sorry," says the woman holding the baby. She's gorgeous, that's for certain, with chocolate-brown hair falling in soft waves and the bluest eyes I've ever seen. I've also never met her before. "I didn't know what else to do."

My eyes drop to the child in her arms. *What the hell?* It looks like... a baby. I don't know ages. Not a newborn. Its cheeks are chubby and full, glistening with drool. Given the pink on its outfit, I'm guessing it's a girl.

Note to self: Don't call a baby an "it."

"Can I help you?" My voice comes out in a croak.

I don't know this woman or what she wants from me, but as a professional hockey player, I've been warned about the manipulative people who will try to sink their money-hungry claws into me.

"You don't know me," she says, bouncing the little girl. "But you might remember my sister. Carter Matthews?"

I shake my head. "You've got the wrong guy."

"You're Alberto Gonzales. You're a hockey player, and you used to play for Arizona." Her mouth twists in a frown. "Fifteen months ago, you slept with my sister."

"Okay, and...? What do you want?" I'm trying not to sound petulant or rude, but as a professional athlete, I've heard plenty about guys who fall for the sob story hook, line, and sinker, and then it turns out the entire thing is fabricated.

The woman takes a deep breath. "Last week..." She swallows hard, her face crumpling. "Carter was in a car accident. She didn't make it."

My stomach knots at the pain on her face. If I'd lost either of my siblings... "I'm sorry for your loss."

"The thing is..." Her blue eyes meet mine, her unshed tears squeezing my heart in a vise. "I promised I wouldn't do this, but legally, I'm not her guardian."

"I'm not following." I glance down at the baby, who's happily sucking on a toy, then back to the woman.

"You're her father."

It's like a sucker punch to the face. The three words I never expected to hear.

I shake my head, trying to process, but this still isn't making sense. "What are you talking about?"

She hefts the baby in her arms. "This is Emmy. Meet your daughter."

Panic rises in me, threatening to send me over the ledge into a full-blown panic attack. Black dots hover in the corner of my eyes and I swallow, hard, against the bile in my throat. If this is my kid... I need to be strong. She's already missing her mom, so the last thing she needs is a father who can't take care of her.

My stomach twists, half dreading and half accepting this as my new reality. I don't want to believe it's true, but I have to hear out this woman. I have to give her a chance.

With my foot on the threshold, I stumble back, nearly tripping and falling flat on my ass. I catch myself on the doorframe. "Why don't you come inside?"

The Mattapan townhouse I grew up in feels even smaller than usual, the walls closing in on me. As the woman steps into the house, I practically sprint to the kitchen, where I pour myself a shot of tequila. Fire licks down my suddenly dry throat as I swallow the burn of the alcohol, and I reach for a glass, filling it with water. I down that, too.

She stands by the door, shifting her weight from one foot to the next like she's waiting for me to stop freaking out. The baby babbles, completely unaware of the tension, waving around a hot-pink silicone toy.

Meanwhile, I'm trying not to pass the fuck out. Or throw up. Or crumble under the weight of *what the fuck*?

Filling my water glass a second time, I gesture for her to sit down. I take the armchair as she settles on the couch, her shoulders tense.

"Why don't we start with your name," I suggest.

"I'm Riley," she says, giving me an awkward wave. "Riley Lucas. And this is Emmy."

My stomach clenches, and I force myself to blow out a breath. "Okay."

"Carter was my sister. We live together in Phoenix." Her face creases with pain. "*Lived.* She was on her way home from work when some asshole ran a red light and T-boned her car. The only saving grace is she went instantly. S-she didn't suffer." Sniffling, she clears her throat, then looks down at her —niece?

"I'm sorry for your loss," I say again. The words aren't enough. How can they be?

"Thanks." She drags her finger beneath her eyes, catching the moisture.

An awkward beat passes between us before I twist in my seat and grab the tissue box off the end table, handing it over.

I want to give her time to gather her composure, but I can't help asking the one question pounding in my brain. "Why didn't she tell me she was pregnant?"

I have no recollection of this woman—either of them. Was she at the bar the night I met Carter?

"She wanted a baby. She didn't want a baby daddy." Riley shrugs, her face tinged with sadness. "I don't agree with her choices, but she didn't know you were famous until after. You were just a guy in a bar."

"I'm surprised she didn't contact me, ask for child support." My stomach twists once more, all the warnings from my agent ringing in the back of my head. "Not that I believe you."

Tearing her gaze off me, she stares down at the floor and shakes her head. "Carter didn't want money. We grew up in the foster system. She wanted someone to love her unconditionally, and I wasn't enough for her. The only way she knew how was with a baby."

"Why not foster herself? Or adopt?"

Riley scowls. "I'm not here to defend her choices. They were hers to make, not mine."

Holy fuck, okay. I lift my hands in surrender. "Got it. Sensitive subject."

Sighing, she roves her hand over the baby's back. "I'm sorry. I don't mean to bite your head off. I just… I don't know what else to do. Carter and I, we were foster sisters. Not blood. I was granted a temporary placement by Social Services, so I can keep her for now, but I'm not a suitable guardian long term. I can't afford our apartment on my own, much less day care."

… And there it is.

"How much do you need?"

But she shakes her head again. "It's not about the money. I—Emmy is your daughter. She's yours. She's not mine."

"What are you saying?"

"I can't keep her. Legally, financially…" She blows out a breath. "I have no right to keep her, and I can't justify keeping her from you. My feelings on Carter's decision aside, Emmy's *your* kid. She deserves to know her father."

Everything blurs as my head spins, and a faint ringing fills my ears. I stare unseeingly at the baby.

My baby.

"I'm guessing you'll want a paternity test," Riley continues. "Carter was convinced she was yours."

"Why didn't she tell me?" How could she rob me of the opportunity to know my kid?

"She found out she was pregnant the same day Arizona traded you to Boston." A sad, bitter smile tips the corners of her lips. "She was afraid you'd sue for custody and take the baby away from her. And it's not like a transcontinental living situation is good for an infant. We have no money. You'd win, hands down."

"My living situation isn't… ideal." I glance around my childhood home. The shabby, worn carpet, the walls that could use a fresh coat of paint. Last summer, I bought a new couch and TV, but this is very much a bachelor's house, not something suitable for a child. Growing up, it was close quarters with my parents, brother, sister, and I filling the house with love and laughter. And fighting. There was a lot of that. Good-natured tussling, but *loud*.

Now, there's just… me. Tony moved to Denver over the summer, and Cari is across town living with her rugby teammates, leaving me alone. Sure, it's *home*, but it feels so… empty. I've finally gotten used to the quiet. Am I ready to add a screaming child to the mix?

Not to mention my schedule. "I travel for three-quarters of the year. Fuck, I leave tomorrow for Detroit."

"I'm staying in a hotel for a few days," she says. "I know it might take some time for the paternity test results to come through and for you to trust me, so if you want, I can take care of Emmy until you can find a nanny. But eventually..."

Presuming this baby is mine, I'll have to step up. I'll have to be her *father*.

Fuck. I'm in over my head here.

Reaching into my pocket, I grab my phone and then scroll through my contacts. I should probably call McKittrick, my former captain, or maybe even Coach. I should definitely call my agent.

Instead, I dial the only person who can fix this.

"What's wrong?" Vanessa Larsson asks as soon as the call connects.

"Why do you presume something is wrong?" Although I try to tease her, play it off like everything is fine, my voice cracks on the last word. After all, if everything *were* fine, I wouldn't be calling her.

"Cut the shit, Gonzo." A hint of fondness colors her tone beneath her no-bullshit attitude.

"Can you come to my place? Like... now?"

The team's logistics coordinator sighs. "I'm on my way."

On the couch, Riley raises her eyebrows. "So you believe me?"

"I don't know what to believe," I admit. "I don't know you, and I don't remember your sister. I'm sorry for that, I'm sure she was a lovely person, but—"

"She was a bitch," she says with a laugh. "A little rough around the edges, but given the hand she was dealt, she made the most of her life. We were sisters in everything but blood, and I loved her." Riley's face falls. "But because we're not related, I have no legal claim to Emmy. I can't put her on my health insurance, can't take her to the doctor..."

"That's her full name? Emmy?"

"Emilia Riley Matthews." A proud smile curves her lips, the first sign of genuine happiness.

At that, the air knocks from my lungs like I've been cross-checked into the boards. My middle name is Emilio. Did she know? Or is it a coincidence? Was that Carter's way of acknowledging my absence in her life?

But more than Emmy being named for me, I'm stuck on the other half of her name.

"She's named after you." They must have been close.

"Carter was my best friend. She drove me nuts, but we're all each other have." Her face clouds. "*Had*. Emmy is my last tie to her."

"It must be tough. Losing a sibling. I can't imagine…" Tony and Cari make me crazy, but I don't know what I'd do without them.

Riley clears her throat. "Her birthday is April ninth."

I count in my head. We're in the second week of October, just starting our season…

"That makes her about six months old." And conception would have been during the offseason, when I had nothing but time and energy for getting into trouble.

"She's a great baby. Happy most of the time. Usually sleeps through the night. She's… perfect."

The baby stares at me with dark brown eyes. *My eyes.* Wisps of chocolate-brown hair attempt to curl on her head. Her cheeks are round and full, her arms and legs chubby with rolls. Although she's wearing socks, they're slipping off.

"Isn't she cold?" She's only wearing a little one-piece outfit, her limbs exposed. It may be early October, but it's already getting chilly.

"I usually wrap her in blankets. She doesn't like to wear clothes." Riley chuckles. "If I let her, she'd be naked all the time. But that's not a good idea in this weather."

I grunt in agreement. Especially if she's from Arizona, she

won't be prepared for the cooler temperatures in Boston. Every baby I've ever seen has been wrapped in blankets and layers. But what do I know about dressing a baby? Maybe that's how they do it everywhere.

We fall into an awkward silence, interrupted by a knock on the door. I get up to answer it, my heart racing.

Vanessa is tall, blond, and athletic, with the best poker face I've ever seen. She works for the Boston Grizzlies, and she's married to Sven Larsson, my teammate. She also has a kid about the same age as Emmy.

"What did you do?" she demands as she steps over the threshold. "I'm not PR." At the sight of Riley and Emmy, she stops in her tracks. "Gonzo, what the fuck did you do?"

"I need help." It's the truth, but my voice still cracks anyway. I don't like asking for help. I don't want to be the family screwup any more than I want to be the team's laughingstock.

"Hi, I'm Vanessa. I work with this guy," she says, striding past me into the living room. She shakes Riley's hand. "And who is this?"

"This is Emmy. She's my daughter."

two

. . .

Riley

VANESSA IS BEAUTIFUL, but the thing I like most about her is her take-charge attitude. Within ten minutes, we have an action plan and find a lab that will do a same-day paternity test.

I'm positive Alberto Gonzales is the father. I may not have been at the bar that night, but Carter swore up and down it was him. She had no reason to lie—not about that, at least.

Emmy hasn't left my arms this entire time, content to hang out with me rather than explore her new home. What am I going to do when I can't see her every day? When I don't get her chubby baby snuggles each morning. My throat spasms, so tight I can barely breathe. I don't want to cry. I *refuse* to cry in front of this man who gets to keep the last remaining member of my family.

But I'm not above crying where he can't see me. "May I use your bathroom?"

Alberto nods. "Down the hall, to the left."

He doesn't make any move to take his child from me, though, staring blankly instead.

Vanessa stands, reaching for Emmy. "Let me hold her for you."

Somehow, passing over the baby to another woman is ten times easier than the thought of giving her to *him.*

I rush to the bathroom, practically slamming the door behind me, then sink onto the closed toilet seat and cover my face with my hands. I don't want to do this, but I know all the reasons I have to.

A sob bubbles up in my throat, and I move to cover my mouth before it escapes. Tears streak down my cheeks, faster than I can wipe them away with the sodden tissue he gave me. Scrambling for a strip of toilet paper, I wipe my eyes again and again, but there's nothing I can do to stop the flow.

I miss my sister. I *need* my sister. But she's gone. And she's the one who got us into this mess.

From the very start, I told her she needed to be honest with him. Alberto had the right to know he had a child, and she deserved to know her father. But I know how scared Carter was of losing the one person who was supposed to love her unconditionally.

Except me. She was my best friend, my other half, ever since we met while living with a terrible foster family when I was twelve and she was fourteen. I wasn't enough for her, though.

She stayed with the Burkes for seven weeks; I was there for four and a half months. We stayed in touch, and when I went to high school, we reconnected. From that point on, we were inseparable. We looked out for each other.

Fuck, I miss her so much. She was there one moment, and then she was gone. I'm glad Emmy wasn't in the car with her; I don't know what I'd do if I lost them both.

Taking a deep, shuddering breath, I try to pull myself together. I can do this. I can do hard things. *Or so I thought.* The waterworks start all over again, and I can't muffle my choking sob.

A soft knock raps on the bathroom door. "Riley?"

It's him.

"Are you okay?" His voice is quiet, concerned.

"I'm fine."

Through the heavy wood separating us, I hear him exhale a long, drawn-out sigh. "Okay."

His passivity makes my blood boil. He's not behaving the way I expected him to. Every day for the last week, I scripted and replayed this entire conversation in my head, and none of it is going according to plan. He's supposed to fight back. Argue. Do anything besides *accept* this.

I fling open the bathroom door, not making any attempt to hide my tear-stained face.

"What do you *want*?"

His eyes widen as he takes me in, his posture defeated. "I wanted to check on you. I know this must be difficult for you."

"Do you?" I demand. "Do you have any idea what I'm going through?"

"I know if my sibling was suddenly gone, I'd be a mess," he murmurs. His soulful brown eyes catch mine, holding my gaze. "And if I were about to lose my last link to them, I don't know how I'd survive it. So, yeah, I have an idea."

A fresh wave of tears clings to my eyelashes. "I'm not okay," I admit. "I don't know how to be okay with any of this."

He reaches for my hand, tugging me from the bathroom, and I follow him limply. Surprise ripples through me when he pulls me into his arms, wrapping them around me.

"What are you doing?" I mumble into his chest. His hard, sturdy, *muscular* chest.

"You looked like you needed a hug." He tightens his hold around me to the point I can barely breathe, but it's sort of… *perfect*. "Has anyone hugged you since everything happened?"

I shake my head against his pecs. I'm getting tears and snot all over his soft T-shirt, but he doesn't seem to mind.

This man is a complete stranger to me. But I soak in the comfort he's offering.

He smells like cedar and firewood, with a hint of spice I can't identify. Like a bonfire on a warm summer night, or a roaring fire in the cold of winter. His strong arms are wrapped securely around me, and he's not letting go.

This is nice, but it can't last forever.

So I pull myself away, swiping at my eyes. "I know you have no reason to trust me… but Emmy is my last remaining link to my sister. Please don't shut me out of her life."

To my surprise, he takes my hand in his. "Why don't you come chat with Vanessa? She has an idea."

The woman is rocking Emmy as we approach, and her eyes fall to our linked hands. My face heats and I pull my hand free. I don't know this man. I have no claim to him.

But for one moment, one perfect minute, I wasn't alone in this world.

I take Emmy into my arms again, inhaling her sweet baby scent. Her chubby arms cling to my neck, and the tears threaten to fall again.

"Presuming everything checks out with the paternity test," Vanessa says, "we still have a few problems."

My eyebrows dart up into my hairline. "Like what?"

"Like I'm about to leave for a road trip," he says. His voice is rough, and he clears his throat. "If she's mine…" He blows out a breath. "If she's mine, I'll do right by her. I'll do everything I need to. But like I said earlier, I travel for work three-quarters of the year."

Oh. Right. I hadn't thought about that.

"You live in Arizona," Vanessa adds.

My stomach sinks. "I can't afford to fly out here more than once a year. Twice, maybe."

Alberto shakes his head. "How attached are you to Arizona? Would you be willing to relocate?"

"I'm going to need you to spell this out for me." My tone

is slow and measured, each word dragged up from the depth of my heart. I don't want to let myself hope. It would hurt too much if I'm wrong. "Because if you're saying what I think you're saying…"

"I need a nanny, or at least someone to stay with Emmy while I'm gone, and someone else for daytime. And I'm gone a lot," he says. "You don't want to leave her. I get that. And I don't blame you one bit. I wouldn't want to leave her, either."

Swallowing, I study Emmy's perfect little face, then raise my eyes to his. "What does this mean?"

"You would move here. You would live here, so there's minimal disruption to her routine," Vanessa cuts in. "He'd pay you a salary, along with free room and board, and you'd take care of her."

"My job…"

"I can pay you better," he says, full of cocky confidence.

"It's not about the money. I have a career. I have an apartment."

"One you can't afford." His eyes pin me to the spot. "You said it yourself, you don't want to leave her. And I need help."

Blowing out a breath, I consider my options. I don't have very many. Give up my last remaining link to my sister, or a job in a field I've worked my ass off to get to, but don't actually love.

"I don't want to be a nanny forever," I say. "I'm okay with it for now, until she's bigger. But—"

"We can revisit it in the offseason," he suggests. "I'll be home more and won't need as much help. I don't have time during the season to fuck around with someone I don't trust."

"But you trust me?" I scoff in disbelief. He's got to be shitting me; I'm a complete stranger, and he wants to leave his kid with me? Have me move into his house?

He laughs. "No. I don't."

At least he's honest about it.

"But you're all Emmy knows, and I can't disrupt her life any more than has already happened. At least for now, you're my only option."

Somehow, that makes me feel better about this. He's backed into a corner; he doesn't want this, just as much as I don't.

Emmy starts to fuss, and Alberto's eyes widen.

"Can I…" He swallows, his Adam's apple bobbing. "Can I hold her?"

Even though it kills me to let her go, I know it's the right thing to do.

We both stand, and I slowly slide her into his massive arms. He immediately moves to support her bottom and her back, and her chubby hands cling to him. He shifts her, and I'm afraid he's going to drop her, but he adjusts his grasp to hold her more securely. One thick finger runs over her hand, and she grabs at his index finger with her strong grip.

His eyes well up, and his throat works.

"Hi, Emmy," he whispers, his voice thick with emotion. "I'm your daddy."

three

. . .

Al

TWO AND A HALF HOURS LATER, thanks to a friend of Vanessa's at Harvard, we have official confirmation: Emmy is my biological child. It's not enough for legal determination, but it's enough of an answer for me.

Thanks to the magic of a black American Express card, an entire nursery will be delivered in a few hours, and we leave the baby store with a portable crib, a car seat, and a stroller. I don't know how Riley survived carrying Emmy on the T and a bus with her in her arms, but my baby deserves the princess chariot of her dreams.

Vanessa drove us to the lab in her SUV so Emmy could use Leo's car seat, but it's not a long-term solution. She needs to be able to transport her kid, too.

We make a pit stop at the hotel and Riley grabs her suitcase, and then it's back to my place. I guess it's a good thing my sister moved out a few weeks ago, otherwise there wouldn't be enough bedrooms for the three of us.

I suppose Emmy's crib could go in my room, but she deserves a space of her own. Also, what if I wake her up when I come home late from games and road trips? No, it's better for her crib to go in my childhood bedroom, and Riley will take Cari's old room.

That's when it hits me all over again.

I have a kid. A living, breathing human who's dependent on me. What the fuck, man?

Emmy starts to cry as we walk into the house, the first real sounds of annoyance all day. She's been a perfect angel since the moment she showed up on my doorstep, barely making a peep. I don't know if she's usually this chill or if she's as stunned by the day's events as I am, but I won't be upset by the lack of noise. From the few times I've met Vanessa and Larsson's son, he never stops screaming.

"I need to change her," Riley announces. She sets down the diaper bag and pulls out a mat, then gestures for me to hand her the baby.

I don't want to let my princess go, but with the way she's yelling in my ear, perhaps it's for the best.

In less than two minutes, Riley swaps out the soiled diaper for a fresh one, snaps her buttons back into place, and then deposits Emmy back into my arms. I'm surprised at how right it feels to hold her. I've never spent much time around kids, especially not enough to hold them.

But with Emmy… she belongs with me. The lab tests only confirmed what I already knew to be true. She's *mine*.

"Uh, Al?" a voice calls from upstairs. "Are you home?"

My blood runs cold. "What are you doing here?" I don't want to do this now, but I guess she's forcing the issue.

Cari bounds down the stairs wearing only a towel, her long hair wet around her shoulders. She stops in her tracks when she sees the audience.

"Why are you holding a baby?" she demands, her voice rising into a high-pitched screech.

Of course, that sets off Emmy, who cries out. Her screaming sobs ring in my ears as I bounce my knees the way Riley taught me, trying to soothe her.

Riley returns from the bathroom, hands freshly washed, and snatches Emmy from my arms. "You didn't tell me you had a girlfriend," she hisses.

"Okay, everyone needs to calm down," I shout. I don't know whether I'm talking to myself or them. No, definitely them. But also, a little bit me. "Carolina, go put on clothes. Why are you even here?"

"A bird shit on my head on my run. Your place was closer."

Frustration bubbles through me, and I pinch the bridge of my nose. "Great. Get dressed, and then we can talk." Stepping closer to Riley, I run my hand over Emmy's back. "It's okay, sweetheart. It's okay."

Riley looks up at me with her big blue eyes, clearly peeved. "I'm not your *sweetheart*."

"Was talking to my girl," I say with a chuckle. "But glad to know where we stand."

She scowls at me, continuing to sway in place.

After a few moments, Emmy's sobs die down, and she settles against Riley's chest. Her eyes blink slowly, clearly exhausted by the outburst.

I'm exhausted, too.

Cari skips down the stairs, wearing one of my Grizzlies T-shirts and a pair of my sweatpants.

"Hi, I'm Cari," she says, holding out a hand for Riley to shake. "You're the woman trying to baby trap my brother?"

Riley's eyebrows shoot sky high. "Brother?"

"Yeah. So what's the deal here?" She glances between us. "Don't tell me you fell for it."

"We just got back from the lab. The baby's mine." As stunned as I am, I can't deny the bubble of happiness ready to burst inside me. "Cari, I have a *kid*."

Her eyes widen and her mouth drops open. "Are you shitting me?"

"One hundred percent factual."

Still stunned, my sister tugs me into a hug. I lean into her silent support. But I should have known the quiet wouldn't last long.

"Is this what you want?"

I've been over the hookup scene for a while. I want a relationship, a family of my own. Well, it may be unconventional, but I'm getting part of what I wanted. Even though I still want a great love in my life, maybe that can come in the form of a daughter rather than a romantic partner.

I can have my happily ever after. I can have good things in my life. I'm worthy of it, damn it.

"It absolutely is," I tell my sister, but my eyes meet Riley's.

"And you're the baby mama?" Cari asks.

"I'm Riley." Her face crumples, and her eyes well with tears. "Her mother was my sister. She passed away last week."

Cari's smile drops. "I'm so sorry."

"Yeah. It was… well, I'm still processing." She blinks a few times, no doubt trying to prevent the tears from falling. "But I knew that Alberto deserves to know his daughter."

"Call me Al," I interrupt. "Everyone does."

My sister's eyes gleam with mischief. "And who is this little one?"

"This is Emmy," I tell her proudly. "Emilia."

Riley gives me a subtle nod, and I lift my baby from her arms, cuddling her against my chest, facing outward.

Emmy babbles happily, and my heart twists at the look on my sister's face. She's already in love with her, that much is obvious. It's not hard. Emmy's pretty damn-near perfect. I already know I'd commit murder to protect her, and I only met her a few hours ago.

"This is my daughter."

Cari gives a little shriek, then makes grabby hands for the baby. I settle my daughter in her arms, and as Cari's eyes flutter closed, I swear I see a tear escape.

"Are you okay?" I whisper, my hand on Emmy's back. Ready to snatch her back if I have to.

"Al, you have a *kid*," she whispers back. "I never thought this would happen."

I swallow. "Me neither."

"Fuck knows Tony won't give me a baby to play with anytime soon." She laughs. "Crap. I probably shouldn't say fuck around a baby."

"She can't talk yet, but she's definitely aware of her surroundings," Riley says, a smile on her face. "Do you, um, live here?"

"No, I live across town with some of my teammates," Cari says.

"She's on the Boston Revolution rugby team," I say, ruffling her damp hair while smiling from ear to ear. My sister scowls at me, but then her gaze drops to my daughter in her arms, and she grins again. "Our brother, Tony, lives in Denver."

"And your parents?"

"They live in Florida with our abuela. They came for a visit over the summer, but the winters are too harsh for them." I chuckle. "You're going to need a coat."

Cari's eyes ping back and forth between us, then land on the suitcase in the corner.

"Why does she need a coat?"

"I'm from Arizona," Riley says easily, but her shoulders can't hide the tension within her. "I've never actually seen snow before."

"You'll see a lot this winter," I promise.

My sister glances at me again. "Al..."

"Riley's moving in with me," I announce. "She'll take care of Emmy during the day and while I'm on road trips. Basically, she'll be my new nanny."

Cari laughs. Full-on belly laughs, shoulders shaking. I swoop in to take Emmy, but she clutches her tighter.

"You don't do anything by halves, do you? Next thing I know, you'll tell me you're getting married."

I freeze. "Why would you say that?"

"Because all you've ever wanted was to settle down with a family," my sister says, as if it's obvious. "Boom, instant family for you."

"We are *not* getting married," Riley blurts out. "I was planning on going back to Phoenix until he made me an offer I couldn't turn down. I don't want to leave her, not if I don't have to."

My sister laughs again. "Of course he did."

This time, when I go to take Emmy from her, she lets me, and I'm instantly settled by holding my kid in my arms.

"What am I going to do with you?" I murmur, taking in her sweet, chubby cheeks and innocent brown eyes.

"Love her," Riley says, stepping beside me. She wipes a spot of drool off Emmy's chin. "All you have to do is love her."

"I already do."

four

. . .

Riley

TWO AND A HALF HOURS LATER, thanks to a friend of Vanessa's at Harvard, we have official confirmation: Emmy is my biological child. It's not enough for legal determination, but it's enough of an answer for me.

Thanks to the magic of a black American Express card, an entire nursery will be delivered in a few hours, and we leave the baby store with a portable crib, a car seat, and a stroller. I don't know how Riley survived carrying Emmy on the T and a bus with her in her arms, but my baby deserves the princess chariot of her dreams.

Vanessa drove us to the lab in her SUV so Emmy could use Leo's car seat, but it's not a long-term solution. She needs to be able to transport her kid, too.

We make a pit stop at the hotel and Riley grabs her suitcase, and then it's back to my place. I guess it's a good thing my sister moved out a few weeks ago, otherwise there wouldn't be enough bedrooms for the three of us.

I suppose Emmy's crib could go in my room, but she deserves a space of her own. Also, what if I wake her up when I come home late from games and road trips? No, it's better for her crib to go in my childhood bedroom, and Riley will take Cari's old room.

That's when it hits me all over again.

I have a kid. A living, breathing human who's dependent on me. What the fuck, man?

Emmy starts to cry as we walk into the house, the first real sounds of annoyance all day. She's been a perfect angel since the moment she showed up on my doorstep, barely making a peep. I don't know if she's usually this chill or if she's as stunned by the day's events as I am, but I won't be upset by the lack of noise. From the few times I've met Vanessa and Larsson's son, he never stops screaming.

"I need to change her," Riley announces. She sets down the diaper bag and pulls out a mat, then gestures for me to hand her the baby.

I don't want to let my princess go, but with the way she's yelling in my ear, perhaps it's for the best.

In less than two minutes, Riley swaps out the soiled diaper for a fresh one, snaps her buttons back into place, and then deposits Emmy back into my arms. I'm surprised at how right it feels to hold her. I've never spent much time around kids, especially not enough to hold them.

But with Emmy… she belongs with me. The lab tests only confirmed what I already knew to be true. She's *mine*.

"Uh, Al?" a voice calls from upstairs. "Are you home?"

My blood runs cold. "What are you doing here?" I don't want to do this now, but I guess she's forcing the issue.

Cari bounds down the stairs wearing only a towel, her long hair wet around her shoulders. She stops in her tracks when she sees the audience.

"Why are you holding a baby?" she demands, her voice rising into a high-pitched screech.

Of course, that sets off Emmy, who cries out. Her screaming sobs ring in my ears as I bounce my knees the way Riley taught me, trying to soothe her.

Riley returns from the bathroom, hands freshly washed, and snatches Emmy from my arms. "You didn't tell me you had a girlfriend," she hisses.

"Okay, everyone needs to calm down," I shout. I don't know whether I'm talking to myself or them. No, definitely them. But also, a little bit me. "Carolina, go put on clothes. Why are you even here?"

"A bird shit on my head on my run. Your place was closer."

Frustration bubbles through me, and I pinch the bridge of my nose. "Great. Get dressed, and then we can talk." Stepping closer to Riley, I run my hand over Emmy's back. "It's okay, sweetheart. It's okay."

Riley looks up at me with her big blue eyes, clearly peeved. "I'm not your *sweetheart*."

"Was talking to my girl," I say with a chuckle. "But glad to know where we stand."

She scowls at me, continuing to sway in place.

After a few moments, Emmy's sobs die down, and she settles against Riley's chest. Her eyes blink slowly, clearly exhausted by the outburst.

I'm exhausted, too.

Cari skips down the stairs, wearing one of my Grizzlies T-shirts and a pair of my sweatpants.

"Hi, I'm Cari," she says, holding out a hand for Riley to shake. "You're the woman trying to baby trap my brother?"

Riley's eyebrows shoot sky high. "Brother?"

"Yeah. So what's the deal here?" She glances between us. "Don't tell me you fell for it."

"We just got back from the lab. The baby's mine." As stunned as I am, I can't deny the bubble of happiness ready to burst inside me. "Cari, I have a *kid*."

Her eyes widen and her mouth drops open. "Are you shitting me?"

"One hundred percent factual."

Still stunned, my sister tugs me into a hug. I lean into her silent support. But I should have known the quiet wouldn't last long.

"Is this what you want?"

I've been over the hookup scene for a while. I want a relationship, a family of my own. Well, it may be unconventional, but I'm getting part of what I wanted. Even though I still want a great love in my life, maybe that can come in the form of a daughter rather than a romantic partner.

I can have my happily ever after. I can have good things in my life. I'm worthy of it, damn it.

"It absolutely is," I tell my sister, but my eyes meet Riley's.

"And you're the baby mama?" Cari asks.

"I'm Riley." Her face crumples, and her eyes well with tears. "Her mother was my sister. She passed away last week."

Cari's smile drops. "I'm so sorry."

"Yeah. It was… well, I'm still processing." She blinks a few times, no doubt trying to prevent the tears from falling. "But I knew that Alberto deserves to know his daughter."

"Call me Al," I interrupt. "Everyone does."

My sister's eyes gleam with mischief. "And who is this little one?"

"This is Emmy," I tell her proudly. "Emilia."

Riley gives me a subtle nod, and I lift my baby from her arms, cuddling her against my chest, facing outward.

Emmy babbles happily, and my heart twists at the look on my sister's face. She's already in love with her, that much is obvious. It's not hard. Emmy's pretty damn-near perfect. I already know I'd commit murder to protect her, and I only met her a few hours ago.

"This is my daughter."

Cari gives a little shriek, then makes grabby hands for the baby. I settle my daughter in her arms, and as Cari's eyes flutter closed, I swear I see a tear escape.

"Are you okay?" I whisper, my hand on Emmy's back. Ready to snatch her back if I have to.

"Al, you have a *kid,*" she whispers back. "I never thought this would happen."

I swallow. "Me neither."

"Fuck knows Tony won't give me a baby to play with anytime soon." She laughs. "Crap. I probably shouldn't say fuck around a baby."

"She can't talk yet, but she's definitely aware of her surroundings," Riley says, a smile on her face. "Do you, um, live here?"

"No, I live across town with some of my teammates," Cari says.

"She's on the Boston Revolution rugby team," I say, ruffling her damp hair while smiling from ear to ear. My sister scowls at me, but then her gaze drops to my daughter in her arms, and she grins again. "Our brother, Tony, lives in Denver."

"And your parents?"

"They live in Florida with our abuela. They came for a visit over the summer, but the winters are too harsh for them." I chuckle. "You're going to need a coat."

Cari's eyes ping back and forth between us, then land on the suitcase in the corner.

"Why does she need a coat?"

"I'm from Arizona," Riley says easily, but her shoulders can't hide the tension within her. "I've never actually seen snow before."

"You'll see a lot this winter," I promise.

My sister glances at me again. "Al…"

"Riley's moving in with me," I announce. "She'll take care of Emmy during the day and while I'm on road trips. Basically, she'll be my new nanny."

Cari laughs. Full-on belly laughs, shoulders shaking. I swoop in to take Emmy, but she clutches her tighter.

"You don't do anything by halves, do you? Next thing I know, you'll tell me you're getting married."

I freeze. "Why would you say that?"

"Because all you've ever wanted was to settle down with a family," my sister says, as if it's obvious. "Boom, instant family for you."

"We are *not* getting married," Riley blurts out. "I was planning on going back to Phoenix until he made me an offer I couldn't turn down. I don't want to leave her, not if I don't have to."

My sister laughs again. "Of course he did."

This time, when I go to take Emmy from her, she lets me, and I'm instantly settled by holding my kid in my arms.

"What am I going to do with you?" I murmur, taking in her sweet, chubby cheeks and innocent brown eyes.

"Love her," Riley says, stepping beside me. She wipes a spot of drool off Emmy's chin. "All you have to do is love her."

"I already do."

five

. . .

Al

TONIGHT IS OUR HOME OPENER, and there's nothing like it. This is my fifth season in the league, my fourth starting in the NHL, and I still get jitters every year when the season officially kicks off. We've been in prep mode for a few weeks already, so I've got my legs back, and I'm itching to get on the ice and play for real.

This is my second year with the Grizzlies. After Arizona traded me last summer, I inked a new seven-year deal with my hometown team. I grew up coming to these games, wishing one day I could skate on this ice. The awe I felt when I pulled on the script Boston jersey for the first time… it was all my childhood dreams come true.

And every day, I get to go to work and live my dream.

MacGregor, our new captain, nods at me as I enter the dressing room. His shocking red hair is rumpled, like he's been running his fingers through it. He's started growing a beard lately, but right now it's still in the patchy, scraggly phase. For his sake, I hope it grows in better soon.

"Morning." I drop my bag in my cubby.

"You ready for this?" he asks.

My stomach twists. Does he know? Did Vanessa tell him? Anxiety swirls in my belly while I look around the dressing room, but nobody is paying attention to us.

I don't want to hide Emmy. I refuse to pretend she doesn't exist. But how do I tell people about her? How do I explain her sudden appearance in my life?

A few of these players have kids. Maybe I should arrange for the wives to meet Riley. Aside from Larsson's kid, Easton has two under three, Henry has a newborn, Lewis's wife is due any day now, and Amelia, our physical therapist, has a niece who recently turned one. I never thought I'd be invited to a baby's first birthday party, but her brother is part of our extended family, so his kid is, too.

McKittrick, our former captain turned player-development coach, enters the dressing room. He's already in his skates, though now he's wearing a team quarter-zip and athletic pants rather than full hockey gear.

"Hey, Cap," MacGregor says, offering his fist for a bump.

McKittrick laughs. "That's you now."

"Yeah, yeah."

More guys filter into the dressing room and start stripping down for practice. Nick Mitchell, the newest player to join our team, gives me a nod as he takes his place at the cubby beside mine. He's a veteran in the league and a lethal goal scorer. I still don't know what New Orleans was thinking, letting him walk in free agency. At least he's on our team now, rather than playing against us.

Coach Turner has been messing with the lines, trying to find the best on-ice chemistry. There's always a bit of turnover at the start of every season—that's part of the game. Easton moved up to the first line, playing with MacGregor and Larsson, leaving Mitchell to center me and Jenkins. But it does mean we need to work a little harder to gel as a line and find our groove. Hopefully, it won't be long until we're able to predict where the others are on the ice, until our connection becomes near-telepathic. We had that last season, and I'm confident we can find it again.

"You ready for this?" the new guy asks, pulling on his gear.

I go to answer him, but somehow, what comes out of my mouth is: "I have a kid."

The room goes silent.

"Uh, what?" Logan asks.

"I have a baby."

Mitchell cocks his head. "Is this news?"

"Yeah. I found out yesterday." My heart threatens to pound itself right out of my chest.

"Like… your girlfriend is knocked up?"

"No, like a woman showed up on my doorstep with a baby." A loud thump sounds as I fall back against my cubby, collapsing into an awkward heap. "I have a kid now. She's six months old."

MacGregor frowns. "Are you sure she's yours?"

I don't blame him for being concerned; I was, too. If it were any of my teammates in my situation, I'd be the first to stand beside them. But now that I know Emmy's my kid, I won't let anyone doubt the truth.

"We did a paternity test, and the lab expedited the results. She's mine."

Larsson clears his throat. "How are you feeling about this?"

My laugh comes out hollow. Forced. "I don't even know."

Stunned. Surprised. Confused. Bitter for having missed out. Tentatively happy… Irrevocably in love with her. I've known about her for less than twenty-four hours, and I'm obsessed with her.

"Why now?" Sinclair asks. "If she's six months old, why didn't the mother tell you before?"

"She died." When I look around the room at my team-mates, my brothers, I see nothing but sympathy on their faces. "Her sister showed up on my doorstep."

"Fuck, man," MacGregor says. "That's a lot to deal with."

"Do you have a nanny?" Larsson asks. "I can see if Brigitte can help out..."

That's the woman who takes care of his son when both he and Vanessa are on the road. She's cut back on travel, but she still comes with us on road trips once in a while.

Brigitte is nice. Pretty. Vanessa tried to set us up last year, but we didn't click. After our coffee date, we went our separate ways, and I haven't seen her since.

"I've... uh, found someone," I say simply, not wanting to get into it.

"Do you need help?" MacGregor pushes. "Do you have everything?"

"Put together the crib yesterday. Spent all night trying to figure out the exerciser bouncy thing." Huffing out a laugh, I run my hand through my hair. "For being so small, babies need a lot of shit."

"And the diapers," Easton adds. "There are so fucking many diapers."

Riley walked me through my first diaper change this morning. There was a fair bit of fumbling, but I'm sure I'll have plenty of practice once I'm home from this road trip.

Luckily, Emmy seems to be a pretty easygoing baby. She sure does love to eat—she really is my kid—and has no problems when I hold her. She fucking loves her new bouncer thing, too.

Crap. I should probably start training myself not to say *fuck* quite so much. The last thing I want is for someone to call social services because the kid's first word is *fuck*.

How old are babies when they start talking? And walking? I need to read all the parenting blogs, stat. Most guys get almost a year's advance notice to prep for this; I got none.

Some of my anxiety must show on my face, because Logan claps me on the shoulder.

"Don't worry," he says, steady and sure. "You'll figure this out. We've got your back."

A lump forms in my throat, and I nod.

My phone buzzes in my cubby, the vibration rattling the wooden shelves. I'm expecting an angry call from my agent or maybe my lawyer, so I'm surprised to find a text from Riley.

It's a photo of Emmy. She's in the bouncing contraption, pure, unbridled joy on her face, and I smile, my heart thumping loudly.

"Oh, fuck," Mitchell says, the sound echoing distantly. "We've lost him."

"That her?" MacGregor asks, nodding to my phone.

I save the photo as my wallpaper, then I turn the screen around to show them. "She's fucking perfect."

Logan leans over MacGregor's shoulder, trying to get a better look. "Yeah, she is," the defenseman says.

"You want one of these?" MacGregor asks, pointing at the phone.

"Nah. I know it's not in the cards for me and Hailey." Logan shrugs. "We're still focused on the service dog thing."

He's dating MacGregor's sister, and they're disgustingly adorable together. She has some chronic illnesses; I'm uncertain of all the details, but she shows up at nearly every game to support him and her brother. She's good friends with Cari, too, having bonded over being sisters of hockey players.

Coach Turner enters the dressing room, and silence falls again.

"Well?" he demands. "Why aren't you on my fucking ice?"

The guys start filtering out, and I hurry to put on the rest of my gear. Shoving my phone back into my cubby, I stick my helmet on my head and trudge after my teammates.

MacGregor catches my arm. "Hey. You good?"

I think of that photo, of the utter delight on my kid's face at her new toy. I will spend the rest of my life and every dollar I earn making sure she stays as happy and carefree as she was in that moment.

"Yeah. I'm great."

six

· · ·

Riley

ON TUESDAY, Al left for his road trip, and the next day, an endless stream of deliveries showed up. The crib and high chair arrived before he left, but I should have known that wouldn't be the end of it. Between the changing table, rocking chair, five boxes of diapers and wipes, and nearly every age-appropriate toy stocked by the upscale baby boutique, I think Emmy will be set for a while.

It took three loads of laundry to wash all the baby clothes and blankets he bought—everything is pink and frilly, and undeniably adorable. She's going to hate it. But I can't deny I admire the way he's dived in headfirst.

I've organized the living room the best I can, but the place is small, and there are a *lot* of toys.

Emmy is on a play mat for tummy time, and Al is lying on his belly beside her, cooing at her. I refuse to melt for this big, burly hockey player going gooey over his baby.

He came home around three o'clock in the morning. I was changing her diaper when he stopped in the doorway, still in his suit, and I swear my heart nearly melted out of my chest when he took over, wrapping her in her sleep sack and rocking her to sleep.

I expected him to sleep in, especially after his late arrival. But to my surprise, he was downstairs with her, making her bottle and preparing a mashed banana, by the time I woke up.

We can do this. We can raise Emmy together, give her the life she deserves.

Right as the thought crosses my mind, a knock thumps on the door, and I blow out a breath, wiping my hands on my pants.

"You ready for this?" I ask.

Al groans under his breath as he lumbers to his feet. "Not at all."

He opens the door, and somehow, my hand finds its way into his. I don't know who needs the support more, me or him.

Joanne, the social worker, looks around the cramped Mattapan townhouse with a pinched look on her face. She's in her late fifties or early sixties, small and hunched over, with her gray hair cut in a bob.

Immediately, I think of every inexperienced, overworked social worker I've ever come into contact with, every single person who has let me down in my life, and I shiver. She has the power to take away my baby—to destroy all of our lives.

I won't give her the satisfaction.

"I hope you're not expecting special treatment," she says right off the bat.

Confusion flashes across Al's face before he raises an eyebrow. "I'm not. Why would I?"

She scowls. "Your job and your money don't matter to me. What's important is Emilia."

"Emmy," I correct helpfully. "We call her Emmy."

Joanne squints at us, her gaze dropping to our joined hands. "Right."

Hastily, I pull my hand free, then hold the door open. "Come on in."

"And you are?" she asks, brandishing her clipboard.

"Riley Lucas. I'm the temporary guardian."

"In Arizona." The distaste on her face makes my stomach clench.

"Yes. But Emmy's father lives here. So we're here."

"Interstate adoptions are… tricky."

"But it's not an adoption," Al says. "I'm her biological father."

"Except you're not on the birth certificate." Joanne looks almost victorious. "I see here that you're suing for custody."

The color drains from my face, and my eyes widen. "What?"

"I'm suing the state to establish paternity and petition for custody, yes," Al states. He squeezes my shoulder. "This is the way we have to do it. Until then, Emmy should remain with Riley."

"Except she brought her to Massachusetts, which means she should be with a Massachusetts foster family," Joanne cuts in.

I shake my head. "No. She stays with me."

"It's not your choice," she says, almost snidely.

I start toward her, ready to give her a piece of my mind, but Al yanks me back.

"The suit includes a request for Emmy to remain in Riley's care," he says. "I have no intention of pulling my daughter away from the only person left in this world that she knows."

"Hmph." Joanne does not look pleased. "We'll see about that."

My hand covers Al's on my shoulder, lending him support. "We only want what's best for Emmy."

"Well, let me take a look around."

We fall silent while she continues the interview, answering her questions without volunteering any extra information. Al's lawyer briefed him, and he relayed the basics to me, but

I've spent enough time dealing with harried social workers to last a lifetime.

I went into the system when I was six years old, when my mom died of an accidental overdose. My father was already in prison on a domestic violence charge, and he's since had his sentence extended another forty years for various infractions while inside. When I was younger, I wondered why he didn't love me enough to come rescue me from foster care, but once I was old enough to know what he did to her, and what he tried to do to me, I realized what I went through was a cakewalk compared to what life with him would have been like.

Every year on my birthday, I'd receive a letter from him, but after I was twelve or thirteen, I started shredding them, unread. I want nothing to do with a person who has that much evil inside them.

Emmy will never suffer the same fate as I did. Not if I can help it. She has a parent who loves her, and she has me. She will *not* have to go through that.

Al swoops her off the floor, booping her on the nose and grinning when she laughs. He's only spent a few hours with her, interspersed across the two days he's been home, but he's clearly a natural with her.

We make it through the rest of the inspection easily enough, and then I put Emmy down for her nap. On my way back downstairs, I'm surprised to find Al opening the door to his sister.

Cari.

I can't believe I thought she was his *girlfriend*. The family resemblance is so strong, it's impossible not to see it now.

"Hey, Riley," Cari says with a bright smile as she settles on the couch. "I wanted to see my niece."

My heart warms at the idea of Emmy having an aunt. *Family.*

"She's napping, but as soon as she wakes up, she's yours," I promise.

Cari pouts. "I don't suppose you'd wake her up to play?"

At that, Al laughs, the sound springing a rogue flight of butterflies in my stomach. "Even I know you don't wake up a sleeping baby."

"Fine." She huffs, but I swear a smirk twitches her lips. "Tell me about you two. When are you getting married?"

I recoil. "What the hell are you talking about?"

Looking to him for backup, I find Al glaring at his sister, almost like he's angry with her.

Then he runs a hand through his hair and takes a deep breath before giving me a pleading look. "Just hear her out."

"Well, you have custody," she drawls. "And Al is trying to establish paternity. If you get married, he'll automatically get custody as your spouse. Isn't that how it works?"

Staring at her, I try to follow her thought process. "No…"

"Well, think about it," Al says, leaning forward. "If we're together, she won't have to go to a foster family. She can stay with us."

Aghast, I stare at him. "But—*married*?"

"On paper only," Cari adds with a laugh. "It looks better if he's banging the new wife than banging the nanny."

"We aren't sleeping together," I insist.

"Right. Definitely not," he says, as equally resolute.

As much as I don't want to sleep with him, his clear rejection stings. Am I that unattractive? Do I exude man repellent from my pores?

"There's too much at stake here," Al continues. "I would never jeopardize Emmy's security for a fling."

Okay, that makes me feel moderately less insecure.

Back to the question at hand… "I can't believe you want to get married."

"I don't want to," he says, blowing out a breath. "But my agent thinks maybe we should."

"This is insane." Pacing through the small living room, I wave my hands in the air. "It's a terrible idea."

"It's only until we get paternity established and Emmy can be mine, officially," he says. "Please. For Emmy?"

I hesitate, latching on to the sincerity in his pleading tone.

"As soon as everything is finalized, you can get divorced," Cari says. "Outside of us and the social workers, nobody has to know you're not Emmy's mother. To the rest of the world, he's just… marrying the mother of his child."

I don't want to be the mother of his child. I'm her aunt. Carter is her mother. My heart squeezes, and my grief threatens to overtake me once again. I don't want to erase her when she's already been taken so ruthlessly from our lives.

But I understand not wanting to get into the whole baby-mama drama with his career in the public eye.

"It gives you more protection than being her nanny. It gives you security." He winces. "There would be a prenup, of course. A few years. Maybe two? Just so it looks legit and not like…"

"I don't want your money." I wave the concern away. "I don't want to be separated from Emmy."

"You don't have to be." Al rises from the couch and approaches me. He takes my hands in his. "Marry me, Riley, and you'll never have to be separated from Emmy again."

seven

. . .

Al

EMMY BABBLES HAPPILY at me as she lies on my chest, her sticky fingers grabbing at my beard. We're having some daddy-daughter time. Very important business being discussed.

"Am I doing the right thing?" I ask the six-month-old, running my hand over her back. "We just want to protect you."

She giggles and tugs at my beard.

"I don't feel like I'm making a bad decision. It might be quick, but we know where we stand. This isn't an emotional decision. It's a logical one."

Normally, I run into everything headfirst, consequences be damned. But this time... the repercussions are pretty damn scary.

I've only known Emmy for a few days, but I would already fight tooth and nail to keep her. She's *mine*. Nobody can take her away from me.

Not even Riley.

But if marrying a complete stranger is the only way I can keep Emmy... I'll do it in a heartbeat.

The prenup came in this morning, and even though I encouraged her to find a lawyer of her own to review it, she signed it with the notary a few hours ago. She says she trusts me, and I insisted my lawyers were generous, but we both know what's at stake if this marriage dissolves.

I may be Emmy's father, but Riley is all she knows. She shouldn't be separated from *either* of us.

No matter what happens between us, we'll have to find a way to coparent her together.

The front door opens, and I turn, expecting my soon-to-be *wife*.

But it's my brother.

"The fuck are you doing here?" I demand, sitting up and clutching Emmy to my chest.

"The fuck are you doing with a baby?" Tony smirks at me.

"Don't say fuck in front of my baby." Standing, I bound over to him, and he tugs me into a hug, Emmy crushed between us. She shrieks with delight.

Behind Tony is his partner Viv, who's a former rugby player—she used to be Cari's team captain—and even grumpier than my surly brother, which I didn't think was possible.

They moved to Denver over the summer when Tony enrolled in veterinary school, and Viv is exploring life as a content creator and motivational speaker.

"You look good, Al," Viv says, giving me a hug as well. "You holding up okay?"

"I'm fucking fantastic. I've honestly never been better."

Tony takes off his leather jacket, hanging it on the hook beside the door, and then hangs Viv's jacket, too.

"Well, of course. You're getting everything you ever wanted," he says. "Just... a little backward."

"Cari told you, then." With a sigh, I turn back to the couch, settling again.

"Dude. You're getting *married*. Of course I'd be here,"

Tony says, like he can't imagine any other option. "I'm just surprised you didn't call me yourself."

"Didn't know what to say." I run my hand over Emmy's wispy hair, trying to tame it a bit. "Knocked up a stranger, didn't find out until over a year later, and, oh yeah, I'm marrying her sister."

Viv laughs. "When you commit, you go all in." Whereas I might be offended if one of my siblings said it, with Viv, I know it's a compliment. My chest warms with affection. I'm so glad she's become part of our family.

My brother claps me on the shoulder. "Okay, now introduce me to my niece."

"Emmy, this is your Tio Tony. He's an asshole," I tell her. "Tony, this is… This is Emmy."

My brother is a surly butt face. He's shorter than me, stockier, with the body of a professional gymnast rather than a hockey player. The only time I ever see him smile is when he's talking about Viv or occasionally gymnastics.

But when I hand over my kid, and he wraps his muscular, tattooed arms around her, he fucking *melts.*

"Hi, baby," Tony coos. His thumb traces the apple of her cheek, and she grins her gummy smile, and we watch as he falls head over heels for her.

Viv settles on the sofa beside me, resting her head on my shoulder. Her hand falls to mine on the cushion between us, and she squeezes my palm.

"You did good, kid," she says. Her unwavering support reassures me I'm making the right decision.

"She's pretty great."

"She's beautiful."

"Makes you think about having one of your own?" I ask.

"Maybe we'll steal this one," Tony says.

"Not on your life." My growl rumbles through the room. "Gimme back my baby."

My brother laughs, but he places her back into my arms.

Viv, still curled beside me, runs her fingers over Emmy's back, like she's afraid to break her.

"I love her already," she says.

"So do I," I admit.

"Where's the wife?" Tony asks.

"Not my wife yet. And I'm not sure. She said she had to run some errands." I check my watch. "Our appointment isn't for another four hours…"

"An appointment at city hall." And just like that, my brother's signature frown is back in place. "You sure you want to do this? We could get Mom and Dad up here, find a church…"

I shake my head. "No. This needs to be quick and efficient. And you know if Mom and Dad get involved, the entire family will be invited, and I just… no. That's not what I want. Not what *we* want."

"Okay," he says, and that's that.

"Do you have everything you need?" Viv asks. "Diapers, formula, toys?"

I wave a hand at the toys strewn about the place. "She has plenty of toys." I nearly bought out the entire boutique, and I'd do it again in a heartbeat. Anything my girl wants, she gets. As soon as she's old enough, I'll buy her a fucking pony, if that's what she desires. There's nothing I wouldn't do for this little girl.

She starts to rustle around, getting antsy, and I force myself to my feet again.

"Come on, Tio Tony. Do you want to feed her?"

My grumpy asshole of a brother lights up. "I can?"

"Yeah, and then it'll be time for a nap."

"Me too!" Viv says, raising her hand in the air. "I claim dibs on the couch."

"Or you could go back to your hotel room," I mutter.

"Hotel? We're staying here," Tony says.

Jerking my head back, I stare at him. "There's no room."

"You mean you aren't sharing a bed with your new *wife*?"

My glare could burn straight through him. Sadly, he doesn't spontaneously combust.

"Relax, we've got a room," Viv says. "We'll be meeting up with some of my teammates tomorrow for brunch while you're at practice."

Rolling my eyes, I hand off the baby before getting her bottle ready. I show him how to hold her and angle the bottle so she gets the milk and not air. Before long, she's kicking her feet and going to town. Her little glugs of delight never fail to bring a smile to my face.

The front door opens, and I turn, expecting Riley again. What I'm not expecting is for my sister to follow her over the threshold.

My future wife freezes in the doorway, her eyes widening. "Uh…"

"Hey. You guys were out together?" My gaze pings between her and my sister, trying to put the pieces together. I'm glad they're getting along, but it's weird they're hanging out without me. Isn't it?

"I'm going to put this upstairs," Cari says, and it's only then that I notice the garment bag in Riley's hand. My sister eases the hanger free, then drapes it over her arm and all but runs up the stairs.

"Come meet my brother," I tell Riley, coaxing her closer with an outstretched hand.

I'm gratified when she takes my hand in hers, and I squeeze, trying to reassure her. The hand-holding is not something I anticipated, but she seems to like it, so I'll keep doing it.

"This is Tony and his girlfriend, Viv."

"It's nice to meet you," Viv says. "We've heard nothing but good things about you."

Riley's mouth pops open. "Y-you're Viv Gallagher."

Tony smirks while staring at his woman. "She's pretty damn awesome, isn't she?"

"Are you a rugby fan?" Viv asks.

"Not exactly," Riley says. "I saw that talk you gave to the women's soccer federation six months ago, about self-limiting beliefs. It was amazing. I just—wow."

"You weren't this starstruck with me," I pout. "I'm a famous hockey player."

"There, there," she says, patting me on the shoulder with a patronizing smile. "I can't believe I didn't connect the dots."

Before anything else can be said, Cari thunders down the stairs, then launches herself at Viv. "You're here!"

"Like we'd miss this," she says, hugging her former teammate back.

My sister moves to Tony next, giving him a hug with Emmy trapped between them.

"I'm glad you guys made it," Cari says. "I've missed you since you abandoned me."

Beside me, Riley stiffens. But Tony laughs. "We didn't abandon you. We moved to Denver. And you moved out."

Cari huffs. "Shut up."

He tugs at her ponytail until she drops the petulant act and grins.

"We have to do something fun while you're here," she continues. "Maybe tomorrow we can—"

"We leave tomorrow night," Tony says, eyes downcast. "I have school."

"Right." Cari swallows. "Tonight, then. After the wedding."

"Definitely," Viv says. "We'll celebrate."

Riley pulls her hand free. "Here, I'll burp the baby and get her down for her nap."

I frown at her withdrawal. Does she not want to celebrate? Does she not want to do this? If she has doubts about this marriage, we need to get to the root of them now. I certainly don't think I'm hideous. I'm a decent catch, a nice guy. Is my family too much for her? We're a package deal; I couldn't get rid of them even if I wanted to.

What's holding her back?

eight

. . .

Riley

WHEN CARI TOLD me she wanted to take me wedding dress shopping, I wasn't sure what to expect. I've never even thought about my future wedding, not with any concrete plans. I've never had a guy stick around long enough to dream about happily ever afters.

The one thing I planned on was Carter standing beside me, and now I'll be the one marrying *her* baby daddy.

The three Gonzales siblings, plus Viv fucking Gallagher, talk around me as I burp Emmy and clean up. She babbles, trying to keep up with them. Crap. Even my baby is more a part of this family than I ever will be.

"Wait," Al says, before I can take her upstairs. "I need a kiss first."

My eyes widen. What's he talking about? We don't do this.

With the baby in my arms, I approach him, and he bends down until his face is level with her full belly. He hesitates for a second, building the anticipation, then leans and gives her a raspberry while she giggles and kicks her feet. Laughing, he stands and drops a kiss on her chubby, sticky cheek.

"Okay. Now I'm good," he declares. "Have a good nap,

princess." He chucks her chin before his gaze meets mine. "Do you have everything you need?"

"Yep. I'm good." The words come out in a squeak, my throat inexplicably tight. "I'm going to put her down, then get ready."

"Great." His eyes soften. "You sure you want to do this?"

Do I want to? No. But it's the right thing to do.

"I'm in this," I swear to him, and he nods.

"We'll leave as soon as she's up from her nap."

Dismissed, I take Emmy upstairs, change her, and settle her in her crib. And then I start to cry. This is not what I wanted for a wedding day. This is not what I wanted for a *wedding*.

I knew I'd never get the happily ever after in the storybooks, but I at least thought I'd end up with someone who likes me for me. Someone who cares about me and is interested in my life. Not a paper marriage to a man who doesn't know the first thing about me.

His siblings might know the truth, but the judge and the rest of the world need to believe this is real. If social services think anything hinky is going on, they'll pull Emmy from our care faster than we can blink. I wouldn't put it past Joanne to do it just for shits and giggles.

No. This is what's best for Emmy. That has to be my focus. Everything I do is for her.

So, I get to work.

First, I take a shower to scrub off the day's grime, and then I blow-dry my hair until the waves look somewhat decent. The top-of-the-line hair dryer in the guest bathroom makes the process easy. I'd certainly never pay seven hundred dollars for one, but since it's here, I'll use it.

And fuck, does it work well. My chocolate-brown waves fall to right beneath my shoulder blades, and I twist the front back and secure it with pins. As much as I love playing with bright and colorful makeup, today's the day for simple, demure. Although I do go a little heavy on the smoky eye for daytime.

Safe in the sanctuary of my room, I pull the dress from the garment bag. I've never spent this much money on a single piece of clothing, but when I saw it on the mannequin, I knew I couldn't bear the thought of wearing anything else.

The dress might be lilac, or maybe periwinkle; it's that in-between shade that's hard to label, but whatever it's called, the color flatters my skin tone and makes me feel like a princess. It's light and gauzy, with a simple slip underneath to cover all the important parts. Fluffy chiffon sleeves fall to my elbows, and it drapes over my body to the floor. With a pair of three-inch heels, it's the perfect length.

The part that caught my eye was the intricate embroidery. Floral stitchwork covers the dress, with little wildflowers and vines from head to toe. It's a little more bohemian than anything I've ever worn, but as soon as I put it on, I knew it was the one. I felt confident and in control of my emotions.

From the next room, Emmy stirs, but heavy footsteps on the stairs tell me Al's got her. He talks to her, or maybe to his siblings, his deep voice indistinct through the two closed doors between us.

A quick *tap, tap* sounds on the door, hesitant, like he doesn't actually want to bother me. I slip on my shoes before I open it.

Al's wearing a suit and holding his daughter, who immediately squirms, reaching for me. He starts to hand her over before he freezes, and his mouth drops open, Emmy suspended in midair.

He hates it. He hates *me*.

"Wow," he whispers. "You look beautiful."

Oh.

Heat rushes to my face, pooling in my cheeks. "Thanks."

She squawks, upset at being ignored, and I pull my niece into my arms, giving her a quick snuggle. Although I suppose she'll be my daughter now. Stepdaughter. Does it matter? She'll be mine, and that's all I care about.

Al clears his throat. "We're getting ready to go."

"Okay. I'll change her."

"She's clean. I just did."

"I got her an outfit." One singular baby dress shouldn't cost over a hundred dollars, but if he and I are getting dressed up, so should she.

His eyes soften. "You did?"

"She's part of this. Hell, she's the whole reason we're doing it."

I squeeze into the doorway and he takes a step back, letting me pass. His cedar-and-firewood scent lingers in the air as I enter her room, and he stands in the threshold, watching while I pull out the light purple dress. It's frilly and full of taffeta, and I anticipate she'll hate it—she hates most clothes—but it has delicate embroidery that coordinates with my dress. I even found little ballet slippers.

Emmy whines as soon as I take off her onesie, and she is definitely not happy to wear the dress. She kicks her feet and screams while I struggle to put on her shoes.

But when I scoop her into my arms and deposit her into Al's, suddenly she's happy as a clam. She grabs at his beard and he chuckles, kissing her palm before tucking her more securely against his broad chest.

"My princess," he murmurs into the top of her head, and my heart squeezes, filling it with warmth and reaffirming my decision to do anything to protect her. Even if it means the death of my dreams for love. Her happiness comes first— always.

We make our way downstairs and into the car. He has a top-of-the-line SUV, sleek and black, with a car seat already installed in the back.

"Where are your siblings?" I ask as Al gets Emmy situated.

"Cari drove them, since we don't all fit in here." He rounds the hood and slides into the driver's seat beside me. "Any news on your car?"

I blow out a breath. "I don't know if it'll survive a trip out here." I bought it from a guy I used to work with, and it had already been through a few owners. "I guess I should find a new one. With my savings, I should be able to afford it in a few months."

I still have to figure out what to do with my apartment. All I have with me is a few days' worth of clothes. Most of my singular suitcase was packed full of baby things, as I certainly wasn't planning to move here last week.

Al grunts. "I'll get you a car."

"You don't have to…"

"Riley, you'll be my wife," he says, turning to glance at me before focusing on the road again. "What's mine will be yours. But more importantly, you need a way to get around, and to get Emmy to doctor's appointments and the park or wherever you want to go. You shouldn't be trapped at the house all day, every day. That's a surefire path to a breakdown."

Uncomfortable, I force a laugh. "We take walks with the stroller."

"Great. Still buying you a car." He clears his throat. "I ordered a credit card for you, and I trust you'll be responsible with it. Household supplies, groceries, formula, diapers, whatever you need… Most of my meals are organized by a dietitian, but if you want Tyler to make you meal prep, too, just let me know. I'll ask him for his menu. I know he has a special offer for his athletes' partners so you don't have to eat the same healthy slop we get."

There is a stack of glass containers in the fridge, but for some reason, I thought he prepared them. It makes sense they come from a dietitian, though. He doesn't exactly get a lot of time off to cook.

We arrive at the courthouse and, of course, Emmy has fallen asleep, so I pull out the stroller while Al wrangles with the car seat. He clicks her into place and then takes the wheel.

Cari, Tony, and Viv meet us inside. I still can't believe *Viv Gallagher* is at my wedding. They're dressed up for the occasion, and I'm suddenly glad I chose to buy a new dress rather than wear jeans and a T-shirt.

After what feels like forever, we're called back to the judge's chambers. Al squeezes my hand, then grabs hold of the stroller, and Emmy stirs, looking around with her wide brown eyes.

Judge Alexander McCall is younger than I expected, maybe in his forties, with salt-and-pepper hair and a kindness in his expression. He's wearing one of those robes you see on Court TV, and as he stands from behind his desk, he shakes both Al's and my hands.

He flicks through the packet of paperwork I hand him, then says, "Everything seems to be in order. Let's get married, shall we?"

nine

. . .

Al

I TAKE Riley's hands in mine, staring into her baby blues. They're wide and scared, and I squeeze her hand, trying to reassure her.

"Do you, Riley Anne Lucas, take Alberto Emilio Gonzales to be your lawful wedded spouse, to live together in marriage? Do you promise to love, honor, comfort, and keep him, in sickness and in health, forsaking all others, for as long as you both shall live?"

She swallows, the sound loud in the small room, and pulls her hands from mine.

"Riley—" I don't know what to say. Did I push her too fast?

"Your middle name is Emilio?" she whispers.

Slowly, I nod. My kid's name is Emilia. We're matching.

Did Carter know? I never told her. It's not on my Wikipedia page, but I'm sure it's somewhere deep in the Internet.

Something shutters in her eyes, and her face falls. She looks over at Emmy, safe in Tony's arms, and sniffles a few times, swiping beneath her lashes, before she lets out a gusty sigh and squares her shoulders. "Okay. I can do this."

She takes my hands again, then nods at Judge McCall. "Say it again."

He quirks an eyebrow. "If you're being coerced…"

"Only by a ghost," she says with a bitter chuckle. "But my sister's already dead, so I can't kill her for getting me into this mess."

The judge chuckles awkwardly, then repeats the vows.

"I do," she says, her voice steady and sure. She squeezes my fingers, staring me straight in the face. "For as long as we both shall live."

My heartbeat thuds in the back of my ears. This is temporary. This is for Emmy.

But as Judge McCall says my part of the vows, I know deep in my bones this isn't temporary. This may be fake, but it's real life.

"I do," I say, loud and clear.

"The rings, please," the judge says, and Cari hands over a small box.

Riley looks alarmed. "I didn't—"

I open the velvet box, withdrawing two rings. Mine is a simple white-gold band, not too thick, with a flat finish. The other is more ornate, matching white gold with an eternity band of diamonds surrounding the entire thing. It's understated, simple, not flashy. It won't scratch Emmy's delicate skin.

"It's perfect," she breathes.

"Repeat after me," Judge McCall prompts.

"With this ring, I thee wed," Riley says, and she slips the plain band onto my finger.

It feels heavy. Weighty. Right.

"With this ring, I thee wed," I repeat, as I slide hers into place.

"Congratulations," Judge McCall says. "I now pronounce you husband and wife. You may kiss your bride."

Oh.

Oh, shit.

I hadn't thought about that.

Riley stares up at me with her big blue eyes, hesitation on her face. She goes to pull her hand from mine, but I cling to it tighter for one second, before letting go.

Nervous energy crackles in the air between us and my pulse thrums in my ears. She leans closer, hesitating just long enough for me to catch the warmth of her breath and the faint pressure of her mouth on mine. Time stretches thin, suspended on the edge of something new, inevitable.

Before I know what I'm doing, I cup her cheek, then lean down and brush my lips against hers. She gasps against my mouth, hers parting, and I swallow the sound, bringing her closer until we're flush together.

Her hands curl into fists, grabbing the lapels of my jacket. My chest tightens with the ache of possibility, and in that singular heartbeat, I swear I can taste forever.

Emmy cries out, and I jolt back, stunned. Riley lets go of me, smoothing the fabric she bunched up, and takes a step back. She goes immediately to the baby, taking her from Tony's arms and soothing her. Her face is flushed as she devotes her entire attention to Emmy, ignoring me.

What the hell was that?

I clear my throat, shoving my hand into my pocket. The new ring catches on the fabric. That'll take some getting used to.

"Congratulations," Cari says, stepping forward and tugging me into a hug. Pain ripples through the back of my neck where she pinches the skin. "What just happened?" she hisses into my ear.

"I don't know," I whisper back.

She releases me, and Tony takes her place, slapping my back.

"I'm happy for you, chimuelo," he says.

Toothless. My childhood nickname. With that, I know all is forgiven for not telling him about the wedding and my baby. I'm glad Cari had the courage to do it for me, but she won't be fighting my battles anymore. I've got this.

Viv squeezes me into a forceful hug. "I'm so proud of you," she says, linking her arm through mine.

We watch as Tony approaches Riley, setting his hand on her shoulder. She looks up at him, uncertain, and when he opens his arms for a hug, her lashes flutter shut. She buries her face in his neck, mumbling words I can't make out.

The judge's chamber seems impossibly smaller. Are the walls getting closer? It's only now hitting me—the gravity of what I've done. Married, to a virtual stranger. Married, in a civil ceremony. Secret, so my parents don't even know. How do I tell them I took this step without them? My mother will cry, and my father will frown, and there will be endless guilt trips for the rest of my life, even when this marriage is over and I've hopefully found my real happily ever after.

But I can deal with all of that later. This is about Emmy. It's about me and Riley protecting my kid. I can handle the guilt trips. What I can't tolerate is anyone taking Emmy from me.

My brother folds his arms around my wife, speaking into her ear. And my heart twists at how effortlessly he's welcomed her into our family. How accepting he is. Both my siblings are.

He holds her for a long time, Emmy trapped between them. My princess lets out a squawk, clearly annoyed, and everyone laughs. When Tony lifts her into his arms, completely smitten, she giggles and kicks her feet. Watching my brother fall in love with my baby is almost as magical as falling for her myself. My eyes get watery when Cari and Viv lean in to wrap Riley in hugs, too, and I blink a few times to clear the moisture away. She's one of us now, whether she's prepared for it or not.

My wife turns to me, extending her hand. The band on her

finger glitters, and a primal sense of satisfaction settles deep in my chest at my ring on her finger. She's mine, and I'm hers, and even though it's purely in a legal, non-romantic way, I like the idea of belonging to someone. Being part of a unit, together against the world.

Even if the first and hopefully only nemesis we're battling against is social services.

"Let's go home," she says.

The drive back to the house passes in the blink of an eye. My ring glints in the late-afternoon sunlight, and I keep running my thumb over it, getting used to the feeling.

"I don't expect you to wear it," Riley says into the silence between us.

"Hmm?" I glance over at her while we're paused at the red light.

"The ring. I know it's not…"

"I have no problem wearing a wedding ring," I tell her. "It's a sign to the world that we've taken this step. I can't wear it on the ice or in the weight room, but the rest of the time, I plan to wear it."

She opens her mouth, but I cut off whatever she's about to say.

"We're married," I repeat. "That means something."

"I'm just trying to give you an out," she whispers, like she's afraid of my reaction. "I'm sure it'll be hard for you to pick up women if you're wearing a ring."

"What makes you think I'm trying to pick up women?" Despite trying, I can't keep the incredulity out of my voice.

She snorts. "Please. You're a hotshot hockey player. Until a week ago, you were single and carefree. You can't tell me you don't have a list of women in your phone, down to fuck at any given moment."

"I've been over the hookup scene for a while." Flexing my hands around the steering wheel, I exhale slowly. "Since I've been back in Boston, I haven't dated, haven't gone partying, haven't hooked up. That's not what I'm interested in. While we're married, I'm committed to you. To us."

"So what is it you want?" She shifts in her seat, facing me.

"I wanted a family. I wanted my happily ever after."

I want a great love, like the one my parents share. Like the relationship my brother has found with Viv. A true partner, in every sense of the word, ready to support me, and willing to let me support her in turn. Sure, sex can be important in a relationship, but it's more than the physical that goes into having a strong, healthy marriage. I can't imagine not wanting to spend time with my wife, to live as strangers in the same house.

But we *are* strangers. Only now, we're married.

"And instead you got me."

"And Emmy." I glance back at her in the rearview mirror. She's babbling while she plays with her toes, content now that she's finally free of her shoes. "I've got everything I need."

ten

. . .

Riley

LIFE SETTLES INTO A ROUTINE. Al goes to the rink every day. On nights when he has a home game, he gets back to the house a little before midnight. He takes care of any middle-of-the-night diaper changes, and for the first time since Carter died, I finally get to sleep through the night.

He has road trips. Some are only two nights, some are longer. His game schedule is taped to the fridge, which is full of prepared meals. A man comes by every Monday with a cooler, delivering the glass containers and taking away last week's empties.

Some of the meals are for me, so I don't have to worry about cooking every night. They're pretty tasty. It's a far cry from the ramen, beans and rice, and canned-tuna diet I survived on until payday each week.

One day, a sleek brand-new black Audi SUV arrived, and the delivery person handed me the keys. *Me.* I called Al, but all he said was *I promised I'd get you a car*, and hung up. A top-of-the-line car seat was already installed.

It's isolating, being home alone with a baby all day. My schedule revolves around hers, naps and bottles and diapers,

58

and whenever Al is home, I try to give him as much space as I can.

But I'm fucking lonely. Aside from a few walks around the block, I haven't gone anywhere or done anything by myself in the last three weeks.

I miss my sister. She was the other half of my heart. And now it's like a piece of me is missing. She wasn't a perfect person, not by far. But she was *mine*.

And now Emmy is mine.

An authoritative knock sounds on the door, and I freeze. What if it's Joanne, coming to take my baby away?

For one second, I consider not answering. Just because someone knocks doesn't mean I have to answer. But I know if it truly is social services, I stand to risk more than I have to gain by ignoring them. I blow out a breath, then trudge across the room and open the door to my fate.

Vanessa stands on the stoop, holding a baby with round cheeks and white-blond hair. He looks to be about eight months, chubby and cute. A brunette carries a car seat with an infant, and another woman stands beside her, tall and redheaded, holding a diaper bag.

"Sorry for dropping by unannounced," Vanessa says, a smile stretching her face. "I thought maybe you might like a playdate."

I blink a few times. "A playdate?"

The redhead holds up her diaper bag. "I brought wine."

A laugh bubbles up from inside me. "In that case, come on in."

Vanessa sets her son down on the play mat near Emmy, and I disappear into the kitchen, retrieving four wineglasses.

"I don't have much in the way of snacks," I apologize. "The grocery delivery is supposed to come in a few hours."

"Don't worry about it," the brunette says, scooping her hair into a ponytail. "We're the ones barging in on you uninvited. Hi. I'm Audrey. I'm married to Seb Henry, the goalie."

"And her dad's the coach," Vanessa adds with a smirk.

Audrey rolls her eyes, shoving her playfully.

"Nice to meet you. I'm Riley."

"I'm Bex Whitney," offers the redhead. "Van and I went to college together, and my brother plays for Austin, so I'm basically part of the team."

"We'll find you a hockey player one of these days," Vanessa teases.

But Bex shakes her head. "Nope. Been there, done that. Don't need to go down that road again." A loud *pop* echoes through the room as she opens a bottle of white wine, pouring a generous serving into each glass. Every cliché about wine moms pops into my head, but after a few weeks of solo parenting, I'm starting to understand the stereotype more and more.

"How are you settling in?" Audrey asks.

"Uh…"

"It must be difficult, suddenly having to be responsible for a baby. Especially one that's not yours." She clucks her tongue sympathetically. "I chose this, and it's still hard sometimes."

"It gets easier," I assure her. "That's what they tell me, at least." I reach for my wineglass, taking a sip.

"Holy hell," Vanessa says, grabbing at my hand. "You guys got *married*?"

My face heats under her shocked, inquisitive stare. "Um…"

"Congratulations," Bex cheers. "Weddings are exciting."

"It wasn't exactly a wedding." I force my gaze to the babies. Vanessa's son is trying to crawl, rocking forward on his hands and knees, but not yet ready to commit. Emmy is on her tummy, watching him with fascination. She hasn't been around many other babies. "We just… got married. It's no big deal."

"It's definitely a big deal," Audrey argues. "Gonzo is the

heart of the team. We love him, he's the best. I'm glad he has you."

The heat radiating off my cheeks could fry an egg, so I distract myself with another sip of my wine, hoping to cool my body temperature. I'm not much of a drinker, though, especially these last few weeks.

"So. Tell us about yourself," Bex says, leaning back on the couch and drawing her leg up.

"What do you want to know?"

"Well, you're the baby's aunt," Vanessa says. "That's pretty much all we know."

"I'm twenty-five, I'm from Arizona, and Carter was my foster sister," I say simply. "We met when I was twelve and she was fourteen, and she's looked out for me ever since." I swallow, trying to dislodge the ball of emotion that always lodges in my throat when I think of her. "She was in a car accident on her way to pick up Emmy from daycare. We lived together, and I'm her only family, so I was awarded temporary guardianship. But social services…" I shake my head. "So we got married. They can't take her away from me."

"Oh, honey." Bex touches my hand. "Who are you? Without the baby, without your sister. We want to get to know *you*."

My eyes well up with tears. "Really?"

"It's easy to lose your identity when you're married to a hockey player," Audrey says quietly. "I have a career, and now I'm a mother, but my entire life has to revolve around Seb's schedule and his needs. For now, his career is more important."

"It's shitty, but it's true," adds Vanessa. "I still work for the team part-time—I didn't want to give that up. But I can't travel as much as I used to. Hell, I can't do half of my responsibilities I handled pre-baby. My entire life changed."

I blow out a breath. "I worked at a beauty counter at the

mall, and I did makeup on the side. Now I have no clients, no time to work, nothing."

Bex grins. "You don't know who you're talking to, do you?"

Blinking a few times, I shake my head.

"You're a hockey wife now," Vanessa says. "We can put you in contact with the rest of the squad. There's a group chat and everything. When we have events, it usually requires a full glam squad for the red carpet." She pauses. "Of course, you'll be attending them, too, so you might not want to work the glam squad. You'll finally be the one sitting in the chair."

"I don't know about that... I'm not really a red-carpet kind of girl."

"That ring on your finger means you are now," Audrey says. "Trust me, I resisted for as long as I could. It was definitely not the future I planned on when I started library school. But it's what fate planned for me, and now I can't imagine anything else."

"It's just something to consider," Vanessa tacks on. "We'd love to have you in any way you want to participate."

"I'll think about it," I promise.

"You'll have to bring the baby to the next matinee game," Audrey says. "I haven't brought Cora to any yet. I'm a little nervous."

"Is that a thing? Bringing the kids?"

"Oh, yeah," Vanessa says. "We usually only do it as a group for matinee games, but Mel will bring hers to nighttime games, too. We hang out at the ice level for pregame skate, let the boys see the babies, then we retreat to the suite and hang out. There are toys and play mats and a changing table, everything we'd ever need."

"Really?"

"The happier the babies are, the happier the wives and partners are," Bex says. "And the happier the partners are, the happier the players are. Management wants to take care of the team. They want the guys to want to play here." She scowls. "My brother's played for a few different teams, and it's definitely a different culture here. They're accepting in a way other teams aren't. They've even accepted me as part of the team, even though I'm not actually related to anyone on the Grizzlies."

"Now we just have to convince management to trade for Wyatt, and he and Elsy can come here," Vanessa says.

"I'll drink to that." Bex laughs, lifting her wineglass. "My best friend moved to Austin and started dating my brother. I'd love for them to be in Boston long term," she says, filling me in.

"It'll happen one of these days," Vanessa says with a grin. She sips from her wine, looking over at the kids, who are rolling back and forth. Leo gets up onto his hands and knees again, then collapses onto his belly with a chortle. "Everything is so different now. I almost don't recognize myself. But then I look in the mirror, and I realize this is my life now, and I'm so fucking happy, I don't know what to do with myself."

She looks at me, her blue eyes bright. "I don't have any contact with my family. I don't have any siblings. And now I have this huge family of friends and players and their partners, and I wouldn't have it any other way. This team, the culture they've built… it's special. You'll see. You'll be at home here before long."

"I've never had a home before. Not really," I admit quietly. "I bounced from foster home to foster home. The first time I ever put down roots was with Carter, and that was yanked from beneath me."

"And now you have Emmy and Gonzo," Audrey says. "You'll put down new roots. And you'll make a new life for yourself. You get to start over, on your terms, with all these resources at your disposal. You can do anything."

"So," Bex says, looking at me expectantly. "What do you want to do?"

"I don't know." The words come out quietly, just above a whisper.

The redhead reaches over and pats my hand. "It's okay. You have all the time in the world."

eleven

. . .

Al

THE ICE IS my happy place. I love hockey, getting to play the sport I've devoted the last twenty years of my life to. There's nothing like skating out onto a clean sheet of ice, the crisp scent settling my nerves and pumping adrenaline through my system. Even when we're in enemy territory, nothing can bring me down.

After this game, we're home for six days. That's six mornings I get to spend with Emmy. We've got three home games, so I won't be able to put her to bed *every* night, but I can do bath time and bedtime at least a few of those evenings.

I expected to be a hands-on dad, but I'm continuously surprised by how much Riley does, how little she needs me. Still, I participate as much as I can with my schedule, and I try to get up with Emmy every morning I'm home.

Home. I'm ready to sleep in my own bed, rather than another shitty hotel room. Ready to be reunited with my girls.

MacGregor skates past me, giving me a nod. "You ready?"

"As I'll ever be." We're playing Montreal, and it's sure to be a bloodbath. It always is, given our century-long rivalry.

He nods again as he moves on to Mitchell, who's warming

up a few feet away. The new guy is settling in well. He's a veteran in his early thirties, so he knows the score.

And score, he does, five minutes into the first.

Montreal does *not* like that, challenging the play. But the goal was clean, and we go on the power play.

I set up shop at the left point. Logan quarterbacks the play, Sinclair straddling the blue line in support, and Mitchell and Jenkins get all up in the crease.

Logan passes the puck to Sinclair, who saucers it over to me, and my slapshot lands squarely on the goalie's pads.

But Jenkins is there to clean up the play. Even though he can't seal the deal on the rebound, he's able to kick the puck back, and Logan scoops it onto his blade and back to me.

This time, my shot lands in the back of the net, and the lamp lights up red. The guys crash tackle me into a group hug, and then we zoom past the bench for celebratory fist bumps.

Coach Turner pulls me off the ice, and I grab for a nearby bottle, spraying some of the electrolyte drink into my mouth.

"Good job," Coach says, clapping my shoulder. "Now do it again."

I grin. "You got it."

Larsson scores a goal, and in the second, so does Jenkins, off an assist by Mitchell. In the third, Montreal scores two dirty goals, but a bullet from Sinclair seals the deal.

We win, 4-2. It's a buoyant mood in the room as we cool down and clean up. Rock music blares, and guys chat and laugh as we get dressed in our suits. I grab my ring, slipping it onto my finger. I'm surprised by how natural it feels after only a few weeks.

"Hang on," MacGregor says, catching my shoulder.

"What's up, Cap?"

He grabs my arm. "What's that?"

I cock my head. "What are you talking about?"

"The thing. On your hand."

"Oh, that. Riley and I got married."

The room falls silent.

"Are you kidding?" MacGregor's quiet voice echoes through the room. His deadly calm face does little to lessen his intensity, his ice-blue eyes boring into me.

"Why would I joke about this?" I glance at my teammates, but they all look as confused as our captain.

"Do you even know this woman?"

"I know she was awarded custody of my child, and I have to sue the state for her to be mine," I finally say. "I also know social services is trying to take her away from me, and if I have to marry a complete stranger to keep my kid, I will. I did. I'll do anything for Emmy."

"But she's your baby mama's sister," Mitchell says.

"And?"

"Isn't that… weird?"

"Not for us." I'm firm about that. "Marriage doesn't have to be all about love and rainbows. It's a business transaction."

MacGregor shakes his head. "That's sad."

Fists clenching at my sides, I turn on him. "What does that mean?" I would never take a swing at him, but I still don't have to stand here and tolerate his accusations.

He doesn't know half of what I'm dealing with. The doubts running through my head at all hours of the day. He's saying my inside thoughts out loud. It's not what I wanted for myself, but it's the hand I've been dealt. Now I have to live with it. I don't need him calling me out.

"Marriage should be about spending your life with someone who makes you happy. It should mean something," he says. "Sure, there are business deals and political alliances that happen behind closed doors, but that's not what it should be about."

"Who knew you were a romantic?" I throw a nearby towel at him. "This works for me. It works for us."

But hours later, as I take my seat on the team plane, I whip out my phone and pull up my messages with Riley. It's all fairly straightforward. Everything is about Emmy or the house. The day the maid comes, when Tyler will drop off the prepared meals, when I'll be back.

She doesn't share anything personal. Neither do I.

And for some reason, that leaves me feeling hollow. We're married on paper, but we don't act like a married couple. We don't do anything together, like ships passing in the night, trading the baby back and forth between us.

Until MacGregor brought it up, I tried not to let it bother me. Doubts are one thing; regrets are another. Now, it's the only thing I can think about. For so long, all I've wanted is a family, someone to come home to. And boom, now I've got it. But it's not at all what I thought it would be. I like belonging to someone. I like knowing someone belongs to me. That we're a unit, however it happened.

And even though I'm surrounded by teammates, I go home to Emmy and Riley, and I'm still lonely. I never thought I could be so alone when I'm constantly around people.

Something has to change. *I* have to change. I need to do something.

The flight is only an hour and a half, but by the time we deplane, grab our bags, and I drive home, it's past midnight. Riley should be asleep, so I'll have to talk to her in the morning.

But when I walk in the door, her light is on, and I find her in Emmy's room, changing her.

"Hey," I whisper so I don't spook her.

Riley looks up, exhaustion etched into her face. "Hey. How was the game?"

Part of me is disappointed she didn't watch. But I've never asked her to. It didn't occur to me until just now that it's something I need.

I want my wife to care about me. I want her to show an

interest in the things that are important to me, beyond our daughter.

"We won. I scored a goal." I lean against the door, my gaze raking over her body. Dark circles crease under her eyes, and she's wearing sweats and a baggy shirt, her hair tied up in a messy ponytail. I wonder what would happen if I pulled the hair tie out, letting her waves cascade around her shoulders. She looks gorgeous with her hair down. She also looks gorgeous with her hair up. Basically, she looks gorgeous all the time, even when she's exhausted.

She'd probably slap me, though. They taught us in kindergarten not to pull pigtails, but still, I haven't learned. My fingers twitch, and I shove them into my pockets so I don't inadvertently reach out. It's really inconvenient being attracted to my wife.

"Nice." She grins, then zips Emmy's pajamas closed.

The baby lolls her head to the side, and when she sees me, she lets out a happy shriek, going from snoozy to wide awake in an instant. Her smile spurs one of my own, and my heart pangs. I love this little girl so fucking much.

"I guess it's my turn," I laugh. I discard my suit jacket, then roll up my sleeves. "Gimme my girl."

"I'll grab her bottle," Riley says. She shoves Emmy into my arms and practically bolts from the room.

"Guess it's just you and me, then, kiddo," I murmur to my daughter as I settle in the gliding chair. "You like me, don't you?"

Emmy grabs at my beard, rubbing her hands against me. She kicks her feet and squeals, happy as can be.

"I missed you, little one. Did you miss me?"

She doesn't answer me, of course.

"We're going to have to do something about your mommy. I need her to like me. What do you think I should do?"

Because Riley *is* her mother now. She may not have given

birth to her, but in the month since Carter passed, she's stepped up and parented her expertly. And now that we're married, Emmy is technically her stepdaughter.

It feels right, calling Riley her mother. Now I have to convince her to accept the title.

She returns with the bottle, and as I feed my baby, I feel Riley's eyes burning into me from the threshold.

"You have perfect timing," she says around a yawn. "She's been waking up at this time every night. It's like she knows you're on your way home."

"I'm sorry."

She waves it off. "I know it's her system. She doesn't actually realize yet."

Especially since I can get home at different times. After a home game, I'm usually back by eleven, but when we're flying back, we get in at all times of the night. Sometimes after dawn if we're coming back from the Midwest or West Coast. Every once in a while, we fly in the daytime rather than after a game, but not too often. The team would rather we sleep on the plane than in another hotel and waste a day.

She looks dead on her feet, her eyes struggling to stay open.

"I'm home now. You're off duty. Go get some rest."

Her nod is brisk. "Got it. Goodnight."

My stomach twists, knowing I pissed her off. That wasn't my intention.

"Riley."

She turns back, her hand on the doorjamb. "Yeah?"

"I'm home for the next few days. What do you think about going to the children's museum?"

Her frown makes my stomach clench. "She's a little young for something like that. She won't be able to see much beyond the stroller."

"Oh. I hadn't thought of that." It's clear I'm in over my head.

"Maybe you can take her to the Common," she says. "She'll like the duck statues."

"Great idea. They dress them up for winter. It's pretty cute." One of my earliest childhood memories is trying to ride the duck. I was maybe three or four and didn't understand why it wouldn't move.

"That sounds nice."

"Will you come with us?" I hold my breath, then exhale. "It would be nice to do something as a family."

She bites her lip. "You sure you want me to come with you?"

"Yeah. I want you there."

I may not be able to verbalize the chaos on my mind, but I can show her I'm serious. That I'm in this.

Riley stares at me in the dark room, her gaze pinning me to the spot.

"All right," she finally says. "We can go."

twelve

. . .

Riley

A MAN in a Boston Grizzlies hoodie stops us in the middle of the Common. "Gonzo!"

Al slows his pace, offering a friendly smile to him. "Hey!"

I wish I could say this is a surprise, but after the third stranger accosted us, I stopped keeping track. We can't go more than a few feet before someone else approaches us. Al isn't wearing any identifying apparel, so how these people recognize him is beyond me. On TV, he simply looks like a beard and a helmet.

Every single person, he gives them his undivided attention. Not once has he said to leave us alone. He treats them like they're special, like they *deserve* access to him at all times. Doesn't he want a break? It's his day off. He should be allowed to have downtime.

He chats with the fan, his eyes flicking down to Emmy every few moments. Always watching, always protective. She's content in her stroller, surrounded by warm blankets. A chilly breeze kicks up, the wind rustling through the trees. In typical Emmy fashion, she jerks her feet, dislodging her blanket and a tiny bootie. Without pausing his conversation,

Al reaches into the stroller and fits the shoe back onto her foot.

Why is him being a competent, caring father so charming?

"I didn't know you had a kid," the man says. He glances down into the stroller. "Hi, baby."

"Yep," Al clips out, his tone a tad strained. "We try to keep her out of the spotlight."

The stranger looks between us, no doubt wondering who I am. I guess he presumes I'm the baby's mother, which makes me uncomfortable.

For all intents and purposes, I am now. But Carter was her mom. And she'll never get the chance to know her.

Emmy wails, and Al gives a forced laugh. Maybe he doesn't like interacting with his fans, either. "Gotta take care of this. Nice meeting you, man."

The fan waves as we walk away, and after a few paces of movement, Emmy calms down. She sucks on her fists with a serious expression, her brown eyes trained on her father.

"You're certainly popular," I comment blandly while we make our second loop of the park.

"Part of the job." He steers us to a nearby bench, then pulls Emmy from the stroller, wrapping her in his arms. Giggling, she smacks her sticky hands on his cheeks, and he grins. "Do you know why they call me Gonzo?"

"I'm guessing because your last name is Gonzales."

"Nope. Because I look like a Muppet." A short, sarcastic laugh rumbles from his throat. "I've got the eyes and nose of a puppet. That, and when I was younger, I flopped around on the ice."

I grin. "I like your eyes." They look just like Emmy's.

"But not my nose?" He glances at me out of the corner of his eyes, his mouth twitching.

"I mean…"

His bark of laughter makes me giggle, filling me with a

sudden burst of joy. But I wasn't lying. He has a big, honking nose that's clearly been broken more than once.

He sets an arm on the park bench behind me, his body radiating warmth. I scoot a little closer, trying to steal some of his heat.

"Cold?" he murmurs.

"Just a bit."

His arm slips from the bench to curl around me, tugging me into his side. The familiar scent of his soap washes over me, making my gut clench and my heart skip a beat. *That's a weird reaction to have.* Maybe I'm coming down with something.

Emmy squeals, reaching for me, and I pull her onto my lap to give her a snuggle. She looks so cute with her little hat and pink cheeks, even if she did throw her mittens out of the stroller, directly into a puddle.

"She's getting so big." He catches her little fist with his index finger, and the sun glints off the white-gold band he wears. I'm struck by a bolt of possessiveness. He's mine, and I'm his, and we belong to each other. On paper, that is. "It's all happening so fast."

"Yeah, she'll be crawling any day now."

"How are you holding up? Anything I can do?"

I shake my head. "I'm fine."

"I heard Vanessa and Audrey came by. I should have arranged something for you. I'm sorry."

"It's fine. It was nice to be around other adults for a bit."

I don't have a support network here. Outside of Al, I don't have anyone.

His arm tightens around me. "We'll have to find you some new friends."

"You don't need to set up playdates for me."

My scowl makes him laugh. "Noted. Maybe you can try some Mommy and Me meetups? Or Cari can babysit so you can go to Vanessa's book club?"

I'm stuck on the suggestion. "I'm not a mom, though."

Al nudges me. "You are."

"Carter's her mother."

"But you're her *mom*. You're the one doing the work, day in and day out." He pauses. "And technically, she's your step-daughter now. That makes you Mom."

"I hadn't thought of it that way," I admit.

"I don't want to push you into a label you're not comfort-able with. But you belong in those spaces. It's just a matter of whether you want to be there."

"Vanessa was telling me how Sven takes Leo to the pool. I thought that might be fun." Nerves swarm in my stomach, and I bite my lip. "I didn't learn how to swim until I was an adult. I don't want that for her."

"We'll take her," he promises. "We can all go together."

"You want to come with us?" I think of Al shirtless, his ripped, muscular body on display as he treads water with his baby in his arms, and my heart beats a little faster. Is it wrong to wish my husband weren't as gorgeous as he actu-ally is?

"We're a family now," Al says. He catches my gaze, main-taining eye contact. "However this all happened, we're married, we're raising a baby together. We should spend some time together."

"I'm not going to sleep with you."

He laughs. "I'm not propositioning you. The last thing I want is to make you uncomfortable. Nobody has to know what goes on behind closed doors. But it will look odd if we are never seen together."

"I'll think about it," I finally say.

"There's a matinee game on Saturday. Some of the wives and partners bring the kids." His throat works as he swal-lows. "I... I'd like it if Emmy were there."

"Vanessa told me. I wasn't sure if you wanted to go public with... everything." A violent shiver shakes my frame, but with Emmy on my lap, I can't put my hands in my pockets. Hastily, I tuck them under her blankets.

Turning on the bench, Al tucks me further against his side, rubbing his hand over my upper arm to keep me warm.

"To the outside world, you're Emmy's mom," he murmurs. "If you want me to tell the world about Carter, I will. But if you're okay with it, when people start asking, all I want to say is that I've married the mother of my child. Because to me, that's who you are. You're Emmy's mom in both name and act. I can't bring Carter back. All we can do is move forward."

"I don't want to lie to her." My eyes well up with tears when I think of my sister. "I don't want to erase her."

"And when Emmy's old enough, we'll tell her all about Carter. I will never erase her birth mother," he promises. "I'm talking about what we say when this gets out. You and me."

"I thought your agent made a plan?" That was the deal; he makes the plan, and I follow through. There wasn't anything on the brief that I disagreed with, at least not enough to back out of this thing.

"Yeah, but I want to run it by you. It's more than only me impacted now."

"My social media is locked down, I deleted any inappropriate photos, and I'm... well, prepared isn't the right word, but I'm resigned to this. The partner of the hockey player thing."

Al chuckles. "Resigned?"

Shrugging, I pull my coat tighter around me. "I don't want to be famous. I don't want the attention. All I want is Emmy."

"You've got her. Even if—when—we get divorced, you'll still have her." His eyes meet mine. "She's yours as much as she is mine."

I shake my head. "I can't take her away from you."

He nudges me again, my arm lighting up from the contact.

I guess I was colder than I thought. "Guess that means you're stuck with me, then."

"Guess so."

But somehow… that doesn't feel so scary anymore. We've survived the first month of being coparents. Maybe this will work out after all.

Emmy squirms in my arms, trying to take off her booties. When I cover her foot with my hand, she squeals with frustration.

"We should get her inside where it's warm," I say, getting to my feet and settling her in the stroller.

Al takes the handle, pushing her along the path. Emmy babbles at us, tucked into her blankets again. When we get to the car, he gets her into the car seat, then rounds the SUV and opens my door for me.

"Thanks," I mutter, my stomach fluttering.

"Do you want to head home?" he asks. "Or how do you feel about lunch?"

"I could eat. I brought a bottle and a pouch for her." Glancing in the rearview mirror, I find she's content in the back seat. "I'm game if you are."

The grin he sends me makes my heart thump loudly in my chest, so I focus on the road ahead. I can *not* have a crush on my husband. No. That's against the rules. Nothing can ever happen between us. I can't go back on our deal.

Al shifts the car into gear. "I know just the place."

thirteen

. . .

Al

AFTER PRACTICE, Coach Turner calls me into his office. With lightning speed, I shower and change into a pair of athletic shorts and a quick-dry shirt with the team logo before knocking.

"What can I do for you, Coach?"

"Sit down and close the door," he says, looking up from his computer with a frown.

As I take a seat, I fold my hands in my lap, my thumb running over the ring on my finger. The second I was out of the shower, I put it back on. I feel naked when I'm not wearing it.

"You've had a lot of changes lately. How are you holding up?"

My announcement—both of them—must have reached his ears. I'm certainly not trying to hide either Riley or Emmy.

"I'm fine."

"Not distracted?" He studies me.

"I'm on a points streak, the second longest in my career."

"Hmm."

"I'm good, Coach."

He picks up his tablet, tapping on the screen, before he hands it to me.

"There's a Grizzlies Foundation gala next week. You need to bring your *wife*."

"Right." I glance at the photo on the screen. It's me and Riley on the park bench, my arm around her as she holds Emmy. We look… like a family. Like we belong together.

After our walk in the park, we went to a nearby bistro. It's one of only a handful of meals Riley and I have shared. Emmy fell asleep in her stroller, so we didn't have to rush home, and our quick meal turned into a leisurely two-hour conversation. I can't deny it felt nice to sit in public with my wife like all the other guys do, chatting and relaxing.

Coach scowls at me. "I don't care if this is a business deal or if it's the real thing. There will be fans at this event, and they're paying a thousand dollars a plate to see you. It's got to look real."

"Got it."

We were already planning on her bringing Emmy for her first game… I guess now we've got a doubleheader. Two public appearances in one weekend.

Passing the tablet back to him, I lift my chin and meet his eyes. "Anything else?"

"Dismissed."

I head back to the players' lounge, where most of the guys are hanging out. Stomach growling, I grab a plate from the stack and fill it from the chafing dishes laid out, then settle at a table with Mitchell, Jenkins, and Logan.

"Where's your shadow?" I ask Logan, and he scowls.

"MacGregor's getting treatment with Amelia."

They're usually attached at the hip. During practice, they're on separate squads, but they sit side by side on every bus and plane ride, and they spend all their time together.

I chuckle. "But you knew who I was talking about."

"Fuck off," he says, rolling his eyes to take the heat out of the words.

"Are you and Hailey finally going to tie the knot?"

He's been dating MacGregor's sister since last winter. They're disgusting together.

Logan cocks his head. "You seem oddly invested in my life today."

"Nah. Just wondering when you're going to join the ranks of the married men. The grass is greener, my friend."

Mitchell laughs. "You fucked your wife yet?"

It's my turn to scowl. "Fuck off."

"You might be married on paper, but it's not a *real* marriage," he says.

"You ever been married?" Jenkins asks him.

"Nope. Came close, but we called it off." He shrugs. "It's for the best. She hooked up with my teammate, and I can't be sure the timelines didn't overlap. Last I heard, they have three or four kids and split up six months after he retired."

"They split up? With little kids?" I can't imagine that. Sure, it's better to be alone than be miserable in a relationship, but I can't imagine only being with my kid part-time. I already get so few moments with her as it is.

"She wanted to be a WAG. She didn't care which guy she had to screw to get a ring." Mitchell scowls. "Watch out for your girl. She might not want to be a WAG now, but they all want that lifestyle, and they'll do anything to keep it."

"Riley's not like that."

He grunts. "If you say so."

"She's not," I say firmly.

"Hailey's not interested in being a WAG, either," Logan says.

"That's because she's family," Jenkins says. "She's basically been one all this time."

He's a few years younger than me, and in the year and a

few months I've been with the team, he's gone through four or five girlfriends. They're all the same: tall, blond, super thin, and gorgeous. He clearly has a type, and I'm not about to judge him for it.

Blondes have never done it for me, which is funny, because Carter was blond. I found her social media profile the other day, and although I still don't remember her, a part of me was settled by seeing her face.

She will always be the mother of my child. No matter my residual anger, she's dead, and I can't change that. As sorry as I am for her passing, if she hadn't, I never would have known about Emmy.

Logan kicks me under the table. "You okay, man?"

I nod, turning my attention back to my plate. "I'm fine."

The house is loud with the chaos of twenty-five hockey players, a dozen partners, and five babies.

Riley looks alarmed as Jenkins shows up on our doorstep with a case of beer in one hand and a giant shopping bag in the other.

"What is all this?" she asks.

"This is your baby-slash-wedding shower," he cheers.

She glares at me. "When you said you invited a few people, I thought you meant, like, four. Maybe five. Not… this."

"Relax. I've got it handled." I set my arm around her shoulders and steer her into the living room. "Grab a drink, hang out. They want to get to know you."

Spoiler alert: I do not have this handled. We're only forty-five minutes into the party and I'm already crawling out of my skin. Generally, I'm energized being around people, but cramming everyone in my small house was not my best idea.

Luckily, I set up a few folding tables and chairs outside, and even though it's cold as fuck, half the team congregates there. I throw Jenkins's beer into a cooler. Sinclair, Clark, and Schwartz all had the same idea. We have an early game tomorrow, so we can't go *too* crazy.

Inside, Emmy is being passed around like a hot potato, charming everyone who holds her. She's loving the attention, clapping and babbling and showing off her gummy smile with two little teeth.

She's been grumpy as fuck the last few nights, inconsolable, screaming her head off all night long, but as soon as the tooth poked through, she calmed down. I don't like when my princess is upset, and I definitely don't like not being able to soothe her. All she wanted was Riley, and it was a kick in the nuts that I wasn't enough for her.

The doorbell rings again, and I open it to find a woman I don't recognize. She's not accompanied by any of my teammates, and I stare at her, trying to figure out who she is and why she's here. She's carrying a canvas grocery tote with wine bottles sticking out the top. Did someone order more alcohol? The metric fuck-ton we already have should be enough.

"Can I help you?" I finally ask.

"I'm here for the baby shower," she says. Her wavy red hair glints in the late-afternoon sunlight. Dressed in a simple sweater and jeans, she's not glammed up like some of the WAGs are. She seems down-to-earth. Normal. But what's she doing here? "Vanessa invited me."

"Right…"

"I promise I'm not a stranger," she says. "I'm Bex Whitney. My brother Wyatt plays for Austin. Van brought me to meet Riley a few weeks ago."

I've played against Whitney over the years, and her having Vanessa's seal of approval is enough to assure me she's not a puck bunny trying to manipulate access to my teammates.

"In that case, come on in."

She passes by me, and to my surprise, Riley hugs her. Good. She could use some friends.

Taking a lap of the party, I check on everyone. The guys are enjoying the onesie decorating station, and although a few designs are definitely inappropriate for a seven-month-old baby to wear, I'm touched they're putting an effort in.

Inside, Emmy starts to fuss, and I scoop her out of Lewis's wife's arms. Rachel is nice enough, but I don't know her well. She's wicked smart, a nuclear physicist. That doesn't mean she can take care of my girl.

"My turn," I announce. "We'll be right back."

Sneaking upstairs, I change Emmy's diaper, but she's still cranky, so I sit in the glider and hold her close.

"Are you done with all the people in your house?" I murmur, running my finger over her downy-soft cheek. She turns her head, drawing my finger into her mouth, and then she *chomps* down on it. "*Fuck.*"

"What did we say about saying *fuck* around the baby?" Riley stands in the doorway with her arms crossed over her chest, looking equal parts amused and peeved.

"She bit me!"

"Your fault for putting your finger in her mouth." She laughs. "She's still fussy?"

"Her mouth probably hurts. I know my finger does."

She smirks. "Bet you won't do that again."

The pinprick of her razor-sharp tooth presses into my skin again, and I wince. "If it makes her feel better…"

Riley rolls her eyes, picking up a teething toy. Warmth shoots up my arm as her hand covers mine and slowly pulls my finger out of Emmy's mouth. My angry little tooth-growing princess throws her head back, ready to scream, before Riley slips the toy into her mouth.

Emmy lets out a grunt, her teeth gnashing into the toy.

"I'm in awe," I confess as Riley lifts her into her arms.

"Had a lot of practice the last few weeks. You done hiding up here?"

"Whose idea was this?" I ask rhetorically.

Her bright blue eyes narrow into slits, and a chill runs down my spine. *Happy wife, happy life,* I remind myself.

"Right. Mine. Sorry."

"You know, if you'd *told* me about this, we could have gone somewhere else to host a party. Somewhere that isn't our house, so we'd have somewhere to escape to," she says. "Why'd they bring so much stuff?"

"Because they're idiots with more money than brains." I force myself out of the glider, otherwise I'll be in it all night. That thing is *comfortable.* "Anything we don't want or need, we'll donate. The only rule I gave them was no Grizzlies merch. The team already gave me everything she'll ever need."

She rolls her eyes, before turning to go down the stairs. "Should I expect a baby hockey toy, then?"

"Oh, like, four of them. And about a thousand stuffed animals."

Her laugh echoes through the stairwell, announcing our return, and our guests turn to look at us. Riley skids to a stop, and I nearly run into her. My hand falls to her waist, steadying myself. The heat of her skin radiates through her simple T-shirt, and my palm itches to touch her bare skin.

That's a weird thought to have about my wife. I've been doing a decent job of tamping down my attraction to her, but I'm terrified one of these days I'll say the wrong thing and make her uncomfortable. Our marriage works because it's a business arrangement, purely platonic; the last thing I want is for her to think I'm pressuring her into taking it to another level. I'm fine with things the way they are. I'm *happy.*

Mostly.

"What's up?" I whisper, as my gut coils with tension.

She shakes her head, walking down the last two steps. After a few moments, chatter resumes as everyone goes back to ignoring us. Riley strides through the party to the kitchen, and I do my best to keep with her rapid pace. Maybe I *should* have asked my wife if inviting everyone over was a good idea. I wanted to make her feel like part of the team, like she's one of us now. They're my family as much as my siblings are.

Riley attempts to make a bottle one-handed. Without asking, I scoop Emmy into my arms, and my wife gives me a whisper of a smile. Maybe she's not as pissed at me as it seems. My heart picks up speed, and I distract myself by dancing with the baby, twirling her around and around while she shrieks with giggles.

"You're good at this," Mitchell says from behind me, and I turn to face him. He's leaning against the wall, arms crossed over his chest. He gives me a nod as he stares at Emmy, an inscrutable expression on his face. "When you said you had a kid you didn't know about, I wasn't sure what to think. Seeing you with her... it's like you were made to be her dad."

Riley hands me the bottle and I adjust my hold on Emmy, tilting her at the right angle. Her little hands clutch at the bottle as she suckles at the plastic nipple.

"Best thing that's ever happened to me," I tell him, my attention stuck on my wife as she puts away the can of formula.

Footsteps announce the arrival of another person, and I turn to see Bex approaching, two empty bottles of wine in her hand.

"Riley, do you have—" She stops, her gaze falling to Mitchell. Anger clouds her face in an instant. "What the hell are you doing here, *Nick*? Why don't you go back to New Orleans and ruin someone else's day?"

"I could ask you the same thing," he snaps, his entire body

coiled with tension. He looks like an animal backed into a corner, ready to lash out and attack to defend himself.

"Fuck you." She hands Riley the empty bottles. "I'm out. See you at the game."

"Coming to watch me play?" Mitchell smirks, his dark eyes bright with a challenge.

"Not on your life." With that, she spins on her heels and stalks out.

I don't miss the way Mitchell's gaze lingers on her ass as she grabs her purse and coat before wrenching open the front door and disappearing.

"What's that about?" Riley asks.

He drains his beer and tosses it into the nearby recycling bin. "Nothing."

"Didn't look like nothing." Raising my eyebrows, I wait for him to elaborate, but he doesn't say anything. "You two have history?"

"Something like that," he mutters. He grabs a bottle of Gatorade off the table, cracking the lid and taking a gulp. "Cute kid. I'm leaving."

"You can't go after Bex. She'll kill you."

"Why would I go after her?" He snorts. "I don't hate myself that much."

Emmy finishes her bottle, and I hoist her onto my shoulder to burp her. Riley tucks a cloth under her face, her fingers brushing the nape of my neck, and a shiver zaps through me.

A few good pats later, Emmy is content again, and I shove her into Mitchell's arms.

"Here, hold the baby," I say. "It'll make you feel better."

His eyes widen with alarm. "I—I can't. I'll drop her."

My hands on his upper back, I steer him into a nearby chair, and he sinks into it automatically. I adjust his hold on Emmy, who giggles with delight at a new face. She claps her hands on his bearded cheeks, and he flinches.

"Feel better?" I ask with a smirk.

There's still a line of tension in his shoulders, but the anger on his face has receded.

"I'm fine," he snaps. Emmy squeals happily and his dark eyes soften. "She is pretty cute."

"She's fucking adorable. Doesn't it make you want one of your own?"

Mitchell laughs. "Yeah, no. Not interested."

fourteen

. . .

Riley

I'VE NEVER BEEN to a hockey game before. Watched it on TV, sure, though not often. We didn't have cable in our apartment, and until Al, I'd never known anyone involved in the sport.

Carter didn't know he was an athlete when they hooked up, and once she got pregnant, she was content to forget the man who'd helped create her child. He was only a guy in a bar. As she said once, his job was done, and she wanted nothing to do with him. It wasn't until she saw his post-trade goodbye video to the Arizona fans that she realized who he was and the implications of his career—and his access to resources we'd never be able to compete with.

Every day, my frustration with my sister increases as I see Al with Emmy, how much he loves her. She robbed him of so much in her selfishness. I understand she was scared, but he had every right to know he had a child, and it wasn't her place to unilaterally cut him from Emmy's life.

But I can't focus on that. Carter is dead. All I can do is move forward.

Vanessa pulls up in her enormous luxury SUV, and I realize with a jolt it's the same one Al bought for me. We settle Emmy in the back seat beside Leo, and both babies let out screeches of delight at having a new friend. When we get to the arena, she waves a pass and parks in the family parking structure with a valet.

"Thanks, Teddy," she says, as a man helps take out both strollers from the trunk.

The man gives me a nod as I get Emmy into her chariot. We even have matching strollers, top of the line from a luxury brand.

Having grown up with everything secondhand, never getting anything new and shiny, I'm glad Emmy doesn't have to know that life. The little princess will be spoiled and I'll enjoy every moment of it.

Vanessa leads me into the arena, the temperature immediately dropping several degrees. I shiver in my puffy down coat. Everyone says the key to staying warm is layers, but as soon as I enter a building with the heat on, I start sweating. How do people deal with this? Life in Arizona didn't prepare me for living in snow country.

Before he left, Al handed me a security badge to allow me into the behind-the-scenes areas. I don't have access to the locker room, but I can go pretty much anywhere else that the general public can't. We show our security badges and are waved through. They rifle through the diaper bag, but we're not limited to the little clear bag policy.

"We'll drop off our stuff and then head down to meet the girls," she says, as we step into an elevator, and she presses the button for the eighth floor.

"I don't know if I'm ready for this," I admit.

She squeezes my arm, and her unwavering support helps soothe my nerves. She's been nothing but kind since the moment we met. "You've got this."

The suite is nothing like I expected. It's huge, with a separate room screened off and a second area with cocktail tables and a bartender before the steps down to the plush leather seats.

A changing table takes up space in the corner, stocked with a ton of supplies, and a playpen sits next to it, with a shelf full of toys beside it. The second room is essentially a parking lot of strollers; there are already four of them.

Following Vanessa's lead, I deposit my things and the diaper bag here, lifting Emmy into my arms. She's still drowsy from the car nap, not quite ready for the day's excitement. I fit the giant earmuffs onto her ears and she whines, but doesn't try to take them off like she did her mittens.

She looks adorable in her little Boston Grizzlies jersey. The back has Al's number and DADDY on the crest. I found little black-and-gold booties to match, and she's wearing a gold headband beneath her earmuffs. I'm in a bedazzled black-and-gold Grizzlies sweatshirt with his name and number. Vanessa has a matching one with Sven's name.

Thank goodness she warned me this would essentially be a fashion show; I was ready to show up in jeans and a hoodie, my hair tied back in a ponytail. Instead, I took the time to do my hair and makeup for the first time in way too long, and I feel almost like myself, if the old me was married to a hockey superstar.

We head down to the ice level, and Vanessa smiles and chats with the people we meet in the hallways. It makes sense; she works for the team, and she's been with Sven for three years, so she knows basically everyone.

Downstairs, we run into Mel Easton and her two kids, and Audrey with her newborn. There are a few other wives and partners I met at the baby-slash-wedding shower, and they nod and smile as they hold their kids up to the ice. The biggest kid is about six, and the littlest one is baby Cora Henry, only two months old.

Vanessa perches Leo on the ledge where the boards connect to the glass, and he gives a squawk of delight, so I do the same with Emmy. Her chubby fists bang on the glass and she throws her head back with giggles.

"It's contagious, isn't it?" Bex says from behind me. I turn to see her standing beside Rachel Lewis, who's hugely pregnant and clutching at her swollen belly while looking miserable.

"What's contagious?" I ask, against my better judgment.

"The baby fever." Bex smirks at me. She's wearing a navy Austin Aces sweater and her wavy red hair is tied up in a sleek bun, tendrils falling loose. "Maybe you'll be next."

"I don't know about that."

That would require me and Al to be more than we are. I like what we have… for the most part. Is it lonely? Yes. Am I going to hook up with my husband because I'm in my feelings? No. I still have to live with the man. I won't ruin our fledging friendship for a fling.

"We can still set you up with someone," Vanessa sings, turning to face Bex with a teasing smirk. "Maybe… Nick Mitchell?"

Bex's cheery smile drops in an instant. "No thanks."

"Come on. You don't know—"

"I do know, actually," she says. "Not going there. Not again."

Vanessa nods. "Okay. You know I love you. I only want what's best for you."

"And reliving the worst mistake of my life is not what's best for me," she says with finality. "Drop it. Please."

"Consider it dropped," Vanessa says. "Come hang out with your godson."

Bex squirms between us, hip-checking the blonde as she reaches for the baby. "Come to Auntie," she says, snuggling him. He goes into her arms willingly, his chubby cheeks pressed into her neck.

"It's the best, isn't it?" I ask.

"Hmm?"

"Baby snuggles."

Bex grins. "Yeah. Especially when I get to give him back at the end."

I laugh. That's what I used to say. I loved playing with Emmy, but I would hand her back to Carter for the diapers and dirty work.

Now, it's all on me. And, well, Al too. But with his practice and game schedule, he's barely home. Eighty percent of the childcare falls to me.

And I'm not complaining. I wouldn't change it for the world. I love Emmy. But I'm also losing sight of who I am as a person. I'm starting to feel like a babysitter and not like *me*.

Who am I? I don't even know anymore.

There's commotion at the other end of the ice, and Emmy squeals and bangs her hands on the glass as men in black and gold skate out of the chute. The players take a few laps of the rink, skating by fast as lightning. I can't find Al, until a figure zooms up to us, skidding to a stop barely a foot from the glass.

He's even taller on his skates, broader from the padding, and his helmet strap hangs loose. With all the gear on, he looks big and imposing, but he's still the same goofy, kind man with a heart of gold. I thought he was good-looking in general, but on the ice... My husband is *hot*.

Emmy screams when she sees him, trying to break through the glass to get to him.

"Hey, baby," he says, pressing his glove against the glass.

I move her hand to his, so they can touch through the inch-thick plexiglass barrier.

The smile that lights up his face nearly brings tears to my eyes. He's so in love with her, and she adores him.

Another player skates up to us, then a second, and before I know it, all the fathers have joined us, saying hello to their children.

Seb Henry, one of the goaltenders, looks comical in his

extra-large padding beside his two-month-old daughter. Sven Larsson is playing peekaboo with Leo, and Mark Easton is waving at his two kids, a huge smile on his face.

Al catches my eye, and his happy grin makes my heart pound. He pokes at the glass, as if he's tickling Emmy in her belly, and she shrieks with giggles. She can't hear anything, not with the ear protection, but he's talking to her as if she can.

With the noise of the arena, I can't quite make out his words, but it almost looks like he's saying *I love you.*

He's talking to Emmy, of course. Not to me. That wouldn't make sense.

Still, my heart aches. The only person who's ever said those words to me is Carter, and now she's gone.

Al raises his eyebrows at me. *Are you okay?* he mouths.

I force a smile onto my face, but I can't fool him. His brown eyes are so expressive, clearly calling me on my bullshit.

The buzzer goes off, signaling the end of warm-ups, and Al lifts his hand, blowing Emmy a kiss. My face heats. What if it were me he was kissing? What if what we had was real?

Vanessa nudges me, and I follow her lead as we head back to the suite. A few of the women have beaten us here, and as I settle Emmy on my lap, Bex sits next to me and hands me a glass of wine.

"You look like you need this," she says with a grin.

"That obvious?" Taking it from her, I purse my lips at the mangoes, pear, and cantaloupe floating in the white wine before taking a sip. Much to my surprise, the flavor is actually pretty decent, and the sharp taste of the alcohol is barely noticeable. I take another, larger drink. This could be as dangerous as jungle juice.

"Hey, you survived. The photos will be adorable."

The blood drains from my face. "Photos? What photos?"

She stares at me. "You mean you didn't notice the team photographer?"

"No..." My eyes fall to my ring. It's simple, an eternity band of small diamonds. Will they wonder why I don't have an engagement ring? Did our interactions look *real* enough? What if the social worker sees the photos and decides I'm a bad influence and not fit to be Emmy's mom?

Bex places her hand on my arm, squeezing. "Breathe. It's okay."

"It's not."

"Everything is fine," she whispers. "Just breathe."

"What if they take Emmy away from me?" My heart breaks just thinking of it, and I hug her tighter, breathing in her sweet baby scent.

"They won't. Nobody's going to take that kid from you," she insists. "You're her mom now."

"I—" My throat feels thick, like I can't swallow. I can't get enough air.

"You're her mom, and Gonzo's her dad, and you guys are married. Nobody is going to take a baby away from her parents, especially not two people who love her as much as you do." Bex squeezes my arm again. "Everything is going to be fine. People bring babies to hockey games every day. Sometimes, they even sit in the stands."

I stare at her, unseeingly. "But what if—"

"You love her, and he loves her, and nobody is mistreating her. There have never been two people who love her as much as you do. Everything is going to be fine."

I want to believe her. I do. But there's something in the pit of my stomach telling me this was a terrible idea.

fifteen

. . .

Al

I SCORED A FUCKING *HAT TRICK*. I haven't managed three goals in a game in the last year and a half. And today, with my kid and my wife in the stands, I was able to score three times. If this is what having my family in attendance will do for me, I need them to show up to every game from now on.

Early-2000s emo music rocks the dressing room as we cool down, shower, and change. The guys are rowdy, pumped up after our win, laughing and joking. I much prefer when the room is like this than the somber air after a loss. Lewis and Henry are dancing like they're in a two-person mosh pit, and Easton is scream-singing to Simple Plan. I'm buoyant like Elphaba, like nothing can drag me down.

"Gonzo, MacGregor, Logan!" Coach calls before I can whip off my shirt. "Media!"

Okay, that might do it.

I salute him before following my teammates to the room where the team holds post-game press conferences. Some reporters will be let into the dressing room for a sound bite, but the formal question-and-answer session is for the full press pool.

I don't particularly enjoy talking to reporters, but I can hold my own... mostly. My agent put me through media training when I first got into the league, and after a few years of doing this, I've got it handled, more or less.

"Gonzo, tell us about your game," asks the hockey writer for the Boston Union. "What was different about tonight?"

"Having my family in the stands, cheering me on," I say honestly. "Seeing them during pregame warm-ups lit a fire under my skates. I think I was showing off a little for them."

Forcing a laugh, I'm gratified when I get a few chuckles in return.

"Sounds like your family will need to be at every game from now on," he says.

"I'll see what I can do." I scratch at my beard with my left hand.

A shout goes through the room. One of the indie blog writers stands up.

"Gonzo, is that a wedding ring?"

I glance at my hand in confusion. "Yes?"

"When did you get married? Who is she?"

Thankfully, my agent prepared a script for me. "My wife enjoys her privacy, and I won't be going into details of our relationship. We were married at the start of the season, and I am incredibly lucky to wake up each day knowing I get to spend the rest of my life with her."

At least for the rest of the next year or two, until Emmy is officially mine and enough time has passed that nobody can comment on our quick divorce.

He opens his mouth, but another reporter beats him to the punch, asking Logan about his diving save in the second and subsequent absence for most of the third period.

Coach catches my eye, and he nods, pleased. A warm glow settles over me at his approval. We survived round one of the inquisition. Now, it's only a matter of how many more.

As the press conference wraps up, we're dismissed back to

the dressing room. I waste no time in stripping down and hopping into the shower. By the time I'm dressed in my suit and out the door to the friends and family suite, I'm late—very late.

The suite is starting to empty as guys retrieve their families. I catch sight of Larsson with Leo and Vanessa, and Easton is giving his kid a piggyback ride.

Riley has her back to me, and I stop in my tracks. She's wearing my name and number. Holy *fuck* is that hot. Hopped up on adrenaline from the game, my cock twitches, and I inhale sharply at the endorphins careening through my system.

I cannot act on this attraction to my wife. No. It's not going to happen.

She turns, and I catch sight of Emmy in her arms. My little princess is crying, soft, snuffling sobs that tug at my heart.

Crossing the room, I set my hand on Riley's back, and she jumps.

"Hey," she says, swaying with the baby. "Good game."

"Thanks." I duck down, kissing her cheek, and her skin heats beneath my lips. "How was the view up here?"

"Eh."

I stare at her. "Eh?"

Riley's cool facade cracks and she bursts into giggles. Instantly, I'm warmed from the inside out, her happiness radiating through the room.

"It was really cool. Now I see what all the fuss is about."

Emmy hiccups, catching my attention, and I reach for my daughter. "Is she still fussy?"

"A little. She doesn't like that I won't let her take off her shoes."

With a chuckle, I kiss Emmy's forehead. "I'm sorry, my princess. Your mommy only wants to protect you."

Heat radiates off her forehead where we're connected, and I frown, pulling away to check out her flushed skin. At first, I chalked it up to her crying fit, but she's calm now and still pink in the cheeks. She slept through the night, the first time since her last tooth broke through.

"What's wrong?" Riley asks, setting her hand on my forearm. Warmth spreads through me at the innocent contact.

"Does her skin feel warm to you?"

"A little. And she's been grumpy..." She runs a finger over the baby's cheek, and when Emmy doesn't even smile, I know something's wrong.

"We need a doctor. Is her pediatrician open today?"

It's a Friday, but it's also a holiday. I don't even know the doctor's name off the top of my head; her number is saved in my phone contacts. Riley knows, though. She took her to a well-baby appointment while I was on a road trip two weeks ago. I wanted to be there, but it's not like I can change the league schedule, and this doctor is in high demand. I only want the best for my girl.

Riley shakes her head. "We can go to urgent care. The pediatrician recommended one for situations like this."

"Okay. Perfect."

Without realizing what I'm doing, I duck down and kiss her. It's just a quick brush of lips, completely innocent.

But when I hear her sharp intake of breath, I know I've messed up.

Fuck.

"Sorry," I mutter, shifting Emmy in my arms. "Let's get out of here."

Heat floods her cheeks and she steps away. I'm kicking myself for ruining this when she comes back with the stroller and diaper bag. Once Emmy is settled, I sling the pink quilted bag over my shoulder and take over pushing the stroller.

A few staff members give us weird looks as we navigate through the arena, but I don't pay them any mind. The only thing I can think of is ruining the fragile friendship Riley and I have.

And tomorrow night we have the gala… I shake my head. Coach will understand if I don't show. Emmy comes first. She has to.

The pediatric urgent care is only a few blocks from the house. I've never noticed the building before. Not that I would've had a reason to. Until now. We rush inside, Emmy sniffling and crying, and I go straight to the front desk. A harried-looking nurse glances up from her computer with a frown.

"Something is wrong with my baby." I shift Emmy in my arms, until she's peeking over my shoulder, but even her favorite position doesn't soothe her.

The nurse's eyes widen. "Did they fall or hit their head?"

"No. She's warm and grumpy and I—something is *wrong*."

Riley sets her hand on my arm, and instantly, some of my panic recedes. I don't know what I'd do without her.

"She's seven months, her last shots were two weeks ago, and she's generally pretty happy. No colic or reflux. This has been going on for less than twelve hours."

The nurse nods. "Fill this out, and someone will be right with you." She hands the clipboard to Riley.

We sit in the crowded waiting room, surrounded by coughing, sneezing, sniffling children. Everyone looks miserable.

"I have a bad feeling about this," I mutter, and Riley chuckles, but her smile doesn't reach her eyes.

"She'll be fine."

It feels like a year before we're called back and shown to an exam room. A nurse in dark purple scrubs takes Emmy's vitals while she screams and screams. Nothing we do can calm her down. She's red in the face, her cheeks streaked with tears as she fights against the nurse.

My own eyes well up. My baby is in pain, she doesn't feel good, and I can't do anything to make her better. I'm *useless*.

Riley answers the nurse's triage questions, which is good, because I wouldn't know the first answer. I've been busy all day with the game; I haven't spent time with Emmy since I left the house at nine o'clock this morning.

For the first time in my life, I think I hate being a hockey player. Especially if it means I can't be there for my kid, for my family.

"I should quit my job," I tell Riley.

She blinks at me. "What are you talking about?"

"I should retire. That way I won't miss out on Emmy's life. I'll be there if she gets hurt or sick."

"You love hockey. It's your life," she says.

"But Emmy is more important."

Her laughter is tinged with mania. "She'll be fine. She probably has a cold. You can't freak out about this."

"I—"

"She's a baby. Kids get sick. They get hurt. It's part of life. You can't put yours on hold. You have to live your life, too."

sixteen

. . .

Riley

SHE HAS A COLD. A stinking cold.

"She'll be fine," Cari says, from where she's sitting on the closed toilet-seat lid.

"Maybe I should stay home…"

"No, you need to go out with Al," my sister-in-law says. I still can't believe I *have* a sister-in-law, much less that she's interested in me and my problems. "His coach already said you have to go. You don't have to be there long, just enough to get photographed."

I make a face in the mirror. "I hate pictures."

"Should have thought of that before you married my stupid brother," she sings.

"I married him for Emmy."

"For better or for worse, right?" She smirks at me. "This is the worse."

"If going to a charity gala is the worst part of being married to him, I think I can get used to this," I admit.

"I'm so glad I don't have to do that anymore."

"What do you mean?" I rake my fingers through my hair, then lift a chunk and wrap it around the curling wand.

"Before you came on the scene, I was Al's date to all the team events."

"Oh. I didn't realize." Does she want to go in my place?

"He didn't want to lead anyone on," Cari says. "It was kind of fun for a little while, but it got old, fast. I love the other wives and partners. Hailey MacGregor is one of my best friends. But I never really fit in. I'm a sibling, not a wife."

"I would hate for you to think now that I'm around, you can't hang out with the team." My eyes meet hers in the mirror. "You are *always* welcome."

"I know. I would have been at the game yesterday if I didn't have practice. I can't believe I missed my niece's first hockey game!" She laughs. "There will be plenty more of them if Al has his way."

"He's already talking about ways we can make it to more games. Maybe he'd get a hat trick every game if we were in the stands."

"So? Are you going to?"

I'm not sure how I feel about it. As much as I want to support him, I don't really want to be in the public eye, and every time I go to a hockey game, I'll be there as *Gonzo's wife* and not me, Riley. The other wives and partners are nice enough, but aside from Vanessa and Audrey, they aren't my friends. More like colleagues; our husbands work together, so in a way, so do we. Even though they added me to the group chat, I still feel like I don't belong there. Like any second now, they'll realize it's all fake and I'm an imposter and they'll kick me out.

On the other hand...

"The games start right at Emmy's bedtime. Maybe when she's bigger and can stay up later." Right now, keeping her on her routine is the priority. She needs stability.

A grin stretches Cari's lips wide, and I'm nearly bowled over by her resemblance to her brother. "Don't let the fans hear you say that."

And just like that, the dread curdles in my stomach again, and I groan.

"What?"

"The fans. They're going to be everywhere tonight."

If tonight is anything like our walk in the park, I'll be standing awkwardly on the sidelines as Al schmoozes with the guests. I know it's part of his job, but I don't want to be relegated to a piece of arm candy.

"Just smile and nod," she states. "They don't care about you. Essentially you're there as window dressing. It's not like you'll actually spend quality time with him."

Blowing out a breath, I grab the last chunk of hair to curl. "This sounds like *so* much fun."

Maybe Vanessa, Audrey, and I can form our own little party with some of the other partners. We can hide out in the corner while the guys do their thing.

She laughs. "It's not. But it is a night out, and you guys haven't had very many of those."

"None, actually."

"See? You need this."

"But Emmy—"

"Will be *fine*," she says again. "She needs to get used to being around other adults. Besides, I've barely gotten to spend any time with my niece with fall conditioning taking up all my time. It'll be good for us to bond a bit."

"If you're sure…"

"You aren't going to scare me off." Cari stands, dusting off her hands. "Now come on. I want to see the dresses he picked out."

"*He* picked out? Or the boutique?"

She grins. "Oh, this was all him."

Al said not to worry about finding something to wear, but I wasn't expecting a rack of gowns to be delivered yesterday while we were at the game. I took one look at the contents and immediately walked away, overwhelmed.

Now, as I flick through the hangers, I find myself wishing I could wear my wedding dress again. I loved the way it made me feel, the way I looked in it.

There are eight dresses on the rack, all in various jewel-toned shades. Maybe he recognized that I typically wear the color profile, or maybe it's just coincidence. They're all boho-chic, upscale versions of the dress I wore to the courthouse.

My hand stops on a lilac dress with a rose-gold overlay. It's nothing like anything I would ever pick out for myself, sleeveless with a very deep V and a high slit, and a heavy material with a tulle overlay. The fabric is frilly and fussy. It looks itchy.

But when I put the hanger up to my chin, imagining myself in this dress, I know I won't be happy until I at least try it on. It will probably be awful. It'll be too tight, or too long, or just… not *right*.

I step into the dress, and to my surprise, the tulle isn't nearly as scratchy as I thought it would be. The hem skims the floor, and when Cari passes me my heels and I slip them on, the gown is the perfect length for my five-foot-four height.

"You look gorgeous," she says, from where she's sitting on the bed behind me.

"I don't know…"

"Gorgeous," she says again.

"It's missing something." I wish I had a necklace, or maybe a bracelet. Something to add a little sparkle. We hired someone to pack up my apartment in Phoenix, and half my things are still in boxes. Including my jewelry and accessories.

Cari vaults off the bed, opening my door and bellowing, "Oye, pendejo!"

I jump at the loud, unexpected noise. Since most of my Spanish consists of ordering off a menu and dirty words, I know she's calling him an asshole, and I grin at the fondness of her tone beneath the volume.

Heavy footsteps sound on the stairs as Al joins us upstairs, Emmy in his arms. He's already wearing his tux, and if I thought I was immune to my husband, I'm quickly corrected. Al is hot. Al in a tuxedo is *holy fuck* hot.

"What do you want, pinche hermanita?" He stops in the doorway, his mouth going slack. His eyes widen and he swallows, hard. "Wow."

I can't deny his reaction sends warmth flooding through me, but it's a bit weird for my platonic husband to be looking at me like he wants to strip me bare and eat me for dinner.

She smacks him on the arm. "Do you have the thing?"

He blinks at her. "The thing?"

"You know, the *thing*." She raises her eyebrows.

"Right. Here, hold the baby."

He thrusts Emmy into her arms, and she coos at her niece, who immediately grabs hold of her hair and tugs. Wincing, Cari settles on the edge of the bed.

"Now, now, be nice to your Tia Cari," she says, extracting her ponytail from the baby's grip. "We're going to have so much fun together, you and me. Aren't we?"

She tickles Emmy's tummy, and the baby lets out a loud, wet fart.

I laugh. "Don't worry. We'll change her before we go."

Al returns in the doorway, a long black velvet box in his hands. Cari lets out a quiet squeal, and he glares at her. "Do you mind?"

"Come on, Emmy, I know when we're not wanted," she teases the baby. She hip-checks her brother on her way out the door.

He shakes his head, a smile twisting his lips, but when I sit to fasten the buckle of my shoe, his smile fades, and he adjusts himself in his pants. I don't know if he's aware of it, or if he's simply not trying to hide it. Knowing he's having a reaction, even if it's purely physical and not emotional, has my heart fluttering a little faster.

"You look… I have no words," he says.

"That bad?"

"That *good.*" The thick column of his throat works, and the bob of his Adam's apple sends heat radiating through me. Why is that so sexy? "I got this for you. I thought you might want to wear it?"

"Is that a question?"

Seeing my big, strong hockey player so unbalanced, so off his game, makes my stomach flutter. *Maybe I'm not the only one in this thing.*

Al takes my hand, pulling me upright. His hand feels right in mine, warm and solid. Even with the help of my heels, I only come up to his chin.

He opens the jewelry box, revealing a large square amethyst on a delicate white-gold chain.

My eyes dart up to his, and he swallows again.

"Do you like it?"

"It's beautiful. I—I can't wear this." Deep in my soul, I know this isn't costume jewelry like everything else I own. This is the real deal.

"It matches your wedding dress." He pulls the necklace out of the box, opening the clasp and drawing it around my neck.

Bowing toward me, he fastens it while holding my hair out of the way. I catch a whiff of his cologne, cedar and firewood, and inhale deeply. Something settles deep within me. The base level of anxiety I didn't even realize was plaguing me soothes into abeyance.

"You ready for this?" His eyes search mine. "Last chance to back out."

As much as I don't want to leave Emmy, especially while she's sick, I know Cari is right; we need to go out together. This is a command performance, and there will be repercussions if we're not in attendance. Al needs me by his side for these types of things. The way he's supported me the last two months, the last thing I want is to make him think I don't have his back, too.

I shake my head. "We're going."

We can do this.

seventeen

. . .

Al

THE BOSTON GRIZZLIES FOUNDATION'S Fall Gala is held in a swanky hotel ballroom in the historic Back Bay neighborhood. Some of my teammates live on this side of town, but even hockey players with our salaries can barely afford to live here.

The thing about these charity events is they're all the same. Sure, they all support worthwhile causes, and yes, it's exciting at the start, but rubbing elbows with the Boston elite is not my idea of a fun time.

These are the same people who look down on me for the part of town I grew up in and the secondhand gear I wore growing up. Between Tony's gymnastics fees, my hockey equipment, and all the sports Cari played, money was tight. My parents worked tirelessly to make sure we could do the things we loved.

And look how it turned out; all three of us became professional athletes. Tony's had a successful decade and a half elite gymnastics career, he's in veterinary school, and he has two Olympic medals to his name. Cari's nascent career is off to a booming start. She competed at the same Olympics as our brother, and nabbed a team gold medal.

I don't begrudge my siblings' medals. I know that in two years, when the Winter Olympics come around, I'll get my shot. I didn't make the team's short list last quad, but I've been working my ass off the last few years to get to where I'm at now. My time will come.

"We can do this," I mutter under my breath, and Riley glances at me with her eyebrows raised.

"What was that?"

"We can do this." I offer her my hand, and when she takes it, warmth floods through my entire system. "We can escape at any time."

"I'm sure it won't be that bad… Right?" She doesn't look certain, though.

"Oh, it'll be hell. But we can do it together."

"We need a code word," she says. "If you're in over your head or need a break, just say… pizza. And I'll find a way to excuse us."

"Fuck, that's brilliant. I could kiss you right now."

She frowns, a little wrinkle forming between her brows, and I want to kiss it away.

"Better not."

My stomach sinks. "Right. We have a good thing going." I already fucked it up by kissing her in the suite yesterday. The last thing we need is to make our working relationship even more awkward.

Riley touches the amethyst around her neck. "Exactly."

Squeezing her hand, I urge her forward, and together we enter the ballroom. It's decorated in black and gold everywhere—the team's colors.

"Do you want a drink?" I ask, as a waiter beelines for us.

"Oh. Yes, please."

We untangle our hands as I take a champagne flute from his tray, her fingertips brushing mine as I pass it over nearly making me slosh the alcohol all over us. I clear my throat as I take a second flute for myself, then my hand finds the small of her back.

"Thank you," she says, offering a smile to the waiter, who nods and moves on. She takes a sip and wrinkles her nose. "I always forget how much I hate champagne."

"There's a bar. I can get you whatever you want."

She laughs. "I don't think a place like this will have jungle juice."

"Hey, if that's what my wife wants…"

Her hand lands on my chest. "I'm kidding. But I won't say no to a vodka Sprite or a rum and Coke. Something sweet so I can't taste the alcohol, but not so sweet I'll get wasted."

"You got it. Let's do a lap, then we'll find our way to the bar."

After we set our still-full champagne flutes down on a nearby table, my hand lands on her back again. The innocent contact grounds me as we join the party.

We've barely made it five feet when a fan accosts us. For some reason, I like the dude-bros who find me on the street better than the slick guys in suits at these types of events. They're authentic in a way these guys are not.

Maybe because if I hadn't made it, I would be one of those dude-bros. Living in my hometown, working my ass off to make ends meet, all so I can play a few games of beer league hockey and watch the matches on my TV.

It's still such a foreign concept to me to have money in my bank account. The two years I played in the AHL, I was lucky to afford rent on the house I shared with five other guys on the team. Once I was called up to the big leagues, I earned the league-minimum salary. It was still above the average salary in Phoenix, but nowhere close to the millions I earn now.

When I signed my big contract last summer, I paid off my parents' house, and they were able to retire with my abuela to Florida and escape the harsh winters. I have enough in the bank to be comfortable, but if my career winds up in the toilet, I'll need to rely on those funds to support my family.

My daughter. My wife.

"Do you have a favorite pizza place around here?" Riley asks the fan, and I startle back to the conversation.

The fan responds with the name of a bougie pizzeria, and I clear my throat.

"It was great chatting with you, man. I need to get my wife a drink. Excuse us."

Grabbing hold of Riley's hand, I lead her away, and she lets out a sigh of relief.

"Sorry I left you hanging," I apologize as we head to the bar—for real, this time. "I got a little overwhelmed."

"You're fine."

I stop in my tracks, turning to face her. "It's not fine. This is my job, and I didn't hold up my end of the bargain. You shouldn't have to—"

"Al." She lays her hand on my arm, and I feel her touch like a brand straight through to my soul. "It was small talk. I can handle that in small quantities. It's fine."

"But—"

"Are you going to do it again?" She raises her eyebrows expectantly.

"No."

"Then it's fine. It won't happen again."

Blowing out a breath, I tug her into a hug before I can recognize what I'm doing. But it feels *right*. Her small body pressed to mine, her soft curves against my hard muscles.

Slowly, her arms come up to wrap around my waist, and I bury my face in her hair. Her perfume, sweet and floral with a woodsy undertone, tickles my nose in the best way possible.

"There you are!" MacGregor's voice calls from behind me. I cling to Riley tighter, not ready to face the music.

My captain claps me on the shoulder. "You can't hide all night."

"Watch me," I mutter. But I disentangle from my wife, immediately reaching for her hand. "You remember MacGregor, right?"

"Aidan," he says, offering his hand for a shake. "Nice to see you again."

"This is some party," Riley says, gesturing at the room.

"My sister's on the foundation board," he boasts. "This event is her baby. They put on three a year, all supporting different causes."

"That's admirable," she says. "It seems like a lot of work."

"We work hard, but we play harder." He winks, and she giggles.

Red-hot ire floods my system. How dare he flirt with my wife right in front of me. My hand curls into a fist, and I take a deep breath.

Before I can do or say anything rash, Riley squeezes my hand. "We were on our way to the bar. Do you want to join us?"

"Sure." MacGregor tips his head in that direction, and the three of us finally reach the drink line without further interruption. "How did you like the game?"

"It was fun. I'd never been before."

I stare at my wife. "To the Grizzlies?"

"To a hockey game. In real life." Her cheeks flush a pretty pink, and I want to know what else I can do to make her blush. "I'm from Arizona, which isn't exactly a hockey hotbed, and it's not like there was a lot of leftover money after bills and everything…"

"We'll fix that," I promise, squeezing her arm. "Any game you want to go to, we'll get you there."

MacGregor laughs. "We get comped tickets to each game," he adds.

I shake my head. "It's not about that. I'll pay full sticker price. What my wife wants, she gets."

Riley's eyes widen. "You don't have to do that."

"I want to." The bartender nods us forward, and I nudge her. "Vodka or rum?"

"Vodka, please."

"Coming right up. A vodka Sprite, and an Old Fashioned." I turn back to MacGregor. "What about you?"

"I'm good," he says, holding up his glass of clear liquid with a lime wedge. He never drinks when we go to the bar after a game, so that he has one now is unexpected.

Unless he's drinking something nonalcoholic. That's an option, too.

The bartender pours our drinks and I stuff some bills into the tip jar before handing Riley her glass. She gives me a shy smile as I knock my glass against hers.

"Cheers."

Taking her first sip, she hums with pleasure, the sound deep in the back of her throat, and I freeze, wondering what else causes her to make that noise. Heat floods my system and I stumble.

"You all right, there?" MacGregor asks, a knowing smirk on his lips.

"Fuck off."

"Hey, look, there's Bex," Riley says, nodding to her friend.

The redhead looks beautiful in a floor-length emerald dress, but there's no comparison. Riley is gorgeous. She outshines every other person at this party. It's like there's a spotlight trained on her, following her around the room. I can't take my eyes off her.

"Let's go say hello." I start after her, but my captain catches my arm, holding me back.

"You like her," he taunts, his voice low.

"Of course I like her. She's my wife."

"No. You *like* her." He waggles his eyebrows. "Anything happen between you two yet?"

"What is this 'yet' business? You know the score as well as I do. That's not what our relationship is about."

"Except you want it to be."

Scowling, I go to shove past him. "Fuck off."

"Hey. Don't blame me for your lack of sealing the deal."

———

By the time we return home, I'm exhausted and emotionally drained from having to interact with so many people. Typically, being around other people energizes me, but all they did was prevent me from spending time with Riley, interrupting and being all needy. Sure, I'm only there to encourage donations. But they didn't have to cockblock me all night.

Not that it was cockblocking, per se. More like conversation blocking.

We send Cari home and both peek in on Emmy, who's fast asleep in her crib. Riley pauses at her door, like she wants to say something, but then she sighs and shakes her head.

"Goodnight."

I want to ask her what's wrong. I need to know what made her sigh. More importantly, I don't want this night to end.

But I don't know how to tell her that without scaring her off.

"Sweet dreams," I murmur, ducking down and kissing her cheek. Her floral shampoo washes over me, settling my nerves deep in my belly.

Her mouth drops open in surprise, her eyes widening. She swallows, the sound loud in the quiet hallway.

"Al..."

"Have a good night."

Wrenching myself away, I stumble back, then force myself to walk the three paces to my bedroom door.

I make quick work of undressing. My suit jacket smells like her perfume, light and refreshing, and my cock hardens in my pants. I debate taking a shower to rub one out, but I don't want to wash her scent away.

The soft flannel brushes against my semi as I slip beneath the sheets, and I squeeze the base of my cock, trying to stave off the blood flowing south.

In the room next door, I can hear the squeaky wheels of Riley's dresser drawers stuttering along the tracks, and the soft *thud* of the drawer closing. I wonder what she wears to bed. An oversized T-shirt? Matching pajamas? A satin nightie? Nothing at all?

I can't be thinking of my wife this way.

She looked drop-dead gorgeous tonight. The way the dress I picked out clung to her curves, my necklace shining in the hollow of her throat, my ring on her finger… I was battling a semi most of the evening, and every time she touched my arm or held my hand, it took everything in me not to lean over and kiss her.

I wish I had. Wish I'd given in to the urges running rampant through me.

My cock throbs, and I might not be able to act on them in real life, but I can indulge in the fantasies in my mind. I give myself a firm stroke from root to tip, pleasure coiling deep in my gut.

We look good together. Our relationship works well as it is. We don't need to change anything.

Even if I desperately want to.

In the next room, the old wooden bedframe creaks, the muted noise barely audible. Riley is in her bed only a few feet away. What if she came into mine? Knocked on my door, crawled into bed beside me, and wrapped her lips around my cock?

I'm rock hard now, and I reach for the lube in my bedside drawer. Can she hear me now? I stroke myself faster, fucking up into my fist. Every sense is heightened, my skin covered in goose bumps. Each breath I take punches from my lungs.

As I touch myself, I think of the way Riley felt in my arms. She fits perfectly against me, as if she were made for me, or maybe I was made for her. My hand moves faster, sensation hurtling through me while I twist my wrist at the head. Sticky precum trails down my shaft, and my gut tightens.

My wife. *Mine.*

I bite my fist to keep from making a sound as pleasure washes over me. Cum fills my palm, and I stroke myself through my orgasm, lightning aftershocks making my thighs tingle.

Breathing hard, I sink back onto my pillows. Did I really just do that? Did I cross eight thousand boundaries by getting myself off to the thought of my wife?

After a few minutes, the stickiness in my hand prompts me to get out of bed. Quickly, I clean myself up, then crawl naked beneath the sheets. It feels empty. Enormous. I wish Riley were beside me.

But that's never going to happen. It's time I accepted that.

eighteen

. . .

Riley

FANCY GALAS BY NIGHT, spit-up by day. The glamour of my life never ceases to amaze me.

Emmy has been miserable for the last week. All she wants is to lie on top of me, and most of the time, she coughs directly into my mouth. It's lucky I'm not a germaphobe, because it would be enough for me to nope out of this.

But when I glance down at the baby sleeping fitfully on my chest, I know I'll do anything for her. Even if she gives me her germs.

I run my hand over her back, trying to soothe her in slumber. She shifts, the congestion turning her snuffling into rattling snores. Sometimes I have to pinch myself and remember this is my seven-month-old daughter and not a seventy-year-old man sawing logs.

The doorbell rings, and Emmy startles awake, letting out a blood-curdling scream directly into my ear.

"It's okay, baby," I murmur as I force myself to my feet. "You're okay."

She continues to shriek as I head downstairs, opening the door to reveal Joanne, the social services worker who haunts my nightmares.

My blood runs cold. This is it. Is she here to take away my baby?

"Can I come in?" It's not a question.

Hugging Emmy to my chest, I step back to allow her entrance.

"I received a report of an urgent-care visit," she says, getting right into it. "Do you want to tell me what happened?"

"She has a cold, but we thought… we were concerned it might be something worse," I admit. Fire licks at my burning cheeks, remembering the way the nurses talked down to us. "First-time parents, you know? Her doctor's office was closed and we didn't know what to do."

I can laugh at it now, but I don't think I can forget that initial panic. Emmy's never been sick like that before. And Al's anxiety only ramped up mine. Now that she's doing better, I can look back with a clear head and recognize all the things we'll do differently next time she's sick.

Because if one thing's for certain, she will get sick again. Kids are like human petri dishes, constantly passing germs back and forth.

Joanne nods, making a note on her clipboard. "Better to get it checked out than have it be something more severe. You did the right thing."

My jaw drops. "Really?"

"Yes. We have to investigate, but this shouldn't impact Mr. Gonzales's custody petition." Her eyes narrow. "That is, if you'd still like to give up custody?"

"I'm not giving up anything. He's her biological father, and I'm his wife. We're raising her together—as a family."

To my surprise, Joanne nods. "Very good."

Confusion muddies my brain, and I stare at her, slack-jawed. "Are you serious?"

What happened to the hard-ass I met that first day?

"The department's goal is reunification with the biological

parent if safe and healthy. You and Mr. Gonzales seem to have a good balance here." She glances at Emmy, snuffling fitfully, then back at her clipboard. "I do have a few questions for you."

"Yes, please, sit."

Emmy whines as I move to the armchair, but as I situate her on my chest, she falls back asleep.

"You said she has a cold?"

"It's been about a week, and she refuses to sleep unless it's a contact nap." I give a self-deprecating chuckle. "Luckily, I don't have anything to do today." *Or at all this week.*

"And Mr. Gonzales?"

"He's away on a road trip, but he'll be back tomorrow night."

He played Dallas last night, or maybe it was Austin. I know it was one of the Texas teams, followed by the other. And then today he's over to New Orleans before he finally comes home.

"And until then, you're alone with the baby?" She raises her eyebrows.

"I have my sister-in-law and a few friends I can contact, and I have her pediatrician on speed dial. I'm nap trapped, but I don't have anything else I need to do other than take care of her."

"No dishes, no laundry?" Her tone is sharp with judgment, and it takes everything in me not to snap back at her.

"I have a baby wrap I put her in, so she's in her carrier as I vacuum or wash dishes, and I do the laundry once she's in her crib for the night."

Baby wearing is safe and good for her, helping her with neck control, but it's also good for me; it strengthens my core, and it gives me my hands back.

I don't mention the housekeeper, who comes twice a week, or Tyler, the private chef who drops off our dietitian-planned meals. I don't want her to think I'm flaunting Al's money, or that I married him for it. Even though I still make a few things for myself and some solids for Emmy, most of my meals are prepared. I didn't realize how much mental energy meal planning and preparation took until it was suddenly off my plate.

"Socializing?"

"We do playdates once or twice a week, and when she's not sick, we go to the park almost every day if the weather is nice. In a few weeks, we start swim lessons."

"Good." Joanne nods. "Water safety is important for children of all ages."

My heart beats a little faster. Is she… approving? What the hell kind of *Freaky Friday* shit is this?

"I didn't learn to swim until I was an adult, so I want to make sure she's comfortable with it. And some of our friends go to a baby swim class, so it's a good way to continue socializing her."

The social worker nods. "Is she eating?"

"Not so much this week, but generally, yes," I report. I'm determined to ace this test. "The doctor says she's meeting all her milestones, and they're happy with her growth. It was touch and go when she cut her first tooth, but the second one was a little easier. And she's growing like a champ. We had to go up a size in diapers. She still hates wearing clothes, though."

The heat is on, warming the house against the winter chill, so she's dressed in only a diaper. Anything more and she screams bloody murder, and given she already feels like crap, I didn't want to fight her. Not on this. We're not leaving the house today; she's fine.

Joanne's pen scratches across the papers on her clipboard. I have a flashback to every overworked social worker I had to deal with in my childhood, and my resolve deepens. Emmy will not know that life. She has two parents who love her.

And yes, I'm including myself as her parent. Al is right;

it's what I am to her. She doesn't know anyone else, not anymore.

My grief for my sister is like a tidal wave, ready to crash into me at any moment. But as each day goes by, it recedes ever so slightly. I'm still grieving, but every day it's a little easier to live without her. To *thrive*. To accept this is my life now.

Emmy lets out a snore, snuggled on my chest, and my heart squeezes tight. It's all for this little girl. Everything she needs, anything she wants, I'll move heaven and earth to give it to her.

Joanne glances up, setting her clipboard aside.

"What happens now?" I ask.

"Mr. Gonzales submitted the DNA sample, and it's still being processed," she says.

The quick test we did in the lab at Harvard was enough to convince him, but not legally acceptable. Our lawyer warned us this could take weeks to be finalized.

"You will continue to have custody until a hearing date is set. At that time, the judge will review the paternity test and determine if he is suitable to be a custodial parent." She pauses. "It helps your case that you are married to the father, that he has been actively involved in her life."

"He's definitely involved. He's devoted to her."

"DCFS will need to observe him with the child, since he isn't here today."

"I can get you a copy of his game schedule. I know your visits are supposed to be unscheduled, but perhaps in this case, you can make a slight exception." I wince, her words from the first time we met coming back to haunt me. *No special treatment.*

"Perhaps," Joanne says with a glint in her eye. Maybe that day was just a fluke. We caught her on a bad day, and she's not as heartless as she made it appear.

Her phone rings, and she checks the display with a sigh. Standing, she tucks her clipboard under her arm.

"You're doing a good job, Riley," she says, as if the words pain her. "Keep doing what you're doing."

Emotion clogs my throat, and I swallow down the lump. I didn't know how much I needed to hear that—especially from *her*.

"Thank you," I whisper.

"Take care, now. I'll be back soon."

Somehow, this time, it doesn't feel like a threat so much as a promise.

nineteen

. . .

Al

THE TEAM JET has never felt more like a prison than it does right now. We're somewhere over the Carolinas or Virginia, and home feels impossibly far away.

"Will you shut up?" Larsson snaps, after I sigh for the fourth time in about five minutes. He's across the aisle from me, sitting by himself since Vanessa didn't make the trip.

"Sorry," I mutter.

"We all want to get home. You aren't making it happen any quicker."

"How do you do it?"

He cocks his head at me, taking off his headphones. "Do what?"

"Being away from your family. Constantly on the road, and then never getting to spend enough time with them when you're home?"

"It's the job," he says slowly. "I like when Vanessa joins us on the road, even though we both miss Leo. But when she stays in Boston, it makes coming home to her that much better."

"I just—I feel like I'm crawling out of my skin. DCFS came by today and—"

Larsson frowns.

"Social services. Because I'm not on the birth certificate, everything is complicated, and…" I sigh again. "I just want my kid to be *mine*. I don't want this constant threat looming over our shoulders."

"It will all resolve soon." His tone is firm. Sure. Like there's not a single doubt in his mind.

If only I could be as trusting.

"But you don't *know* that. They could decide my job means I can't be there for her, or—"

"It will resolve," he repeats. "Will it be difficult? Perhaps. You can get through it. You *will* get through it. Because the alternative…"

"She's my kid. *Mine.* And yeah, maybe the way I found out was a bit unconventional, but I wouldn't trade her for the world."

"You won't have to." Larsson nods, way more confident than I am. "If we have to get team lawyers on it, we will. If we have to go to public goodwill, we will."

"I don't want to air my dirty laundry in public." The last thing I want is Emmy growing up to find her birth mother's name dragged through the mud online. That kind of drama sticks around. No matter how deeply it gets buried, it will always resurface eventually.

"You won't have to. It will all work out."

"I want to believe you. I just…"

"If you don't trust yourself, trust in Riley. She won't let anything happen to your child. She loves her as much as you do."

I'm not sure if he's ever spoken to Riley one on one, but given she and Vanessa are close, it wouldn't surprise me if he were privy to more of the gossip than I am.

Larsson has opened up considerably since I've joined the team, but he still keeps to himself a lot. Outside of Andrews, our equipment manager, and Logan and MacGregor, he doesn't socialize with most of the guys. He's not antisocial, just autistic. On the ice, he's laser-focused, and off it, he keeps it hockey related or talks about Vanessa. It's rare he engages in conversation like this. Since Leo was born, he's definitely come out of his shell a bit more.

"Thanks, man." I reach over to clap his shoulder, then think better of it. He's touch averse, and after he was nice enough to talk me off a ledge, I'd hate to turn around and make him uncomfortable.

He nods, lifting his headphones over his ears again. I guess he's done being supportive.

I try to nap, but sleep eludes me. My skin itches everywhere, all at once, but I know it's not an allergic reaction. I merely want to get home to my girls.

Both of them.

When we finally land, I'm the first off the plane, but of course my luggage is the last to be unloaded. I'm half tempted to leave my suitcase there.

The thirty-mile drive home usually takes me a good forty-five minutes, but tonight, I make it in just under half an hour. I park my car behind Riley's and unclench my hands from around the steering wheel.

She's probably asleep. Both of them. It's close to four o'clock in the morning.

But when I go inside, I find the upstairs hall light on. Riley's door is open, but she's not inside.

I poke my head into Emmy's room, and my heart nearly thumps out of my chest at the sight of my girls. My daughter is lying on Riley's chest, her breathing steadier than it was when I left.

Lifting Emmy into my arms, I hold my breath, but relax when she doesn't stir. Riley does, though.

"Hmm?" Her lashes flutter open, and she relaxes when she catches sight of me. Her sleepy smile makes me grin. "You're home."

"Come to bed," I whisper, trying not to startle either of them.

"But—she'll wake up."

"I've got her. Come lie down."

Offering my hand, I'm gratified when she takes it, and I lace our fingers together. I lead her into my room, and Riley blinks a few times, even as she follows me. She's wearing a pair of sweatpants and one of my Grizzlies T-shirts, and I have to admit, I like the sight of her in my clothes. Maybe a little too much.

"You want me to stay in here?" Her sleepy expression is adorably confused.

"We can all stay here together."

"Co-sleeping isn't safe. We could crush her."

I set Emmy down in the bassinet beside my bed. We don't use it very often, usually she's in her crib in her own room, but right now I'm glad we have it. She's close enough we can check on her, but she won't be in the bed with us. Hopefully, she'll sleep for another few hours.

"She'll be fine. And we'll be right here if she wakes up."

Stripping off my coat and suit jacket, I toss them to the side. Riley stands at the end of my bed, tracking my hands while I unbutton my shirt. Her gaze sears into me like a brand, and my cock pulses, enjoying the frank appreciation on her face.

Discarding my shirt, I work at my belt and then unceremoniously shove my suit pants down, almost forgetting to take off my shoes. Once I've gotten rid of them, plus my socks, I climb into the bed in my boxer briefs.

"Come lie with me," I say again, softer this time.

As I reach out my hand, Riley rounds the bed, pulling back the covers and sliding in beside me.

"Hi," she whispers, rolling onto her side to face me.

"Hi," I murmur back.

Before I know what I'm doing, I cup her cheek and lower

my mouth to hers. It's an innocent kiss, a simple brush of lips against lips. It's not meant to be sexual; I'm not trying to start anything.

I just needed to kiss her. I do it again, and she gasps.

"What are you doing?" she breathes.

But she doesn't pull away. Instead, her hand wraps around my wrist, clinging to me.

"I don't know."

It feels right, though.

She pulls away first. "It's late. You should get some sleep." She rolls over, putting her back to me. But then she scoots closer, pulling my arm around her waist. Her lopsided pony-tail brushes against my face, and the scent of her lavender shampoo fills my nose. I finally feel at ease. Settled.

Her body was made for mine. *Fuck*, her soft curves feel so good pressed to me, but I tamp down my baser urges and indulge in the simple pleasure of holding her. I didn't realize how much I needed to have her in my arms until now.

I want more than a marriage of convenience. I want something real. We're married, and for better or for worse, we're stuck together.

And now I know what I have to do: I have to woo my wife.

She lets out a soft moan, melting into me, and I place a gentle kiss on her nape. My last thought, before I finally drift off to sleep, is that I could get used to this.

twenty

. . .

Riley

I WAKE UP DISORIENTED. There's someone beside me in the bed, and I am most definitely not in my room. It's been a long time since I've slept next to anyone, much less a man, but as I glance over my shoulder at Al's sleep-slackened face, I'm starting to forget why it's such a bad idea.

A rustling sounds from across the room, and I force myself out of bed. Emmy is awake in her bassinet, kicking her feet and grinning.

Rubbing my tired eyes, I yawn, then lift my baby into my arms and give her a snuggle. She's trapped in her sleep sack, her sweet baby scent eclipsed by the stench of a soiled diaper.

Okay. First things first.

"Let's leave your daddy to sleep a bit longer," I whisper to her as I carry her into her room. A few minutes later, I leave her in the crib, freshly changed and dressed in a pink onesie, as I brush my teeth, wash my face, and fix my ponytail.

Fuck, I look wrecked. I'm amazed she let us sleep as late as she did, and that she slept on her own for the first time in the better part of two weeks. Maybe she's finally turning the corner of this thing.

Once we're settled downstairs, I prepare a bottle, and

we curl up on the couch. My mind drifts to last night—or was it early this morning? I don't know what possessed Al to bring me to his bed, to kiss me and hold me all night long.

But I can't deny I liked it.

"What am I supposed to do?"

Of course, Emmy doesn't answer me. She's a baby. She can't talk yet.

After settling her in her bouncer, I clean the bottle, wipe down the counters, and sweep the floor. I don't know what to do. It's weird going about my everyday life while Al's upstairs sleeping.

It doesn't last long, though, because a little past eight, he stumbles down the stairs. Considering he didn't get home until nearly four, I have no idea how he's upright.

"Morning," he says, his voice deep and rumbly from sleep.

"Good morning. Did you sleep well?" There, that sounded normal. Totally normal.

"Like a rock." He ducks down and kisses Emmy on the forehead, chucking her chin, before he crosses the room to where I'm standing. His arm snakes around my waist, his hand on my hip. Soft lips land on my temple, a fleeting kiss. "How about you?"

Before I can blink, he's squeezing past me into the small galley kitchen, pulling a mug off the rack and pouring himself a cup of coffee.

"I slept mine. I mean, fine."

"Good. You needed the rest."

Hands on my hips, I try to glare at him. "Are you saying I look tired?"

Al pauses, the coffee cup halfway to his mouth. "Uh…"

I can't help it; I laugh, and then Emmy giggles too, which makes me grin.

"I'm fucking exhausted. Those three and a half hours is

the longest she's gone without me having to hold her since you've been gone."

"Well, I'm here now. I'll hold her anytime." But then he winces. "I do have to hit the rink for a bit. We've got the day off, so long as we do our weight training."

"I've got her. It's fine."

I know the score. It's part of the gig.

"I was thinking… maybe we can go to the aquarium after? It might be fun for her. They have a children's pool. She can play with the starfish and splash in the water."

My stomach flips. *We.* He wants to do something together.

"That sounds like fun," I manage.

"Great. I should be home by the time she's waking up from her morning nap." He sips his coffee, his dark eyes on me. "Unless you guys want to come with me and she takes a stroller nap?"

I blink a few times. "You want us to come to the rink?"

"We're just getting in a quick lift. I'll be out in an hour, tops. You can see where I go everyday."

"I've been to the arena."

"The rink is different. It's more… intimate."

"Okay," I find myself agreeing. "Let's go to the rink."

He grins at me, and the happiness on his face makes my stomach clench. He's so fucking beautiful. Maybe it's a weird thought to have about my husband. He's not classically handsome, not with the giant nose that's been broken a few times and the deep set of his hooded eyes. His features are striking, sure. But it's his happy-go-lucky, easygoing personality that makes him beautiful.

We get packed for the rink before he changes Emmy into a warmer outfit, and to both our surprise, she doesn't scream bloody murder when he puts on her booties.

The training facility is in Brighton, and with midmorning traffic, it takes nearly half an hour to get there. I'm still not used to the constant traffic in Boston turning a seven-mile drive into something infinitely longer. I thought Phoenix was bad, but now I know there's no comparison.

Al swipes his team badge through the security gate, finding a parking spot near the entrance since there are only a handful of cars here at this time. He pulls Emmy's stroller from the trunk and settles her in it. As I expected, she passed out as soon as we got in the car, and I drape a lightweight blanket over the top of the stroller. Hopefully, she'll sleep better knowing her dad is nearby. I know I did.

He wheels the stroller through the front doors, stopping at a small security station.

"Steve, this is my wife, Riley. This is Steve. He'll get you authenticated so you can come by without me."

"ID please, ma'am," the guard says.

He's tall and wide, with a shiny bald head damp with sweat. I catch sight of a photo on the desk behind him. He's standing with another man, each of them holding tiny newborns. They look happy.

We don't have any photos of both me and Al with Emmy. I have a bunch of him with her, and plenty more by herself, and I've even taken a few selfies while holding her. But there aren't any of the three of us together. Our family.

Steve types a few things on his computer, then gestures for me to stand in front of his booth. He takes my photo, and two minutes later, I have a brand-new security pass.

"This will get you into both the rink and the arena, so you're good to go," he says.

"Perfect, thank you."

"Welcome to the family." He grins. "We're glad to have you."

"Me too."

Al clears his throat. "We've gotta get going."

"Right. Have a good workout, Gonzo. Riley." Steve salutes us both.

"The administrative offices are in the west wing," Al says

as he pushes the stroller down a hallway. "The rink is on the other side of the building. But we're not skating today."

"That might be fun. I've never done that before." When he stares at me, I add, "Ice skating."

He stops in his tracks. "You've never skated?"

My laugh bounces off the surrounding walls, and I cringe for a second, hoping it won't wake Emmy. "Foster kid in Arizona. Never had the opportunity, and even if I had, it would have cost too much."

"Okay, that's it," he says, grabbing hold of my hand. "We're going to skate."

He turns to the right, leading me down another hallway and into a lounge with couches and several long tables, two pool tables, and a giant TV. He stops to grab a bottle of water, handing it to me.

"Any of the drinks and snacks in here are fair game," he says. "Feel free to watch whatever you want on the TV. I'll be back soon."

"I can't watch you?"

His eyebrows dart up. "You... want to watch me work out?"

Suddenly nervous, I nod. "If that's okay."

"It might be loud. There are probably other guys in there."

"Oh." I hadn't thought of that. "I don't want to be in the way."

"You won't be," he says, steady and sure. "Come on. Let me drop my coat."

We go through another hallway to the dressing room. He opens the door, takes a look around, and then beckons me to follow him.

It's nothing like I pictured.

The locker room almost looks sterile. There's worn linoleum flooring and simple metal lockers lining the walls.

"This is the changing room," Al says. "Our dressing room is through that doorway, but this is where we change out of our street clothes." He hangs up his coat in the first empty locker, adding his scarf and gloves to the pocket. His Grizzlies T-shirt clings to his broad back, and as the muscles of his shoulders and lats bunch and flex, my face warms.

He reaches for me, and it takes me a second to realize he wants my coat, too. When he hangs it beside his, I have to admit I like the sight of them together.

Emmy is still snoozing in her stroller as he leads me through the dressing room, past the bikes and treadmills, and down another hallway to the weight room. Three other players are already inside in the midst of their workouts. Pounding rock music shakes the room, and I peek at the stroller, but she's still fast asleep, clutching her favorite stuffie like a lifeline.

"Hey, Gonzo," Logan says, giving him a nod. "Bring your family to work day?"

"Something like that. You okay with it?"

The defenseman nods, going back to his bicep curls. "Sure. No skin off my back."

"Damn," Henry says. "Wish I'd thought of that. Audrey would probably like it."

Lewis laughs. "No, she wouldn't. She'd like watching *you*."

"Yeah, that's what I meant," the other goaltender says with a smirk.

Al positions us in the corner by a soft mat. He drops beside me and runs through a series of stretches.

I'm not shy about watching him, taking in the graceful way his big body moves. His muscles are hot, yes, but so is the rest of him. He's incredibly fluid on the ice, and off it, he's even more beautiful.

After a few minutes, he gets to his feet. He ducks down, kissing me quickly, and before I can blink or protest, he's across the room at one of the machines. I watch with undisguised interest as his strong body lifts incredibly heavy weights. He grows progressively sweatier, and when he whips off his shirt and his broad, hairy chest is on display, I think I might drool.

Fuck, my husband is hot. And with his new penchant for kissing me, I could be in serious trouble.

Emmy makes a soft snuffling noise, and I peek into the stroller to find her stirring. She sighs, shifting, but I know it's only a matter of time before she wakes up screaming.

I wave goodbye to Al, but he's focused on his workout and doesn't see me. As he should be. He has a job to do.

Pushing Emmy through the halls, I find my way back to the lounge. She's fully awake by the time we get there, and I pull her out and give her a snuggle.

"Who's my perfect girl," I coo, tickling her belly, and she giggles, kicking her feet.

After a quick change and a veggie puree pouch, she's happy as a clam. That's where Al finds us, his hair damp, changed into a new T-shirt and athletic pants. The fresh scent of his soap makes my stomach clench and heat rush through me.

"How're my girls?" He chucks her chin.

I'm caught on his words. *Girls*. Plural.

"We're good," I squeak out.

"Awesome. You ready for that skate?"

"Now?"

"Come on." He offers his hand, and I slide my palm against his, surprised by how right it feels. "It'll be fun."

twenty-one

· · ·

Al

WITH A QUICK TRIP to the gear closet, I get Riley into her skates and ready. Kneeling on the mat between her feet, I keep my focus on tying her laces and not on how vulnerable it is to be in this position.

It's only a family skate. That's all it is. It's not like I'm proposing to her. We're already married.

Henry volunteered to watch Emmy, and since he has a young kid at home, maybe two or three months old, I trust him to do the job well. Normally, he's the first one out the door to get home to baby Cora, but he has a PT session with Amelia in an hour, so he's hanging around the facility for a bit.

That gives us plenty of time. I don't think Riley will want to spend a full hour on the ice, especially not for her first time.

My wife gazes down at me with an inscrutable expression on her face. Equal parts fear and excitement and something else I can't identify.

I could ask her. But that wouldn't be half as much fun as puzzling it out myself.

Rising to my feet, I offer her my hand, and when she takes

it, I lace our fingers together. I lead us over to the gate and Riley freezes, clinging to the half wall.

"Don't let me fall," she whispers.

"I won't."

Stepping onto the ice, I turn to face her and take her other hand, too.

"It's going to feel kind of wobbly. That's okay. That's normal." Skating backward, I pull her along with me until we're at the blue line. "Let me guide you."

"What do I do?" Her voice rises into a squeak on the last word as she teeters on the thin blades. "I don't—oh, *fuck*."

"What's wrong?" I glide to a standstill, but she doesn't stop in time, and the forward momentum crashes her body into mine.

Wrapping my arms around her, I hold her securely, our bodies flush together. The scent of her lavender shampoo makes my stomach clench, and my heart nearly beats out of my chest, my blood pounding in my ears. Her smaller body pressed to mine is making me think thoughts I definitely shouldn't be having about my wife.

My mouth goes dry, and I lick my lips, trying to figure out what the hell is happening. Dressed in a T-shirt instead of full practice gear, I barely register the chill of the rink, my skin heating at her touch where we're connected. My cock hardens automatically at her nearness. At how perfect she feels against me. I've gotten myself off to the thought of her nearly every night since the gala, and now I have a new fantasy to occupy my thoughts.

"I'm on the ice," Riley whispers, letting out a hollow laugh. Her eyes dart up to mine, wide and unfocused. "How is this happening?"

My smile stretches my face. "It's just skating. You'll be doing laps of the place in no time."

She giggles, the sound warming me from my head to my toes. "I don't think so."

Slowly, I unwind my body from around hers. She squeaks, stumbling on her skates, and my hands drop to her hips to steady her. Any excuse to touch her.

"You've got this. I've got *you*."

She exhales slowly. "I can do this."

"Yes, you can."

"Okay. Teach me how to skate."

"Keep your knees bent. Push backward with your left skate," I instruct. "Then do it with the right, and then you'll be moving. Don't think of it like walking, it's a whole different movement."

My hands find hers again, and I hold her at arm's length as she tentatively shuffle-glides her skate backward, propelling her forward.

"Good. Just like that. Now the other foot."

She moves a few inches, and I take a few strides backward, pulling her along with me.

"Keep going."

"And you—"

"I won't let you fall," I promise.

Except if she wants to fall in love with me. That, I wouldn't mind.

Slowly, she gains confidence until she's able to take a few strides on her own. At her nod, I release her hands, and she skates about twenty feet on her own. She picks up speed until she's nearly at the half wall, and—

Oh, fuck, oh, *fuck*, I forgot to teach her how to stop.

Snow flying, I race down the ice and pivot in front of her. She throws her hands up over her face, bracing for impact. She crashes into my chest and I cradle her to me. Burying her face in my chest, she wraps her arms around me. She's shaking, her shoulders heaving.

"I've got you," I murmur into her hair. "You're okay."

Riley breaks into a laugh tinged with hysteria. "What the hell was that?"

"So maybe I'm not the best teacher." I chuckle awkwardly. "I'm sorry."

Pulling back, she stares up at me, studying my face. After a moment, she nods, opening her mouth to say something and then looking away. She seems to remember she's still wrapped around me and leans back, but that sets her off balance, and I clutch her to me again.

"Come on. Let's sit for a bit." I lead her over to the gate, and as she steps off the ice, my eyes fall to her ass in those tight jeans that cling to every curve. Biting my lip, I force my gaze to the back of her hair, pushing the thoughts away.

"So that's ice skating," she drawls.

She settles on the bench and I sit beside her, my hand only an inch from hers. I want to reach over and twine her fingers with mine, but it would be weird while we're just sitting here.

"Yeah? What did you think?"

"Different from what I thought it would be." She hums. "I'll probably be sore tomorrow."

"I can give you a massage," I offer, before I can think better of it.

Riley turns to me, her lips parted in surprise. "What? Why?"

In for a penny, in for a pound.

I meet her stare head-on. "If you're sore, I can give you a massage. Or if you want to schedule one with a professional, I can watch Emmy while you take a few hours for yourself. We can get a babysitter if you want."

Her mouth opens, then closes, and she blinks a few times.

"That's not necessary. I'll be fine." She crosses her arms over her chest, a stubborn set to her jaw.

I shrug, trying to decrease the sudden tension. "Okay. But if you ever want some time to yourself, and I'm not available, we can find a babysitter. Even if all you do is go upstairs and take a nap while they play with Emmy. We can make it happen."

"I'm not going to leave my baby with a random stranger."

Lifting my hands into the air, I back off. "I didn't say anything about a random stranger. We'd vet them. Hell, we could probably ask Cari. As long as she doesn't have training, I'm sure she'd love to come over and raid our fridge."

"I'm not going to ask your sister to watch my baby."

My eyebrows shoot up. "*Your* baby?"

Riley's face pales. "I—I mean, she's your child. She's not *mine*. Not like that."

"Face it, babe, she's your kid, too." Enjoying the shell-shocked look on her face, I nudge her ribs with my elbow. "I *like* that you call her your kid. I'm not a fan of unilateral decisions, though. Let's talk this out. Let's figure out a compromise. You deserve to have a break from all of... this."

"I don't want a break from Emmy."

The finality in her tone has me nodding.

"Okay. We'll table this for now. But we do need to have a list of babysitters on hand for emergencies."

Or date nights.

"We can use Vanessa's nanny. Bridget." She frowns as she says the other woman's name.

"Brigitte," I correct automatically.

Riley blinks. "You know her?"

"Full disclosure, we met for coffee once. It didn't go any farther than that." I shrug. "She probably doesn't hate me, but if she's their nanny, she won't be available when they're out of town and I'm gone."

"Oh. I hadn't thought of that."

My hand falls to her thigh, and before I can second-guess myself, I squeeze her leg. "We'll figure it out. I'm sure someone in the organization knows a good nanny."

Her eyes drop to my hold on her leg, and I quickly pull back.

"Do you want to try another lap? Or are you done?" I nod

to the ice. "We've got another half hour before Henry comes back."

Fierce determination shines through her expression as she squares her shoulders, lifting her chin. "Let's do this."

Taking her by the hand, I lead her back to the ice. I'm expecting her to let go, but to my surprise, she's the one who laces our fingers together while we inch our way around the rink.

Her hand in mine feels good. Right. *She* feels right. Like she belongs in my life.

And I'll spend the rest of my life proving that.

twenty-two

. . .

Riley

THE AQUARIUM WAS a big hit with Al, who looked around the place with wide eyes and a smile on his face. Much less so with Emmy. She was not a fan of the touch tank. As much as she enjoys splashing in the bathtub, she hated every second of the petting pool, and she let everyone know. I think people three miles away could hear her displeasure. My eardrums are *still* ringing.

Back at the house, he takes over the childcare so I can have some time to myself. I don't go far, though. He's curled up on the couch, the baby sprawled on his chest and playing with his beard as he reads books to her, and I settle on the floor beside them to paint my nails. It's something I got out of the habit of doing, but I can't deny the sparkly gold glitter polish makes me happy.

There's laundry that needs doing, and I should probably unload the dishwasher, but sitting here like this—like a *family* —feels so nice. I would never want to intrude on Al's time with Emmy. He includes me, though, and has never made me feel like I'm not welcome.

I just don't know why. I don't belong here, not really. Even with his ring on my finger, I know my role is temporary. As soon as Al's officially on the amended birth certificate and custody has been awarded, we can get divorced. I know he says he won't keep Emmy from me, but he'll have to get bored of being married sooner or later. He's a young, hot, soon-to-be single dad *and* a hockey player. I'm sure he'll have women falling all over themselves to be a mother to his child.

… Kind of like I did.

He might need me right now, while I have temporary custody, but as soon as the ink is dry, I know he'll kick me out. Nobody ever wants to keep me. I can't expect him to be any different.

Emmy sits in her high chair and babbles at him as he feeds her. Most of the time, we let her pick up the food directly from the tray table, but tonight he's making airplane noises as he feeds her a veggie puree with a hot-pink spoon.

All of her toys and accessories are pink. Anything that can come in gendered color profiles, she has the pink version. Even her diaper bag. I didn't pick it, Carter did, and the presents from the team were all pink, too. My personal preference is a more neutral color scheme, but he's never shied away from the pink. If anything, I think he's embraced it more than she has.

"Do you mind handling bath and bedtime tonight?" he asks as he guides the spoon to her mouth. "There's something I've got to take care of."

"Oh. Sure."

I thought he'd like to do it, since he doesn't get to most nights, but it's not surprising he's all babied out. Even on his days off, there's usually practice and other things filling up his time. Today has been all Emmy, all day.

Once her belly is full, I take her upstairs and clean her up. She snuggles close to me, clutching at my arm as I read her stories until she finally drifts off. She doesn't stir when I transfer her into her crib or tiptoe downstairs.

The heady scent of garlic perfumes the air. Tyler's meals

don't typically come with a lot of garlic. Maybe he tried a new recipe?

Dim light shines from above, and candles flicker on nearly every surface, casting a soft, romantic glow throughout the room. I count at least seven dancing flames before a sound from the kitchen draws my attention. Al stands in front of the stove, stirring something in an enormous pot. A bottle of white wine sits on the counter next to two glasses, and he's flipping tortillas on a flat skillet.

"What are you doing?" I ask, and he jumps.

"Shit. I'm not ready." He winces. "I need, like, ten more minutes."

"What is all this?"

"I'm making us dinner. Do you want a drink?"

"I can get it. I mean… this." I wave at the candles, the low lighting. "You have prepared meals from Tyler. Why are you cooking?"

"Felt like it." He shrugs, not looking at me. "Is that a problem?"

"No. Just… unexpected." I take a seat at the kitchen table, my eyes roving over his burly body.

He's wearing a dark blue long-sleeved T-shirt, the sleeves pushed up his thick forearms, and a pair of slutty gray joggers with white socks. Casual, comfortable. Gorgeous. I have to force myself not to stare at the impressive dick-print in the front of his sweats.

Al pulls down two bowls from the cabinet. He dishes brown rice into each one, then adds a generous helping of a green stew and tops them both with avocado slices. He brings them to the table, setting one in front of me, before darting back into the kitchen and returning with a tortilla warmer and a bottle of white wine.

"Would you like a drink?" he asks, lifting the bottle.

"Sure." I'm still not sure what's going on. Wine should help.

He pours us each a glass, then settles across from me at the small Formica table. Our knees brush, and I sit up straight, pulling my legs away.

"Smells good," I say, reaching for my silverware. He's even laid out the little fork alongside the little spoon. How does he know I don't like the big silverware, preferring the little salad fork and dessert spoon? We've only shared a few meals together…

"It's my abuela's recipe. Pollo con chile verde. I did cheat and use store-bought sauce, since it's not tomatillo season."

"I'm surprised your abuela taught you to cook. Don't most grandmothers refuse to let anyone help?"

I never had a grandmother, but that's what I've seen in movies and TV shows; the doting older woman who carries the family on her back. Or the evil witch. There really is no in-between. But with the way Al talks about her, I don't think she's a villain in his origin story.

"Oh, no, she didn't teach me. She would kick me out of the kitchen every time I got close. Boys don't cook in our culture, which is ridiculous," Al says, shaking his head with a frown. "Then I moved out for college, and I could barely make a quesadilla or grilled cheese. I had to learn, quick. When I came home for the summer, I sat at this table and watched as my abuela cooked, and I made her go slow so I could write everything down. When faced with the option of teaching me or letting me starve, she came around quick."

"Tyler makes all your food, though."

"During the season, I don't have the time or energy to cook. Last year, when Tony and Cari still lived here, the three of us would rotate meal prep, but once I connected with Tyler, I switched to his service. It's easier. I miss it sometimes, so now I cook because I want to, not because I have to."

"That makes sense." I spoon some of the chicken, rice, and poblano peppers onto a tortilla with a slice of avocado, and nearly groan at the flavor. "This is delicious."

Al chokes, his cheeks going pink. "Thanks."

"One thing I've definitely missed since being out here is the Mexican food. I haven't been brave enough to try it yet."

Compared to back home, where there was a taco shop or truck on nearly every street corner, it's a pretty big culture shock. There are food trucks here, and there might even be a few Mexican food ones, but I'm so afraid they won't compare. Boston isn't exactly known for having a large Mexican population, and other types of Latin and Central American food don't scratch the same nostalgic itch. As much as I love a good ropa vieja or picadillo, nothing beats the northwestern Mexican food I grew up eating.

"There are some decent places out this way. We should go sometime," he says.

Digging into my bowl, I try to pass off my reddening face as a reaction from the spicy chiles. "That would be nice."

"And of course, anytime you want authentic Mexican food, I can always cook for you." His dark eyes meet mine, his gaze lingering. "Anytime."

"I can't ask you to do that. Not with—"

"Riley," he says, reaching across the table and taking my hand. His thumb traces over the ring on my left hand. "This thing we're doing? We're married. My job is to make you happy. If you want authentic Mexican food, the things I grew up on, I'll make it for you. If you want ten million dollars, I'll do a wire transfer. Whatever you want, it's yours. We're together in this. What's mine is yours."

"But—"

He squeezes my hand. "Whatever you want."

"I want Emmy." Once the words are out, I can't take them back. "When this is over, I don't want to lose her. I don't know what I'd do without her."

"Why are you talking about this ending?" His forehead creases. "Do you want out?"

"No. I'm in this until you're ready. Until the custody is transferred and everything."

"But then you want to end it?" His voice sounds… almost hollow. He looks away, his eyes downcast.

"I mean, don't you? You'll have your pick of women. Puck bunnies are probably already throwing themselves at you, but you'll be free to pursue them. You won't need me."

Al pushes back his chair, rounding the table to kneel in front of me.

"Riley, I need you to listen to me very carefully," he says, taking my hands in his. His thumb strokes over the ring on my finger, and my stomach flutters. "I have no intention of ending this until—*unless*—we both want it. We need to stay married until the paternity is resolved and they won't take Emmy away from me. But I will never, ever take her away from *you*. You are her mom now, and the last thing I want to do is take her away from the person who loves her unconditionally."

"But Carter—"

"Is dead."

I flinch at his harsh delivery.

"I know. I'm sorry. But Carter is gone, and you're the only mother Emmy knows now." He sets his finger beneath my chin, tilting my head until I meet his eyes. "I swear to you, I will never take our girl away from you. You have my word."

"But—the divorce. She's your kid."

"And now she's yours," he says, like it's that easy. "She's *ours*. Both of us. Whenever the divorce happens, if it happens—"

I freeze. "If?"

We have an agreement: until his custody is resolved, plus a year. Maybe two. Just long enough that a quickie divorce won't burn him in the press. Then I go back to my everyday life and he… moves on. He finds someone else to take care of Emmy. Someone else to be her mom.

Fuck. Why does it feel like someone just grabbed my heart with icy hands and *yanked*? I don't even want to consider a world in which I'm not her mom. Not anymore.

Al clears his throat. "If you still want out, we'll get you out. But if you want to stay in this…"

Is he saying what I think he's saying?

"You are my wife, and now the mother of my child. We're doing this backward. But just because we're in this situation doesn't mean we can't make the most of it." His face flames, and he looks away. "It turns out, I kind of like being married to you. As long as you're still okay with it, I thought maybe we could table the divorce. Maybe… see where this could go."

My throat feels tight. Itchy. I pull at the V-neck of my shirt. The room seems to close in on me, and it's getting harder to breathe. I exhale slowly, but that doesn't make the nausea recede. If anything, it makes it worse. My stomach turns. "I need to think about this."

Disappointment flashes across his face, and he tries to blank his expression, but he can't hide it from me. "Oh. Right. Of course."

He looks like a kicked puppy dog, crestfallen. The last thing I want to do is hurt him. But I have to protect myself. Nobody else will do it for me. I've learned that lesson the hard way, over and over and over again.

"I'm not saying no. I just need to think it over."

"No, yeah, I get it. It's a lot to spring on you." He releases my hands and settles back in his seat. "Consider it dropped. When you're ready to talk about it, I'll be here. Until then, we just… go back to normal."

Whatever normal is, anyway.

twenty-three

. . .

Al

I'VE NEVER BEEN SO FUCKING happy to go away for a road trip. Things have been tense with Riley since our improvised date night. The evening I'd hoped would end with us taking our relationship to the next level ended with her withdrawing from me even further. I guess it was too much to hope that we were on the same page.

Except last night... my bed felt empty. It's been a long time since I had an overnight bed guest, and even longer since I had a partner I slept beside with any regularity. Years. Typically I prefer to sleep alone. Back in Arizona, I slept around a fair bit, but once I signed with Boston, once I was surrounded by family sticking their nose into my business all the time, I made the conscious decision not to bring anyone home, and they'd be invasively nosy if I didn't come home at night. It was easier not to. The last person I slept with was... Carter.

I'm not sure why I pulled Riley into my room, only that I didn't want to be by myself. Which is kind of ridiculous, because I *like* being on my own. I like being able to starfish in the middle of the bed. I like not having to worry about jostling anyone else, or my snoring keeping them up.

So why did one night change everything I've ever known about myself?

We agreed I'd take care of Emmy's nighttime feeds on nights I'm home, so I didn't expect to see Riley at two o'clock in the morning. But when I crawled back into my bed, a buzzing sounded from the room next door.

A very distinct kind of vibration, a steady *buzz buzz buzz*.

Followed by a moan, breathy and light.

My cock went rock hard in seconds, the rush of blood leaving me light-headed. I definitely didn't shove my hand down my pants and jerk off at the thought of my wife getting herself off with a vibrator only a few feet away.

I did not.

But I wanted to. I wanted to know what she was thinking about. *Who* she was thinking about.

It wasn't me, that's for certain. I might have a healthy dose of self-confidence, but I'm not so full of myself as to think she'd be interested in me that way. If she were, she wouldn't need to think about calling off the divorce. Maybe I should have waited to bring it up. It's still a year or two away; so much can change between now and then.

I don't only want to be married to her, though. I want to date her, spend time with her. For our business transaction to be an actual relationship.

And she… doesn't feel the same. It's a kick in the nuts.

"What's wrong?" Chuck Gallagher, my future brother-in-law, sets a cup of coffee on the table in front of me. We're playing Denver tonight, and ever since my brother started dating his sister, we've made it a point to hang out when we're in the same city. After all, we're family now… or we will be, once Tony gets off his ass and proposes. I don't know what he's waiting for. The ring is already sitting in his sock drawer. Then again, I'm more of a rip-off-the-bandage type and can't wait for a perfect moment.

I shake my head. "Just… thoughts."

"Is this about the wife or the kid?" He slurps noisily at his coffee. "How was the date night?"

"How do you know about that?" The only person I've told was…

He shrugs. "Cari and I chat."

My eyes narrow. "You're talking to my little sister?"

He and I were in the same draft class, so while we went to a few of the same hockey summer camps, we were never really friends. He played college hockey in the Big 10 and I was part of Hockey East, so aside from one year at the Frozen Four tournament where we both lost, our hockey social circles didn't overlap. We were both passed over for the last Olympic training camp, and neither of us made the national team for the big international tournament—something my brother likes to rub in my face.

"I mean, one day she'll be my sister, too, in a way."

"I don't think you understand how family systems work," I mutter. "You don't become siblings like that."

"Okay, so fine, technically she'll be Viv's sister-in-law, not mine, but she's *my* family. I get to choose who's part of my family, and I'm picking her, just like I'm picking you," Chuck says with a grin. "You fuckers won't be able to get rid of me."

Tapping the side of my coffee cup against his in a lukewarm cheers, I force a grin. "Wouldn't dream of it."

He snickers and settles back in his chair. "So. Tell me about the wife. I want to meet her next time I'm up in Boston."

"She's…" I blow out a breath. "I really fucking like her."

I wish that was enough, but I don't think I have the words to describe how I feel about her.

"Riley's sassy and sure of herself, but not in a self-centered kind of way. Like she knows what she wants and goes after it." Although lately, her entire world has been childcare and playdates. I don't know that she has any time for herself when I'm not there to give her breaks. "She built up a successful career in Arizona and left it at the drop of a hat to take care of my kid. *Our* kid. And fuck, man, she's so good with Emmy. That baby adores her. She should. I know I do."

My face flushes and I clamp my lips together. Shit. I wasn't supposed to say that.

His loud laughter draws attention in the small coffee shop, and I pull the brim of my cap lower, hiding my face. I'm not ashamed of being seen with him, but hockey gossip will label me a traitor for daring to spend time with a guy on the rival team off the ice.

"Do you have photos?"

I stare at him. "You want to see pictures of my kid?"

His grin stretches from ear to ear. "Yeah. She's basically my niece, isn't she? Babies are great. Don't want one right now, but eventually, I want an entire hockey team."

"Start with one and see how it goes," I warn, pulling out my phone. I swipe to the album and hand it over.

Chuck hums as he flicks through the first few photos. "Cute kid. She has your eyes."

"She's so sweet. And smart. And she has this little cackle laugh that—" I cut myself off. "I could go on all day about her."

"As you should. If a man can't be proud of his kid, he's a shit dad." Chuck hands me back my phone. "You're doing good, man. You were thrown for a loop and you stepped up. Yeah, marrying the baby mama, if that's what you want to call it, is an extra step, but you did what you had to do for your family."

Shaking my head, I debate glossing over the details, but the truth is going to get out one way or the other. I can't ask Tony and Viv to hide the circumstances from their family. "Riley's not the baby mama, but she *is* Emmy's mom now. I couldn't separate them even if I wanted to."

"So don't."

Frustration simmers right below my skin, and I sigh,

rubbing my forehead. "Except when I suggested we table the divorce, she freaked out."

"The divorce that isn't supposed to happen for another year or two?" He gives me a knowing grin.

My eyes narrow as I glare at him, even though he's not the one spilling secrets. I want to punch the smug look off his stupid face. "Just how much is Cari telling you?"

"Like I said, we talk. She's a nice kid. Fits right in between Frankie and Janine."

His two younger sisters. Janine is a few years older than Cari, and Frankie is about a year and a half younger. Five of the six Gallagher siblings are professional athletes. His twin, Perry, plays football, and only the youngest sibling, Bradley, isn't involved in sports.

"Well, I'm glad she has you looking out for her." Even if I'm peeved about her sharing details she shouldn't be giving out so freely. Then again, there are worse things than Chuck Gallagher knowing my business. I know he would never use it against me.

"Maybe Riley needs some time to get used to things. It can't be easy to leave everything you've ever known for some guy who travels half the time, settle into a routine in his house, taking care of his kid, and he suddenly wants to flip the script. Keep doing what you're doing. Take her on dates. Go out without the baby, do stuff as a family…" He shrugs. "Fuck if I know, I don't have a kid or a wife. Can't convince anyone to stick around long enough to try."

Running my thumb over the ring on my left hand, I consider his advice. "We go out when I'm home. Or, I suggest it, but she never initiates anything. It's all me."

"She's probably afraid of getting turned down," he says slowly. "I mean, you know our schedules. Even our days off aren't truly free. And then coordinating it with the baby's routine… If she's the slightest bit uncertain how she feels, it makes sense for her to withdraw."

I sigh, running my hand through my hair. "I want her to want me, even half as much as I want her."

"Is it only physical? Or do you actually have feelings for this woman?"

"It's not physical. Not purely, at least." The attraction simmering in my veins whenever I see her is only part of the puzzle. How do I act on it without scaring her away, or worse, ruining the fragile relationship we have? "I want us to be married for real. I want us to be a family, and not just for the cameras."

"You want your happily ever after, and you're trying to push the misshapen pieces into a mold that might not actually fit." Chuck stares at me, then lets out a short laugh. "Have you tried simply dating your wife? Taking it one step at a time."

I can't tell if he's being sarcastic or genuine, but I'll take his advice at face value.

"That's what I was trying to do. We spent the day together, then I cooked for us and did the candles and wine thing, and she shot me down. I put myself out there. She's not interested."

He cocks his head. "Did she say that, though? Or did she just need to think it over?"

"I... I don't know." Too blindsided by the hurt of her turning me down, I can't remember the exact phrasing she used. Just the way she recoiled.

"Take it slow. Don't rush into it," he says. "You already got married in the blink of an eye. What's the harm in taking it one day at a time?"

"The divorce?" It's heavy on my mind, making my stomach sink every time I think about Riley walking away. Even if it's not happening anytime soon, it feels like a ticking time bomb, reminding me that one day, this will end. I have no right to ask her to stay forever, but I already don't know what I'm supposed to do without her.

Not as Emmy's nanny. Not even as her mom. Just… her. In my life, being my wife.

"You said it's a year or two away," he says patiently. "When the time comes, you can decide how you feel. It might run its course by then. Playing house might get old by then."

I glare at him. "It's not *playing house* when my kid is in the picture."

A triumphant grin brightens his face. "Then you better treat your wife right. Start by backing off, and then *talk* about things rather than springing them on her. You might have more luck that way."

twenty-four

. . .

Riley

LOUD SHRIEKING giggles of little babies fill the house. Emmy sits on her play mat, grabbing at her blocks and pushing them over, while Leo Larsson chews on a soft book beside her. And Cora Henry, now three months old, naps in her stroller, somehow sleeping through the noise.

The surprise guest today is Ainsley Walker, thirteen months old. I wasn't expecting Tyler to show up on my doorstep with his daughter strapped to his chest, but once he dropped off the week's delivery, I invited him to stay. And I'm glad I did. His sister Amelia is the team's physical therapist, so he's basically already family.

Never in my wildest dreams did I imagine I would find this kind of community. Acceptance.

"Okay, tell me," Audrey says as she sips her coffee. "How have things been? Any better?"

Heat licks at my cheeks, and I look away. "They're fine."

She and Vanessa exchange a look that speaks volumes, and I squirm in my seat as awkward silence falls over us. They're judging me. Hell, I'd judge me too. They know as well as I do that I don't belong here, not really. We're just playing pretend.

"It's fine. I'm fine," I'm quick to add.

Tyler snorts. "Say *fine* one more time. I dare you."

"It's just… I… I don't know," I finally admit. "This wasn't part of the plan."

"What wasn't?" The humor fades from Vanessa's expression as she pats my arm consolingly. "You can talk to us. What's said here, stays here."

"Al doesn't want to get divorced," I blurt, then immediately cover my face with my hands.

"Okay, so what's the problem?" Audrey asks. "It's not like you were planning on doing it anytime soon."

"It changes things."

"Does it, though? Does anything need to change?"

We're married. My job is to make you happy. That's what he said. Am I crazy for reading into it? For thinking he wants more?

It's the only thing I've been able to think about all week. It's almost a relief that he's gone and I don't have a reprieve from twenty-four seven baby duties. The only problem is that when Emmy's asleep, my mind is free to wander, and then…

Letting out a groan, I scrub my hands over my face.

"I don't want things to change, but I think they have to."

"Take it one step at a time," Vanessa says. "It doesn't have to be this big, elaborate thing. Maybe do something just the two of you, without the baby. Not just dinner at home. An actual date."

"He doesn't actually like *me*, though. He wants to *make the most of it*. I'm just the one he's stuck with."

"Or maybe he's catching feelings," Tyler suggests.

"Don't be ridiculous," I say with a laugh.

He shrugs, sipping his tea. "Okay. I don't know him very well. Maybe I'm reading the situation wrong."

"He would never fall for me. That's just… No."

"Why is it so hard to believe?" Vanessa asks, keeping her tone gentle. "You're the mother of his child, you live together, you're *married*. Sure, it all happened a little backward, but it doesn't mean he doesn't want to get to know you better."

"We slept together," I blurt, my face flaming. "Well, not like *that*. It was only sleeping. He got home at four o'clock in the morning and Emmy was sick and… We slept in the same bed. We've never done that before, and haven't since."

"But you can't stop thinking about it," Audrey says knowingly.

"Yeah."

His big, strong body wrapped around me, his hairy chest pressed to my back, the thick length of his morning erection digging into the curve of my ass…

"I kind of want to do it again? But it's weird to ask him to sleep together without *sleeping* together. I don't want to have sex with him, I don't think."

Tyler raises his eyebrows. "Really? Gonzo is hot as fuck." When I stare at him, he laughs. "I'm married, not blind."

"He's gorgeous, but that doesn't mean I would…"

"Hey, there's no rushing any of this," he says. "Ask him for a fully clothed sleepover. He doesn't seem like the type of dude who will push for more. At least, not without your consent."

"Consent is key," Audrey adds. "He wants more with you, but he's asking you before he changes the name of the game. Maybe he's clumsy in the way he's going about it."

He was definitely a little heavy-handed in everything he was saying… Putting my happiness first, wanting us to be a family.

"I've never had a family before," I mumble. "My sister was my whole world, and then Emmy. I've never had a family. Nobody ever wanted me to stick around."

"Al does," Vanessa says. "Marriage doesn't have to mean forever. Yes, most people want it to be, but plenty of people get divorced and move on to happy, healthy lives. You don't have to commit to the rest of your life. Focus on right now. If you want to stay married, stay married. If you decide you're not happy, you can end it at any time."

"Once the threat of social services is no longer hanging over our heads and it won't rake him over in the press."

"If you're really that unhappy, end it now," Audrey says. "If you know you don't want to be with him, end it before he gets more attached. You'll still be Emmy's mom. He can't take that away from you."

"I'm not unhappy. I just don't know what I want." Rubbing at my forehead, I try to explain, but my thoughts are so jumbled, I have no hope of them understanding what I hardly understand myself. "How do we date if we're already married? Do I even want to date my kid's father? What happens if we try and then break up and it gets awkward?"

"There's definitely risk involved," Vanessa says. "You'll have to decide if that's a chance you're willing to take. If *he* is worth the risk."

In my heart, I know he is. But that doesn't mean I can blow up our stable, peaceful life on a crush and a maybe. There's too much at stake. Emmy's health and safety are more important than my heart. They have to be.

twenty-five

. . .

Al

IT'S LATE when I get home from the airport. My entire body aches, my side sore from a brutal hit late in the third period that forced me to miss the last seven minutes of the game. All I want is to crawl into bed and crash.

The hall light is on, but Riley's door is closed. I poke my head into Emmy's room and find her fast asleep, tucked in for the night in her sleep sack. Something in me settles at the sight of her sleeping so peacefully.

My room is exactly as I left it three days ago. Exhaustion weighing me down, I shed my suit jacket and drop the rest of my clothes into a messy pile and climb into my bed.

A part of me was hoping I'd come home to find Riley in my bed, waiting for me. As much as I'd like her to be splayed out for me, naked and ready for me, that wasn't the fantasy. No, I wanted her to decide she wants this, wants *me*.

That was too much to hope for, I guess. I should have known my dreams don't come true. It's like a monkey's paw curse.

Nothing has turned out the way I expected it to. All I've ever wanted is a family of my own, someone to love me unconditionally and support me the way my parents do for each other. The happily ever after they have. Their marriage is stable and unbreakable, the stuff of fairy tales.

My life is good, it's great, even, but I'm not happy. I have a kid, but I missed out on the first six months of her life. I'm married, but my wife can barely stand to look at me. I should be over the moon, but instead I'm deep in my feels.

I don't know how to fix this.

Rolling over, I punch my pillow a few times until the indent is where I want it to be. Even with my head in the divot, it still doesn't feel right. Nothing feels *right* anymore.

I don't remember drifting off, but the next thing I know, daylight is streaming in through the gaps in the blinds. My eyes feel gritty, my mouth gross, and my ribs radiate pain from that hard hit. All I want is to stay in bed and pretend the world doesn't exist.

Emmy wails in the next room, and I force myself out of bed. Throwing the covers off me, I sit on the edge of the mattress for a moment until my equilibrium settles and I don't feel like I'm going to tilt over onto my ass. It's close to eleven, which means her first nap of the day is coming to an end. Padding into her room in only my boxers, I crack open her door to find her sitting up, pulling at the crib's bars.

"Hi, princess." As I reach into the crib, she grabs at me, and I bring her close for a snuggle. "How's my favorite girl doing?"

My daughter babbles while I carry her to the changing table, kicking her legs against my stomach and inadvertently connecting with the bruise. I let out a sharp hiss, and it takes everything in me not to drop her at the explosion of pain radiating through my side.

"That's not very nice," I tell her as I get her settled, running my finger over the tip of her nose. "You're supposed to always be nice to your dad. That's, like, rule number one."

"That's a little advanced for a seven-month-old to remember," Riley says, and I glance over to find my wife leaning against the doorframe, her arms crossed over her chest. She's wearing leggings and an oversized sweater, her feet bare and her hair pulled into a knot on top of her head.

She's absolutely fucking gorgeous, and I hate that I notice. My stomach clenches and I clear my throat.

"Gotta teach her young." My voice comes out mostly even. I finish changing the diaper and snap Emmy's outfit closed. When I lift the baby into my arms, I find Riley's eyes lingering on me, her gaze focused on my side.

"What happened?" She nods to the bruise.

My stomach sinks. Of course she didn't watch the game. I still haven't asked her to. Aside from that matinee game, she hasn't come to any of my home games, either. I'm afraid if I ask she'll turn me down. Again.

"Just a bad hit." I shift Emmy to my other hip, away from the bruise. It hurts like a bitch.

Riley sweeps her gaze over my chest and abs, then down further. I'm uncomfortably aware I'm only wearing my boxer briefs, and even though my morning wood has gone away, her eyes on me make my heart race and stomach flutter. The frank appreciation on her face is only there for a moment before she blinks it away and reaches for Emmy.

"I'll take her," she says, all but snatching the baby from my arms and practically running from the room.

"I'll get dressed, then," I announce to the empty room.

Trudging back to my bedroom, I immediately drop my shorts and hop into the shower before it even warms up. The cool water does nothing to calm my pounding heart.

She clearly enjoys looking at me. So why doesn't she want anything else? Am I that repulsive?

My thoughts swirl down the drain, along with the soap suds, and when I finally turn off the water and wrap a towel around my waist, the last thing I want to do is go downstairs and play happy family with someone who doesn't want the same things I do. I'm low-key dreading spending the day together while pretending I don't want her.

But being an adult means doing things even when we don't want to. And I'll be damned if I miss out on more time with Emmy.

Downstairs, the baby is in her bouncer, kicking her chubby little legs. Maybe she'll turn out to be a gymnast like my brother. Or a track star turned rugby player like my sister. I won't say no if she takes a shine to hockey, either.

And if she decides athletics aren't for her, I'll support that, too. I will always love her unconditionally.

I tickle Emmy's chin before heading to the kitchen. There's a pot of coffee on, with exactly one cup left. After emptying the carafe into a mug, I take a sip and glance at Riley, who's sitting at the Formica kitchen table with a laptop.

"What do you have planned for today?" I ask casually. It takes everything in me not to go to her, to pull her into my arms and beg her to be mine. I heard her loud and clear. Nobody likes a guy who can't take no for an answer.

"Nothing special. Just playing and nap time."

"Sounds like a great day." A nice, chill day is perfect. As much as I'd like to get out and do something together, maybe hanging around the house is what we need. "I've got her for a few hours if you want to take a nap, or maybe a bubble bath."

Riley's eyebrows climb up her forehead. "Trying to get rid of me already?"

"Giving you space. You've been the default parent for the last few days. If you need a break, I'm here. I can handle Emmy today. You deserve some time to yourself."

Fuck knows this weekend will be busy, with the team holiday dinner and then a matinee game a few days after.

A strange look passes over her face. "Okay. If you're sure."

"I've got this," I assure her. "Rest, relax. Do something fun for yourself."

She blows out a breath. "Thanks."

"Anytime." Thinking about my schedule, I laugh. "Well, anytime I'm home, that is. If you want to revisit the nanny situation, I'm still game. It's got to be exhausting being on duty all the time. Everyone deserves a break now and then. I want you to feel supported, not chained to the baby."

She opens her mouth—to argue, most likely—but I raise my hands in the air. "Childcare is a full-time job, and then some. You don't get enough of a chance to decompress when I'm not here. If there's anything I can do to make this easier for you, I'll do it."

Whatever it takes to keep her from running screaming, burned out and exhausted.

Riley shuts her mouth, her nod brisk. "Got it. Thanks." She closes the laptop, pushing back her chair. "I guess I'll get out of your hair, then."

She stalks out of the room and up the stairs, her footsteps echoing.

My stomach sinks. All I wanted was to help, yet I think I made this worse. What the hell am I supposed to do now? How do I fix this?

twenty-six

• • •

Riley

THE GRIZZLIES RENTED out a fancy steakhouse in the Seaport District for the team's Thanksgiving dinner. It's two days before the actual day, but the next game is tomorrow night, so it makes sense to do this now.

When I agreed to marry Al, I didn't know I was signing up for a whole social life revolving around the team. With Vanessa and Audrey dropping by twice a week, plus Bex constantly blowing up my phone, I'm finally finding the social network I thought I'd never have.

This is a baby-free event, so Al corralled Cari into staying with Emmy, and I didn't even cry when it was time to leave. Partly because I didn't want to ruin my makeup. I'm wearing a simple burgundy velvet dress. It's got a high neckline, a cinched waist, and a flirty hem, and even though I've added black tights for modesty (and weather), I've caught Al looking at my legs more than once.

It's hard not to preen at the heat in his eyes. But unless I want to sacrifice my kid's happiness, I have to tamp down the urge to show off for him. Even if I want to.

As we make small talk with his teammates and their partners, his hand splays along the small of my back. The searing heat of his palm against my dress is like a brand, burning me for all eternity. I'm his, and he's mine, and we belong together.

At least for a year. Maybe two.

I can hold out. No matter how much I want to rip that suit off his thick body and nuzzle my face against his hairy chest like a cat, I must resist. I *will* resist. I am stronger than my libido.

Jenkins and Mitchell make their way over to us, giving me polite, perfunctory hugs before tapping knuckles with Al.

"Riley, you look gorgeous," Jenkins says with a smirk. His dazzling green eyes are bright, teasing, as he squeezes my forearm. "You could do so much better than a Muppet like Gonzo."

Al frowns, shoving his teammate. "Knock it off."

"Yeah, it's not his fault he looks like that," Mitchell adds with a grin.

"Fuck off," he mutters, scowling.

I pat his chest, appreciating his rock-hard muscles through his suit. "I like the way you look." Although I try to keep my tone light and even, it comes out breathy, and my face flames. "I mean…"

"Sounds like someone's got a crush," Jenkins sing-songs.

"Leave my wife alone," Al growls. "It's not like that with us, you know that."

We aren't a real couple. He doesn't actually like me, just the idea of me. But for some reason, his shutting down his friends makes my chest ache.

I do like him. If I wasn't in such a precarious situation, I'd throw caution to the wind and make a move already. But if the alternative is losing my daughter, the last remaining link to my sister… No. I can't risk it.

"I need a drink." Pulling away from Al, I start off toward the open bar. Footsteps fall into place beside me, and I glance over to find Mitchell accompanying me. "I don't need a babysitter," I mutter, and he chuckles.

"Hey, I'm only going where you're going," he says, raising his hands in innocence.

"Uh-huh. Sure."

Reaching the bar, I make eye contact with the bartender. "Rum and Coke, please."

She nods, reaching for a glass and the jigger, raising her brows at Mitchell expectantly.

"Whatever IPA you have in a bottle, thanks."

"We've only got cans," she says.

He frowns. "Okay, then I'll take tequila and tonic."

"Going for the hard stuff?" I tease.

"I don't like the taste of cans. It always tastes metallic," he says with a shrug.

"Makes sense."

When the bartender places our drinks on the counter, he picks up his glass and peers at me. As soon as I lift mine, he taps his drink against it.

"Cheers," Mitchell mutters, before gulping down a solid third of his drink in one go.

"Tonight is going to get messy, isn't it?"

A mirthless laugh rumbles from his throat. "Counting on it."

His hand settles on my back, but unlike with Al, his touch doesn't make me feel centered. It's performative at best. Polite. He guides me across the party to my husband, who's scowling as we approach. A line creases his forehead, making his brown eyes glitter darker.

"You two look cozy," Al snaps.

"Relax, Gonzo," Mitchell drawls. "I'm not about to make a move on your girl. I'm dumb, not suicidal."

He turns his glare on me. "You can't sleep with him."

Mitchell sucks in a breath, Jenkins lets out a shocked

laugh, and I want to shrivel up and die with their attention on me. But more importantly…

Irritation flares through me, and my eyes narrow into slits. "Excuse me?"

Dimly, I'm aware of Mitchell dragging Jenkins away. All I can focus on is my stupid fucking husband and his stupid fucking accusations. How can he say he wants to date me and still think so little of me?

"I know you don't want to be with me, but you can't hook up with my teammates. That's, like—"

"Okay, hold the fuck up," I snap. Glancing around, I'm reassured nobody is paying attention to us, but that can change in an instant. I grab him by the wrist and drag him into the hallway between the event space and the main dining room.

Al glowers at me. "What are you doing?"

"I'm not sleeping with your teammates. I have no interest in any of those idiots." Crossing my arms over my chest, I glare up at him. "Do you really think I'm interested in him? In *anyone* else?"

Does he think I'm some kind of whore, offering myself to the closest man around? Doesn't he see *he's* the only man I want to climb like a tree?

Sullen, he bites the inside of his cheek. "Yeah, but you're not interested in me either."

His attitude is definitely not attractive, but I can't deny the hurt in his voice makes my heart beat faster. Maybe I'm more than a convenient option. Maybe there's more to this than I thought.

"Is that what you think?" My bitter laugh echoes in the hallway. "I said I needed time to think. I didn't say no."

He opens his mouth, but I continue before he can get a word in edgewise.

"There's too much at stake for me. I can't do this. There can't be an *us*." I waggle a finger between us. "That day, it wasn't a no. I needed to think it over. But I am saying no now."

His face falls. "Got it. I hear you, loud and clear."

He might hear the words, but he's not listening. Whatever I'm saying, it's not connecting for him.

"I can't jeopardize Emmy's safety for—"

Al rears back. "What are you talking about?"

"When we get divorced, she'll be all yours. I won't have any legal claim to her."

"But you're her mom." He stares at me, his head cocked.

"Not biologically. Not legally."

"I told you, I'd never take her away from you."

"It's easy to say that now, before your shark of a lawyer gets involved. I can't afford—"

"We have a prenup. Everything is outlined there, you can afford whatever you want."

I glanced over the documents, but I didn't pay that much attention. I don't want his money. All I want is my girl, and he can't promise custody of her, not with the courts involved.

"But Emmy—"

"She will *always* be your kid," he vows. "She's yours just as much as she is mine. And no matter what happens with my career, when I retire and don't have to travel every week, I'm still going to need you—need help. Single parents do it on their own every day, but I've never wanted to be a single parent. I want you by my side."

"We can't always get what we want."

He rears back again as if I've slapped him. "Wow. Okay, then."

"I'm just saying—"

"No. I hear you. You don't want this." *Don't want me,* I hear the unspoken words.

"It's not that," I say, awkwardness settling over me like a cloud of discomfort. "What if we start something, and it fizzles out, and then everything is weird?"

"Then we handle it like adults," Al says. "It's not that complicated."

"Except we're *married*."

"So take that out of the equation. It's a legal relationship, not a romantic one. We can simply date and pretend we're not married."

"But—"

He shakes his head. "Either you want to be with me, or you don't," he says flatly. "It's that simple."

"It's not. You're loaded. You can do anything you want. I'm an unemployed, homeless makeup artist with no family. You have—"

"What are you talking about?" He stares at me, mouth agape. "You're not unemployed, you take care of our kid, which is a full-time fucking job and then some. You aren't homeless, you have a house. And we're married, that makes us a family."

It's my turn to take a step back. "F-fam—"

"Riley, you're part of my family now." His voice softens, and when he reaches for me, I allow him to take my hands in his. "For better or for worse. I meant that. Whatever happens between us, I'll stand by you. Do you think I'd really allow you to be homeless? Do you think I'd let the mother of my child struggle?"

I open my mouth to argue, but he continues before I can say anything.

"No matter what happens between us, you will always be taken care of. I can't promise you won't want a job later on, but while Emmy is home every day, when I'm traveling with the team, your job is to take care of our girl. If you wanted to pick up another gig, we could get a nanny. I want you to feel supported, whether you work outside of the house or not."

My lip trembles. "I don't want a nanny. I want to stay home with her."

"Okay. We won't get a nanny," he agrees immediately.

"And even when we get divorced, I want to be in her life. I need to be her guardian in your will so if something happens to you, we don't lose her. Not again."

His eyes soften. "Do you want a postnup?"

"What's that?"

"We'll go to the lawyer and revise the prenuptial agreement. Since we're married already, it's called a postnuptial agreement. We would outline exactly what happens so the divorce is open and shut. Fifty-fifty custody, child support and alimony—"

"I don't need that," I interrupt.

"But I'm offering it," he argues. "We've got eighteen years ahead of us, plus a lifetime of her adulthood. My girl is used to a certain level of comfort. If you're certain you want out, we'll outline it so everything is fair."

"We did that already." I remember signing paperwork, but I didn't pay attention to the financial details. I never actually intended to take his money. I figured I'd walk away and that would be that. It will kill me to lose access to Emmy, but I can't in good conscience keep her from him.

"We can still revise it. The last thing I want is for you to feel cheated, like you've given up something to be with me. I've already updated my will so everything goes to you—"

"You did *what*?" I stare at him.

"You're my wife. You're entitled to it. Most of it is in a trust for Emmy, but if something happens to me, you'll have plenty."

"I—I don't know what to say."

"You don't have to make any decisions right away. But Riley..." His eyes meet mine, the weight of his gaze heavy with meaning. "If you're scared of starting something with me because of Emmy, you don't need to be. I swear, I will never take our kid away from you, and I'll sign anything you need me to in order to make that happen."

"I'm scared." The words fall off my lips as a whisper.

"You don't have to be." Al reaches for me. "We can work this out. Take it slow."

"I like slow."

With the last hurdles out of the way, I finally feel like I can do this. *We* can do this. I squeeze his hand, lacing my fingers through his. The scratch of his calloused palm against mine feels so fucking good. How can simply holding hands feel so monumentally right?

He ducks his head, his warm breath fanning over my lips. I arch my neck, reaching for him, and—

"There you are!" Jenkins calls.

"Fuck," Al mutters, the word puffing over me.

"Come on, we're about to sit down for dinner." Jenkins disappears down the hallway, holding the door open for us expectantly, as if he's afraid we'll bolt if he doesn't escort us.

Not going to lie, the idea of running away doesn't sound half bad.

My husband pulls back, clearing his throat.

"Let's go eat some turkey with my teammates," he says, squeezing my hand. "Make the most of this."

Somehow, I don't think he's only talking about dinner.

twenty-seven

· · ·

Al

RILEY SITS beside me through dinner, and as we're relaxing after the heavy meal, I set my arm on the back of her chair. She leans into me, resting her head on my shoulder and her hand falling to my thigh while she talks across me to Vanessa.

I'm glad they're getting along. It certainly makes my life easier, knowing she has someone in her corner. She shouldn't feel like she has no support network.

Mitchell catches my attention from across the table, a smirk twisting his lips. He's holding a drink loosely between his fingertips, swirling around the clear liquid. I owe him an apology. Riley, too. I know he wasn't trying to make a move on her, and I know she wouldn't fool around with him. It's good that the team has accepted her so unconditionally; I shouldn't try to read into it any more than that.

I give my teammate a nod, and he dips his chin, a satisfied glint in his eye. He tips back his drink, draining the glass, then lumbers to his feet. His gait is unsteady as he shuffles to the bar.

Should I say anything? We're technically at a work event, and we have a game tomorrow night. It's none of my business if he wants to get loaded.

Movement in the corner of my eye steals my focus, and MacGregor shoves back his chair and strides directly to the bar. No pretense. He and Mitchell have a conversation, low and intense, and then Mitchell scowls and turns on his heel. Nobody else is paying attention as the center slips out of the room.

The team captain sinks against the bar, rubbing his forehead. I do not envy his position. Dealing with our cast of idiots is difficult enough on a good day; add alcohol to the mix, and it's sure to be a disaster.

This will be our first Thanksgiving as a family. Cari leaves for Florida early in the morning to be with our parents, and Tony's in Denver, so it'll just be the three of us. Somehow, it feels right. I'll always love my parents and siblings, nothing will fracture our bond, but now that I'm married, I have my own family. Truth be told, I'm looking forward to sitting on the couch with my wife and kid, watching the parade and the football game while the turkey is in the oven.

Well, the turkey is already cooked. Tyler dropped off a giant container the other day, along with all the side dishes, so we don't actually have to *cook* anything, only warm through.

Although, after this heavy meal, I can't imagine eating another bite, much less a second full turkey dinner. I push back from my seat with a groan, and Riley looks over at me with concern.

I lean over and kiss her temple, a soft, innocent brush against her skin. Her cheeks flame red, and a shy smile curves her kissable berry-red lips. Somehow, even with eating and drinking, her lipstick is perfect, the dark color doing dangerous things to my heart rate.

We almost kissed. A real kiss, not the innocent brushes I've gotten away with. If Jenkins hadn't interrupted us, we would have. There's still a lot to discuss, but just knowing she isn't indifferent to me… I can deal with a little more uncertainty if it means we get to the bottom of this.

I want my wife, and I'll do anything to prove myself worthy to her.

Eventually, dinner draws to a close, and we drive home in a comfortable silence. I don't feel that constant pressure to perform, to entertain her. It finally feels like maybe she likes me for me, and not for all the perks of being a rich and talented hockey player. What we have is so different from my other experiences with women. Even the few long-term relationships I had, it was always about what I could do for them, rather than about the two of us as equals.

With Riley, I can be myself.

When we enter the house, Cari is asleep on the couch, the baby monitor on the coffee table. Carefully, I shake my sister awake.

"How'd it go?" I ask.

"She was a perfect angel," she reports with a sleepy smile. "She convinced me to read triple the number of stories, but—"

I laugh. "Oh, the baby who can't talk?"

"Yeah. She's very convincing." Cari yawns, her eyes fluttering shut. "If it's okay, I'm going to stay here. My flight is in… six hours. I can head to the airport straight from here."

"Stay as long as you need," Riley cuts in. "Thanks for staying with her."

"Anything for my favorite niece." She grins.

"Only niece," I add.

"Favorite," Cari says firmly. "Even when you guys have more kids, she'll still be my favorite."

My face heats at the idea of me and Riley having kids. Filling our house with children, her belly swollen with my baby. My cock likes that idea, too, and I swallow loudly.

"Okay. Well. On that note, I'm going to bed."

"Awesome," Cari yawns. "See you when I get back."

"Night." I swipe the baby monitor off the table, tucking it into my pocket. Turning to my wife, I offer her my hand. "Ready?"

Riley nods, her cheeks a pretty pink. She pushes past me, ignoring my hand, and heads for the stairs, my eyes falling to her ass and legs as she walks.

"You're so far gone for her," Cari murmurs.

"Oh, yeah. Totally," I whisper back.

"Does she know?"

"She will soon enough."

My sister makes a face. "Gross. At least wait until I'm out of the house."

Letting out a short laugh, I shake my head and follow Riley up the stairs. Her door is closed, the light on underneath, so I head to my room and start stripping out of my suit. I have enough foresight to hang it up and toss my shirt into the dirty hamper.

Crawling into bed, I pick up the book on my nightstand. The psychological thriller Mitchell recommended has kept me up reading the last few nights. It's the third book by this author I've read in two weeks, and even though it gets my heart racing with the twists and turns, a pleasant sense of relaxation floods my system.

After a few chapters, my eyes grow heavy, and I set the book aside and turn out the lights. Burrowing under my covers, I pull the blankets up to my chest and try to get comfortable.

A quiet knock raps on my door, and I almost think I've imagined it until a second one sounds a few moments later.

"Come in," I call, and the door creaks open.

"Hey," Riley says, shrouded in the darkness.

"What's up?" My voice cracks, and I cough to cover it.

"I can't sleep. Can I…" Her swallow echoes through the room. "Can I stay in here?"

"Of course." I pull back the covers and she rounds the bed, climbing onto the mattress and settling beside me.

Her body is stiff, tension rolling off her in waves.

"C'mere," I murmur, tugging her into me. She's wearing an oversized T-shirt—I think it's one of mine—and a pair of sweats, covered from head to toe. There is nothing provocative about her outfit, and yet it is the sexiest thing I've ever seen. I wrap my arm around her waist and curl my body around hers. "Relax. You're safe with me."

"I'm not so sure." Her words are quiet in the room's stillness, and I freeze.

Propping myself up on my elbow, I stare down at her. "Do you really think I'd hurt you?"

Her bright blue eyes are dark from the shadows let in by the blinds. "Not violently."

A burning sensation rips through my tightening throat. "I would never lay a hand on you. I swear."

After all this, she still thinks the worst of me. She still thinks I'm capable of *that*. My stomach turns, and I exhale heavily.

Her voice is quiet when she explains, "I know you wouldn't hurt me physically. But that doesn't mean you don't have the power to destroy my heart."

"I won't." My own heart pounds at the thought. I would never do that to her.

"You can't promise me that," she mumbles. "You can't control it. Nobody can."

"I will do my best to make sure it doesn't happen. I don't want to hurt you in any way. I'd rather take a thousand cross-checks to the ribs than do that."

She cringes. "Okay, ouch. I know you don't want to. But—"

"All I want to do is love you." The words fall off my lips, and even though I know I should walk it back, I don't want to.

Her mouth drops open. "Love?"

"If we start this… if you let me in, I'll fall for you." I know it in my bones, as certain as the stars in the sky. "If you don't want that, I need to know now, before I let myself fall."

She stares at me for a moment, and my heart races. I'm laying it all on the line. If she doesn't want this, I can't have her in my bed. It's hard enough as it is.

Riley's hand snakes around my neck, pulling me down. I let her manhandle me until I'm half lying on top of her, bracing my weight on my forearm so I don't crush her. Her body feels incredible pressed to mine, all tempting curves and soft sweetness.

Before I know what's happening, her lips are on mine and the world blurs. She tastes like heat and promise, her mouth opening under mine. I sink deeper, desperate, greedy, lost in the rush of her. My cock throbs, hardening in my boxer briefs.

Awareness hits me like a truck, and I pull back. "What are we doing?"

"I'm tired of fighting this," Riley says. "You have the power to destroy me, and I have to trust that you won't."

"You could destroy me too," I murmur. "It's not only you putting your heart on the line."

"I finally understand that." She lays her hand on my bearded cheek, scratching her nails through the coarse hair. "I'm ready to try."

This time, when our lips meet in a hungry kiss, I'm ready for it. Her mouth is soft fire against mine, every brush of her lips unraveling me. I cradle her jaw, angling closer, tasting her sighs. The kiss builds, fierce and unrelenting, until I'm dizzy with wanting nothing but more of her. My cock pulses, and it takes everything in me not to grind against her. That's not what this is about. It's more than sex and getting off; *she* means more to me than that.

The kiss gentles, and I force myself to pull away.

"If you're going to stay in here, there will be no funny business," I say with mock sternness.

"Never?" She wraps her legs around my waist, thrusting her pelvis against me. My eyes roll back in my head, and I take a deep breath. Do I really want to put a stop to this?

She deserves more than a quick, hard fuck. Not for our first time. Not with all the things I want to do to her—*with* her.

"Not tonight," I amend, rolling off her. "Not when we're still figuring all this out, and definitely not with my sister downstairs."

"I can live with that." She squirms closer to me, burrowing her head onto my shoulder and slinging her arm around my waist. "I'm glad we're doing this," she whispers.

"Me too." Drawing my arm around her, I drop a kiss on the top of her head. "Get some rest. Morning will come before we're ready for it."

twenty-eight

· · ·

Riley

THE ARENA IS loud and raucous as I follow Vanessa, Audrey, and a few of the other spouses down to the ice. Emmy is wearing her custom Grizzlies jersey with Daddy on the back crest, her earmuffs firmly in place, and I'm in a matching jersey with Al's name and number bedazzled on my shoulders.

Unlike last time, I finally feel like I belong here, like I have every right to be here. Al is my husband, and we are raising our daughter together. We're a family. Now that I've made friends with the other partners, I'm no longer the odd one out all the time.

It's amazing how quickly it all happened. Yesterday, we spent the holiday lazing around the house, playing with Emmy and watching the football game. While she napped, we made out on the couch. He didn't try to take it any farther than a few wandering hands, and even though it killed me not to rip off all my clothes and sink onto his cock right then and there, I know taking it slowly is a good idea. Just because I'm constantly horny for him doesn't mean I should act on my impulses all the time. It would be highly impractical.

But definitely fun.

The guys stretch and skate around the offensive zone for warm-ups, then drift over to where we're waiting. Al waves at Emmy, his face bright with the biggest grin I've ever seen.

"Hey, baby," he says, his words nearly inaudible through the thick plexiglass.

He's looking at her, but for the first time, I wonder what it would be like if he were actually talking to me.

Emmy babbles and shrieks, trying to get to her father through the barrier. She bangs her tiny fists on the glass, and he grins, pressing his hand flat. She's not coordinated enough to meet him halfway, so I lay my hand against his. I swear I can feel the heat of his skin through the glass.

"Hi," he says, his eyes on mine.

My face heats, and I can't hide my smile. "Hi back."

"I'm glad you're here."

Even though we're in a crowded arena with thousands of people, even though his teammates and their partners surround us, it feels like we're the only two here. Well, us and Emmy.

"Me too," I admit. "Score some goals today."

"Just for you." Al smirks, tapping the glass. His eyes dart down to the baby, then back to mine. "Take care of my girl."

"Always," I promise.

The buzzer sounds, letting the guys know it's time to head off the ice and regroup. I take Emmy's hand in mine and wave it as they skate away.

"Good lord, you guys are sickening," Bex says.

Hefting Emmy into my arms, I glance at my redheaded friend. "Shut up."

She laughs, slinging her arm over my shoulders. "Come on. I need beer and nachos, stat."

"Definitely. I want to hear all about this new research project, too."

Up in the suite, I settle Emmy in a booster seat with a toy and turn back to Bex. She studies something smart at Harvard, and she uses a lot of big words I don't have a hope of understanding.

Vanessa, Audrey, and Hailey join us, and conversation flows easily as the game starts. There's an overwhelming sense of community here. Belonging. I've never had this before. Even with Carter, it was the two of us against the rest of the world; we didn't have a *family* of friends.

Now, I have Al, I have Cari, and I have these women. They've supported me unconditionally since day one, welcoming me to the group with outstretched arms.

Emmy starts to fuss, and I pluck her out of her seat and into my arms. I pace the upper landing of the suite to settle her, smiling at Mel Easton, who's doing the same with her son.

"Kids, huh." She grins, bouncing her knees as she walks back and forth.

"Does it get easier?"

We both look in the direction of where her three-year-old daughter is sitting with a few other big kids, enraptured by the game below.

Mel laughs. "They get more independent, but they still need you, just in a different way. At least at this age they aren't so mobile. It's when they start to run that everything changes."

"Oh, yay," I deadpan.

"Watching them learn and grow… there's nothing like it. It's so rewarding."

"Don't you ever want… more? Outside of the kids?"

She shrugs. "I work part-time with a nonprofit. It's hard with the team's schedule, being the default parent all the time. I was fine with one kid, but when the second came, I knew I needed an outlet outside of the babies. Don't get me wrong, I love my kids to pieces, but I was losing a part of myself. So we increased the hours with the nanny, and I started working again, and I'm much happier."

"I don't want her to think I don't want to be around her. That I'm passing her off to someone else because I can't handle it. That I don't want her."

I chose to be her mother. I chose to stay with her—for her.

"Okay, so on an airplane, they tell you to put your oxygen mask on before the kids' mask, right?" Mel waits for me to nod. "You have to take care of yourself first, or you will burn out, and then it will be even more challenging. Some women don't need an outlet outside of their kids, but others do, and there is absolutely nothing wrong with that. It's not selfish to put yourself first if it means you're a better mother and wife."

"Hmm." Everything she's saying makes sense. It's what I needed to hear, even if I didn't want to.

"And honestly, it's healthy for her to have other adults in her life that she knows and trusts. If anything happens to you…"

I swallow, thinking of Carter. My heart aches, but it's not that sharp, stabbing pain I used to have. The hurt has been dulled by time, and I'm getting better at dealing with it every day.

"She already lost her biological mother. I don't want her to lose me too. Or Al."

"Right. It doesn't make you less of a mother to accept you need help. It doesn't mean you aren't doing a good job. Being a parent is hard fucking work. It's all-consuming. Whatever you can do to make it easier for yourself, do it. If you don't have a village behind you, it's almost impossible."

I've noticed she doesn't come over when Vanessa and Audrey do, and for a little while, I convinced myself it was because she didn't think I was worthy of hanging out with. Maybe it's more so that she doesn't have the bandwidth, either.

"A few of us… we get together for playdates on Thursday mornings, if you'd like to join us."

Mel frowns. "It's hard with a three-year-old and little babies. They can't really play together yet."

"Oh. I hadn't thought about that."

Most of the time, we watch while Leo and Emmy crawl around the living room, and Cora sleeps or eats. Mel's little one is right in the middle, two months younger than Emmy and two months older than Cora.

"When they're a bit bigger, definitely," she says with a smile. "I'd love to attend."

Emmy is snoozing now, snuggling into my neck. If I didn't know better, I'd say she gained about ten pounds in a minute.

"I'm going to set her down before I get nap trapped." I laugh. "Learned that lesson the hard way."

"Do it, quick!" Her knowing smile reminds me I'm not doing this alone. That I'm not the only one in the trenches, struggling day to day.

She's right; I have to put my oxygen mask on first, and I need to take better care of myself. I can't look out for Emmy if I burn out.

There's a harrowing moment when I think she wakes up, but I successfully transfer Emmy to her car seat, then bring her down to where I was sitting. Bex silently offers me some of her nachos, and I dunk a chip into the gooey cheese with a quiet thanks.

"Gonzo's looking good out there," she says. "He's taken four shots on goal this period. Sooner or later, one's going in."

"Let's hope so." He's always in a better mood when he scores a goal. Not that he's ever truly grumpy, just downtrodden. Defeated. I'll do whatever I can to cheer him up.

An idea starts to form. He tried to plan a nice evening for us, with candles and a home-cooked meal. But we haven't gone anywhere together, only the two of us. If we're going to be a couple, an actual couple, we need to do things without the baby.

I nudge Vanessa. "Can I ask a favor?"

"Anytime," she says immediately, and her easy acceptance reassures me that I'm doing the right thing.

"Do you mind sharing your nanny's phone number? I need help."

twenty-nine

. . .

Al

AFTER THE GAME, I'm whistling while I shower and change. Mitchell throws a wet towel at me, but I don't care. Two goals and an assist. I couldn't do it without my wife and kid in the crowd. Tonight, I'm going to order dinner in, light some candles, and seduce my wife. After the absolute fucking torture of spending the last two nights sleeping fully clothed in my bed, I'm hoping she'll be open to taking things a step further.

The guys and I reach the suite, and I beeline for Riley. The sight of her in my jersey makes my heart thump and my cock twitch. Adrenaline from the game still floods through my system, and it takes everything in me not to stalk across the room and claim her as mine like a caveman in front of everyone. As it is, I bite my lip so I don't groan in front of half my teammates.

She turns away from her conversation with Bex and spots me, and a grin spreads over her face. Her eyes are bright as she drinks me in, frank appreciation in her gaze. My stomach clenches.

Desire coursing through my veins, I step right up beside her. I'm not sure who moves first, but the next thing I know she's in my arms, her face buried in my chest. I breathe in her lavender shampoo, the comforting scent soothing my racing heart.

After a few moments, she pulls away, but she doesn't go far. Riley rises onto her tiptoes and brushes her lips over mine in a sweet kiss. It's not nearly enough. I'm addicted to the taste of her, to the soft press of her mouth to mine, to her breathy sighs.

"Hi," she whispers.

My hand finds the nape of her neck, tugging her closer to me. "Hi," I whisper back, before I kiss her again.

This one is decidedly less sweet. I scrape my teeth along her bottom lip, which parts on a gasp. Wasting no time, I slip my tongue into her mouth, hers coming out to tangle with mine. I thread my fingers through her hair, kissing the breath out of her.

A wolf whistle pierces the air.

"Get it, Gonzo," Mitchell calls out.

"Get a room," Logan counters.

When I pull away, Riley's face is flushed red, her chest heaving. Her dark lipstick is smudged, and I trace my finger beneath her lip, rubbing away the berry color.

"Hi," I say again, giddy with butterflies.

She laughs. "We're not starting this again." Emmy is settled in her stroller, playing with her feet. We skipped the booties this time in favor of footsie pajamas, which she seems to hate less. My girl still rebels against most clothes. I guess she really does take after me; I was a naked baby, too.

I reach into the stroller to tickle her belly, and she grins and babbles at me. My heart warms. My two girls, right where I want them to be.

Riley slips her hand into mine. "Let's go home."

Home. That sounds perfect.

We wind through the arena to the parking garage. An attendant has already brought my car around, the heat cranked. I help Riley into her seat and then get Emmy settled in the back.

We chat about the game, casual conversation punctuated by baby shrieks and giggles. My skin feels too tight for my body, like I'm about to burst with happiness.

"I've got a surprise for you," Riley says.

"Oh?"

"Yeah. Don't change clothes."

My eyebrows lift. Usually, the first thing I do when I get home is put on something more comfortable than a suit and tie.

"Okay…"

"Trust me. It'll be worth it."

Once we get to the house, we settle Emmy in her high chair with a mashed avocado and some scrambled eggs. I snag Riley around the waist and pull her into me.

"Have I mentioned how much I like you in my jersey?" I tuck a strand of hair behind her ear, my gaze pinging between her eyes and her lips.

"You do? I had no idea," she teases.

Growling, I dip my head to kiss her again. Her hands fist in my shirt, tugging me closer.

But then the doorbell rings, and I groan as I pull away.

"If it's a salesman, I'm going to be pissed."

She shoots me a grin over her shoulder as she flounces to the door, opening it to reveal—

"Brigitte?" I stare at the blond woman I haven't talked to in at least a year. Maybe longer. "What are you doing here?"

She waves awkwardly. "Congrats on the kid."

"We're going out," Riley announces. "Brigitte is staying with Emmy while we have a date night."

My chest warms with affection for her. She's been so resistant to using a babysitter, even my sister. And she went out of her way to arrange this—a night out just for us.

"Come in, come in," I say, beckoning Brigitte inside. "You can meet our daughter."

"I'm going to run upstairs and get ready," my wife says, patting me on the chest as she passes by.

Since I have no idea what Riley has in mind for the night, I run through the same spiel I gave Cari. Brigitte takes care of Larsson's kid, who's about the same age, plus she's in medical school, so I have every confidence she knows what she's doing. Still…

"We've never left her with anyone before. Anyone who isn't family," I add quickly.

"It's good for you two to get out, for her to see you prioritizing yourselves," she says. "Go. Have fun. Enjoy your night out. I've got this, and if anything should happen, I have your phone numbers."

Relief flows through me with my slow exhale. "Thank you for this. I know you and I…"

She shakes her head. "It was a blind date, and it wasn't a good match," she says simply.

"It's a long story, but we weren't together back then. I don't want you to think I was running around on her. That's not who I am."

Our coffee date was only a few weeks after Carter and I were together, ages before Riley and Emmy came onto the scene.

"I didn't think that at all," Brigitte assures me. "What matters is that you are happy. Are you?"

"Happy? Yes."

"That's all that's important," she says, and that's that. "Now, the little angel and I will have a good time this evening, and she'll be tucked into her crib before we know it."

Footsteps sound on the stairs, and I turn around to see the most incredible vision.

Riley is wearing a short black lacy dress with a floral print, sheer black stockings, and tall black boots with what can only be described as "fuck me" heels. Her hair and makeup are done, amping her pretty features up to a ten. She's wearing the necklace I got her, the amethyst shining in the hollow of her throat.

My mouth goes dry, and my cock pulses behind my suit pants. My wife is fucking *hot*.

She stares up at me, her bright blue eyes lined with dark makeup. The longer I go without speaking, the more her face falls, and her confident mask slips.

"You don't like it?" Her voice is quiet. Small.

That kicks my brain back online. I reach for her waist, pulling her into me. She comes easily, her hand settling on my chest, directly over my heart. Can she hear it beating overdrive, just for her? Can she feel my hard cock pressed into her belly?

"You look beautiful," I tell her, before I press my lips to hers. Her breath hitches.

Mindful of our audience, I pull back, squeezing her waist. "Come on. What do we have planned for tonight?"

"It's a surprise." She grins at me, and then as she turns to Emmy, happily playing with her food, her face falls again. "This won't traumatize her, right? We aren't abandoning her?"

"We'll be back in a few hours," I promise.

Riley takes a deep breath, then bends down, pressing a kiss to Emmy's forehead, and I follow suit.

"Okay, let's go before I change my mind," she says.

Itching to get my wife alone, I open the hall closet and pull out her coat, holding it open for her. Riley smiles up at me, nerves plain to see.

"It'll be okay." Taking her hand in mine, I squeeze her reassuringly before leading her to the door. I help her into the car, and she types an address into the GPS. "You won't tell me where we're going?"

"You'll see when we get there."

The drive is relatively quick, all things considered. As much as I want to reach over and set my hand on her leg, the light snowfall means I'm forced to keep both hands on the wheel.

We arrive at a steakhouse in the Seaport. There's usually a wait list a month long, so I'm surprised when we walk in and are seated at a table right away.

"How did you manage this?" I ask, glancing around the packed dining room.

"I might have pulled a few strings," she says with a shy smile. "Turns out mentioning my husband plays with the Grizzlies opens quite a few doors."

Throwing my head back, I laugh. "Good. I'm glad."

She's not trying to ride my coattails. She's not taking advantage of me. All she wants is to treat me to nice things.

I can live with that.

When the waiter comes, we order a bottle of wine. Conversation flows easily. We talk about where we grew up, how she was bounced around from foster home to foster home. I tell her about my siblings, my parents in Florida, taking care of my abuela. I wish I could spend more time with them, but I know Boston isn't the right place for them.

She tells me about her and Carter, how they stuck together throughout their early adulthood. The one thing she doesn't mention is me and Carter together. I don't blame her. I don't want to think about it. Nor do I want to remember a time when I was with anyone else.

Riley's my present. She's my future. The past isn't important; we've grown from there.

The food is good. The wine is fine. But there's something missing. I don't need fancy dinners. I don't need *this*. All I want is Riley, to spend time with her, to enjoy her company.

But maybe *she* needs this. An outlet outside of our kid, a chance to get dressed up and feel like a grown-up. I leave the house every day for work. She doesn't get the same opportunity.

Maybe now that she's taken the first step of getting a babysitter for a night out, she'll be open to having some more help so she has time to herself, too, before she burns out. Her happiness is my priority. I don't want to do this without her, and I'll do what it takes to prove how much I value her—as a coparent, and as a partner.

thirty

· · ·

Riley

AL IS quiet on the drive back to the house. The snow is falling steadily, so even though I want to touch him, I force myself to keep my hands to myself. I don't want to imagine a wreck where Emmy loses all three of her parents.

When we finally walk through the front door, Brigitte is on the couch, reading a thick textbook, the baby monitor on the coffee table. The faint crackle of the white noise proves Emmy is sound asleep, and I sigh with relief.

"How was she?" Al asks, rushing over to the monitor and peering at the grainy picture on the screen. The tension in his shoulders loosens as the device relays Emmy's soft, steady breaths. My stomach flutters at how adorably overprotective he is.

"She was perfect. Fussed a little at bedtime, since she was off her routine, but nothing I couldn't handle," she reports.

Within a few quick minutes, she has packed up her things, we've paid her, and she's gone.

Al looks exhausted. It's easy to forget he played a full game today.

"Let's head to bed," I say, taking his hand, and his eyebrows shoot up.

All my earlier nerves come flooding back as I lead him up the stairs, bypassing my room and heading directly to his. The *snick* of the door closing after us is loud in the otherwise quiet room, the only sounds his ragged breathing and the pounding of my heart.

I want this. Want him. And that's confirmed the moment I turn to face him, drinking him in. The way his broad chest fills out the custom suit, his thick thighs and powerful frame.

"I have no expectations here," he says, his voice hoarse. "If you want to go to sleep—"

My heels click on the floor as I step forward, reaching for his suit jacket. I slip it off his shoulders, and he helps me shrug it off, then his tie, before I reach for his shirt. Slowly, I unhook each button, revealing his wide, furry chest. Body hair has never really drawn me in, but something about the scrape of his against my knuckles drives me wild.

I turn to give him my back. "There's a zipper."

His thick fingers brush against the nape of my neck, smoothing my hair out of the way. He presses a kiss to the notch at the base of my skull as he drags the tiny metal tab down, down, down my spine. The fabric gapes and I step out of my dress, letting it pool to the floor.

I face him again, and his eyes dart between my lips and my black lace bra. When I reach for him again, he helps me discard his shirt, and then I push lightly on his chest until he sits on the bed. Al stares up at me, his eyes dark.

There's no sexy way to take off a pair of tights. But the heat in his gaze proves he isn't turned off by how the spandex digs into my belly, leaving red marks behind.

He snags my hips, pulling me closer until I'm standing between his spread thighs. His fingertips run over the edge of my panties, leaving tingles in his wake.

"Are you okay if these come off?" he murmurs, his tone husky with need. "We don't have to do anything you don't want to do."

"I want to," I whisper back. I don't know why I'm whispering, though.

This moment feels big. Heavy. Like I'm walking on a tightrope, high above the ground, and he's the only thing keeping me from tipping over. I know he'll catch me if I fall. *When* I fall. For the first time, tumbling off the ledge and into his arms doesn't sound like the worst thing in the world.

Reaching behind me, I unclasp my bra, letting it fall to the floor. Then I hook my fingers in the waistband of my panties and shove them unceremoniously off my hips.

Al is still wearing his suit pants, the crotch tented by his erection. Warmth floods between my legs at the visible proof of his arousal. We have an emotional connection, a legal obligation to each other, but knowing he wants me in this way... I can finally relax a little. I'm not alone in this. Whatever happens between us will happen, one way or another. I don't need to be afraid and hold myself back any longer. He's promised me the moon. Now I have to trust that he'll deliver.

His hands land on my hips, his thumbs caressing the divot of the joints as he pulls me closer. I take a step forward, then another, and straddle his lap, bringing my chest flush with his. The rapid-fire pounding of his heart hammers against mine, sending my own into overdrive. His coarse chest hair tickles my breasts in the most delicious way that makes me wet.

Threading my arms around his neck, I sink onto his thighs, his hard cock pressing against my ass. He lets out a groan, the sound pained.

"Riley..."

Holy fucking hell.

I never thought my name on his lips would sound so good. It soothes my soul in a way I didn't know I needed.

His arms loop around my waist, holding me to him, and then he surges upward, twisting, and tosses me onto the bed. I bounce on the mattress, and he grins, hunger in his eyes.

He wastes no time in whipping off his belt, the whistle of the leather through the loops sending a shiver down my spine. Shoving his pants and underwear down his thick thighs, he steps out of his clothes and stalks toward me, climbing onto the bed and settling beside me.

For a beat, we stare at each other, greedily drinking each other in. His cock bobs against his sculpted, hairy abs, twitching the longer I look at him. I can't decide where I want to start first.

Realization hits me that this might be our *first* time, but it won't be our *only* time. Not when we have forever together. We'll get to do this again, and again, and again, and I can't fucking wait.

He stretches out, lying on his side, and draws one of my legs over his hips, opening me up. There's a good foot of space between us, but it feels like a mile.

I trail my fingers over his pec, down the center of his chest, and over his abs. His body hair scratches my fingertips, the coarse hair tickling. I don't hate it, though. It's sexy as hell. He is one hundred percent confident in who he is and what he looks like, and *that* is the sexiest thing about him. More than his face or his dick.

Although… I quite like his face. And I *love* his dick.

I continue my journey and wrap my hand around his cock, thick and hard, his length throbbing in my grip. Sticky precum gathers at his slit, and I run my thumb over it, spreading the viscous fluid over him.

Al groans, his fingers flexing into my hip before he moves to my ass, kneading the flesh. His mouth seals over mine, kissing the breath out of me. It takes everything in me to remember to stroke him, so overwhelmed by all the sensations coursing through me.

I never thought a kiss could be like this: so right, so perfect. Soul-consuming. His tongue strokes into my mouth, tangling with mine, and I allow myself to sink into this, into him. Giving myself permission to live in the moment instead of hyperanalyzing every fucking second of this.

His fingers tiptoe over the curve of my hip and down to my mound, then lower to my clit. Sparks of pleasure burst through me as his thumb brushes against me, and I shudder, letting out a soft moan in the back of my throat. The touch is too light, too brief. I want more. I *need* more.

Rolling onto my back, I pull him with me. He nudges my hand away from his cock and then brings his fingers between my legs. His fingertips dip low, gathering the wetness at my core, before brushing over my clit again.

"What do you like?" He trails kisses down my neck, over my chest. The soft hair of his beard abrades me, leaving my skin pink and tingly in his wake.

Self-consciousness threatens to take over, but I shove it aside and take his hand, directing him exactly where I want him, with the exact right amount of pressure. He takes over, his fingers drawing quick, hard circles over my sensitive skin.

With his mouth on me, his fingers stroking me, pleasure floods through my system. My body feels disconnected from my brain as the sensations overtake me, and I fall.

I fall and I fall and I *fall*. But he catches me. Just like he promised.

As I come down, he continues to kiss my neck, nibbling at a spot beneath my jaw that makes me gasp. I shake my head a few times, trying to concentrate. We need to have this conversation before I throw all caution to the wind and do something we'll both regret in the cold light of day.

"We should talk," I say, shoving his hand away from between my legs.

His eyes widen. "Now?" His voice is rough and gravelly, but there's no denying the hurt there.

Fuck, I'm doing this wrong. The bed jostles as I sit up, folding my legs, and he props himself up on his elbow. His gaze is heavy on me, the weight of his stare sending warmth flooding between my legs again. Almost against my will, my hand finds his chest, and I lay my palm over his pounding heart. The rapid-fire beats soothe me.

Blowing out a breath, I level with him. "I don't usually come from penetration. It doesn't do it for me."

He hums, thoughtful. "Okay, then."

That's it? That's all he has to say?

"I know it's an ego thing for some guys, to try to make it happen, but it probably won't for me. You can still fuck me. It means I won't—"

His palm lands over my mouth, silencing me. I should hate it, him taking my voice away, but the serious look in his eyes settles something deep within me.

"Do you trust me?" he murmurs.

I nod. Absolutely. With every fiber of my being.

Removing his hand, he kisses me again, quick and hard. "Be right back."

Blinking, all I can do is watch as he pulls away. He gets out of bed, buck naked, and leaves the room. *What the hell?*

But then I hear him rummaging around next door. Why is he in my room? What is he doing in there?

I have my answer a few moments later when he returns, holding my hot-pink vibrator in his hand. My face heats, a flush spreading over my cheeks and down my chest.

"What are you doing?"

He knew it was there. Does that mean he's heard me? *Oh, fuck.*

Al stalks toward me, his hard cock bobbing between his legs. He climbs onto the bed, tossing the vibrator beside me, and covers my body with his again.

"Toys are friends. They aren't a threat. Not to me, not to my ego." His lips twist in a smirk. "If that's what it takes to get you there, I want all the tools in my arsenal."

My heart beats a little faster. He's not offended or put off... but that doesn't mean he'll like what I have to say next. I take a breath, then exhale slowly. The contraception talk might be even more embarrassing than my husband knowing I use a vibrator while I think of him.

But if we can't have these conversations, we have no business having sex.

"My last test results were negative, and I have an IUD."

"Me too." He laughs awkwardly. "Not the IUD part. The test results. But if it would make you feel better..." Leaning over, he rummages in the bedside table, coming up with an unopened box of condoms. "We can be double protected. Make sure nothing happens until we're ready for it."

Until. Like it's a given that we could have children together. Like he wants to expand our family.

Not right now. We can talk about it again later, when we're not so lust-blind to the consequences.

But it doesn't sound terrible. Having more kids. Giving Emmy a sibling—or more than one. I've never really thought about having kids myself, but now that I have her in my life, I wouldn't trade her for the world.

Warmth floods over me, and I heave out a sigh of relief. "I think I want that."

"We're new. Just because we're married doesn't mean we can't use them. It's not a matter of trust or commitment. It's protection—for both of us. IUDs aren't infallible."

He gets me. In a few words, he's summarized what I've been struggling with. He makes me feel seen. Heard. Appreciated.

Taking the box from him, I rip it open and snag a foil square off the strip. I push it into his hand, his fingertips brushing mine and sending shockwaves through me.

All finesse is brushed aside as he tears open the condom, his knuckles brushing the inside of my thigh while he gets himself situated.

I expect him to roll on top of me right away and get down to business, but he surprises me by cupping my cheek, his thumb stroking over my nose.

"You're sure about this?" he murmurs.

"I've never been so sure about anything."

thirty-one

. . .

Al

URGING RILEY TO STRADDLE ME, I wait for her to get into position before I notch my cock at her entrance. My hands on her hips, I let her set the pace as she sinks onto my cock, her tight, wet heat squeezing me with every inch.

Stars burst behind my closed eyelids, and I blindly search the mattress until I connect with the vibrator and turn it onto the lowest setting. The buzz is loud in the quiet room, and her tight pussy clenches around me.

I bring the toy to her clit, slowly pressing it against her. Her throaty moan makes my cock jerk inside her, and she throws her head back, her hips grinding against the silicone wand reflexively.

"That feels so good."

My only objective is for her to come. I want her to feel good. Whatever she needs to get there, I'm game. Tomorrow, we can go to a toy store and buy anything she wants. Fuck, I'll buy out the entire store if it means she'll keep riding me, squeezing my cock.

Her hands settle on my abs, stroking over the tensed muscles while I flex my hips and fuck up into her. She meets me thrust for thrust, rising on her haunches and then sinking back onto me, the vibrations rumbling through her and into me, making my cock throb deep inside her.

The chemistry between us is palpable. We're intimately connected, but it goes beyond the physicality. It's never been like this before. I feel like I'm about to burst out of my skin, like my body isn't big enough to contain my emotions.

I fucking love this woman. I love fucking her, too. She means more than that, though. She doesn't complete me; I am a fully formed person on my own. I wasn't walking around missing half of my heart. But I didn't realize how much *life* I was missing out on until her.

She makes me a *better* person—the best possible version of myself. The love she has for our daughter is only part of it. It's the way she's taken everything in stride, from moving here to marrying me to this crazy found family of the hockey team. The late nights and early mornings and coordinating around my schedule. I've never felt unimportant or inconsequential with her. She doesn't overlook me the way other people do; she *sees* me for who I am—and who I want to be.

I catch her hand, running my thumb over her wedding band. We did all of this so quickly, I didn't buy her an engagement ring. But she deserves the ring of her dreams. Is it less romantic if I ask her to pick it out? She'll be the one wearing it; I want her to be happy.

Riley squeezes her inner muscles around me, swiveling her hips. "You good?" she pants, her chest heaving.

Everything comes back into focus as I blink a few times, concentrating on the task at hand: making my wife come. Ideally, more than once.

The bed jostles as I surge upward and fold her legs around my waist, until we're twined together like a pretzel. The vibrator slips, the curved end positioned lower against her clit, and I groan as the tip brushes against the base of my cock.

With my free hand, I reach for her, threading my fingers

through her dark brown waves. Her hair falls a little past her shoulders, the front pinned back out of her face. The perfect length to wrap around my fist.

Riley's breathy moan goes straight to my dick, and I trail kisses down the column of her neck, tasting the salt on her skin. She smells like lavender and musk. Typically, I'm not attracted to floral scents, but I love them on her.

An emotion I can't identify bubbles up inside me.

I love my wife. Maybe it's too soon. I definitely can't tell her yet. But one day… Maybe I actually can have my happily ever after.

We can have it. Together.

Riley gasps, her walls fluttering around my cock. Her muscles tense and she throws her head back, riding my cock for all she's worth. A long, low groan rumbles through her as she comes, her fingernails digging half-moons into my chest.

The pinprick of pain is enough to tip me over the edge, and I fuck up into her a few more times before my orgasm hits, my entire body overcome with pleasure. I remove the vibrator, turning it off and tossing it aside, the silence without it deafening.

She slumps against me, knocking me back onto the mattress and burying her face in my neck. I run my hand down her spine, caressing each vertebra one by one. As my heart pounds, a staccato beat echoes in my eardrums while I try to catch my breath.

"Fuck," she whispers against my skin.

My entire body freezes. "What's wrong?"

"We're way too good at that for it to be the only time we're doing it," she says, half slurring her words.

"Definitely." I press a kiss to the top of her head. "All day, every day. Who needs hockey when we can do that instead?"

She huffs out a breath of laughter. "We can't lock ourselves away in this room forever."

"Maybe just a little bit longer." I tighten my arms around her, breathing her in.

After a few minutes, she rolls off me, but she doesn't go far. Her head pillows on my chest, her arm slung low around my waist. Even though I know I should get up and deal with the condom, I don't want to leave her. Don't want this moment to end.

"Hey, Al?" she says into the darkness.

"Yeah?"

"I'm glad we went on a date tonight."

"Me too," I confess.

"Can we do it again?"

The hope in her voice makes me grin. "Anytime you'd like."

thirty-two

· · ·

Riley

DAYLIGHT STREAMS in through the cracks in the blinds, and I wake with a start. I'm in Al's bed, naked, but he's not here. The spot beside me is cool when I run my hand over the sheets.

I swallow around the lump in my throat. Why does my stomach clench at him not being around? Why do I miss him? It was just sex; it's not a big deal. Right?

After forcing myself out of bed, I pull a shirt and sweat-pants out of his dresser, his smoky scent calming my ruffled nerves. In the hall bathroom, I wash off my makeup and scoop my hair into a new ponytail.

"No, no, your mommy is sleeping," I hear Al say from downstairs. "Let's give her some space for now."

Emmy whines, the sound punching me straight in the chest. I hate it when she cries.

"Baby, I know, I miss her too," he continues. "She works so hard to watch out for you. She deserves a day to sleep in."

I creep down the stairs, trying not to make too much noise. Al must have supersonic hearing, though, because he looks up as I hit the ground floor, a bright smile on his face.

He's in sweats and a T-shirt, much like me, lounging on the couch. Emmy is sprawled on his chest, pawing at him.

"Good morning," he says. His eyes widen as he takes in my stolen clothes, and the heat on his face makes my sore pussy throb. "There's coffee in the pot. I made chilaquiles, there's a plate warming in the oven."

"Fuck, I love you," I blurt out.

His eyes widen hopefully. "You do?"

Horrified, I cover my mouth with my hand. "I'm sorry. I—"

Al's face falls, but he does his best to hide it. "No, yeah, I get it," he says. "It's way too soon. We just had our first date. It's not… No. I get it," he says again.

My heart breaks at the pain on his face, and I cross the room and perch on the couch beside him, drawing my leg up between us. I pull Emmy into my arms, and she gives a squawk of displeasure at being separated from her jungle gym, but right now, I need the baby snuggles. When she wraps her chubby arms around me and buries her sticky face in my neck, all is right with the world.

"It's too soon," I tell him softly. "Isn't it?"

He swallows thickly, his soulful brown eyes meeting mine. "I think I'm falling for you."

I hold my breath. "Are you falling for me? Or am I convenient?" My heart races. "We're married and we're coparenting. Are you sure it's actually me you have feelings for?"

"Yes, Riley, I'm sure." Al reaches over and cups my cheek, running his thumb over the bridge of my nose. "I see you for who you are. I know it's convoluted, but you are one hundred percent not convenient for me. If we wanted to keep this strictly business, we could have. But I like you too much. Not as my wife. Not as my child's mother. *You*."

My stomach clenches. Everything he's saying sounds great. Almost *too* perfect.

I've never been in love before, so I don't know what it

feels like. I enjoy spending time with Al, and I get those silly little butterflies in my stomach when I think of him, but it's just a crush. It'll fade.

Then again, I've never had a family before, either, and I think we're nailing this thing. So maybe it'll come with time. It's like coffee; sometimes, it takes a while to percolate. That instant stuff will get the job done in a pinch, but a good, strong brew tastes better.

My past relationships... Nobody has ever treated me the way Al takes care of me. Money and physical comforts aside, he goes out of his way to treat me with kindness and respect. He makes food for me and is thoughtful about what I like; he doesn't leave me to fend for myself. He pulls his weight with our child so I can sleep in, getting up with her on the nights he's home and being an equal coparent.

He's a partner in every sense of the word.

But is it *love*?

I don't know what to say. I need to answer him.

But Al takes my silence in stride. He darts forward, pecks my lips in a chaste kiss, and then settles on his couch cushion before I can react.

"Is there anything you want to do today?"

"I just want to spend the day with you," I admit. I run my hand over Emmy's back, trying to settle my nerves. "Maybe when she has her nap, we can have a repeat of last night?"

His eyes darken with desire. "You want to go out?"

"Not exactly." Heat radiates off my cheeks. "If you want to take a nap, too, we can arrange that. Or we can use the bed for... another purpose."

"You want to have sex," he says bluntly.

"Shh!" I cover Emmy's ears with my hands. "You can't say that word in front of the baby!"

Al cracks up. "Okay, okay, got it. We can go have a naked nap while she's in her crib," he says. "Anytime you want to sleep in my bed, naked or fully clothed, I'm game. Even if I'm not here."

At that, my eyes widen. "What are you talking about?"

"When you're ready, I want you to move in with me."

"We already live together."

He fixes me with a pointed look.

"Oh. You mean the spare room."

"I am one hundred percent not pushing you," he assures. His fingers stroke the back of my hand. "When you want to, I'm here."

"And if I'm never ready?"

Al gives me his lopsided grin. "I'll still be here."

"I want that," I admit. "I want us to be together. I'm just…"

"Not quite there yet." He doesn't seem upset, taking it in stride. "That's okay. It's a big adjustment. I want you to be sure."

It's not enough for me to want it; I have to follow through. And that's the part that scares me.

"Now, me and my girl need some important daddy-daughter time," he says, pulling Emmy out of my arms. "Get your coffee, eat your breakfast. We have a full day of playing ahead of us."

My chest warms with contentment. How is this my life? How did I turn out so lucky?

"That sounds perfect."

thirty-three

. . .

Al

IT'S SATURDAY NIGHT, and we're on a national broadcast. As much as I love our local crew, there's something special about being streamed nationwide on mainstream channels. I always want to play my best, but knowing so many extra people are watching pushes me farther.

"You good, man?" Jenkins asks me as we warm up near the left point.

"Golden."

He offers his glove and I fist-bump him. "Your family here tonight?"

"Nah. It's too hard with Emmy's schedule." I shrug. There will be plenty of games where they're able to come, but an eight o'clock start is already past bedtime.

"Too bad. You're always on fire when they're here."

I laugh. "I'm on fire every day."

"Nah, not like you are when they're in the stands." Jenkins smirks at me. "Must be magic, having your wife in the crowd. Maybe I should get one of those."

"You? A wife? Do you really think you're ready to settle down?"

The kid is twenty-four, and even though there's only a four-year difference between us, it feels enormous. He has a new girl on his arm every few weeks. They never last long, and they all look the same: tall, blond, and slim, with no personality beyond what gets them the most likes on social media. It's not the life I want, but hey, if it works for him…

We continue stretching, and I study him in a new light. "What was your longest relationship?"

He scowls. "Fuck off."

"Dude, you are so not ready for marriage."

"I could totally do it. I'd rock the relationship thing." But the fear in his eyes and the way his voice cracks are answer enough.

"There's no need to rush into it. Take your time. Find the right person."

He cocks his head. "Did you? Find the right person?"

I think of this morning, Riley in my bed, her hair splayed across my pillow as she slept. This afternoon, a hasty quickie in the daylight, a stolen moment. The way I'm looking forward to coming home after a hard game and curling up beside her, holding her in my arms all night.

"Yeah. I think I have."

Jenkins grins, clapping me on the shoulder. "Good. I'm happy for you, man. You deserve it."

The siren sounds, signaling the end of warm-ups. We troop back down the chute to the dressing room, where Coach Turner gives us a pep talk, McKittrick gives us some advice, and then MacGregor reads off the starting lineup.

New Orleans plays a heavy-hitting game, and although Mitchell left on decent terms, it's clear his old team isn't taking it easy on him. Their goons are after him all throughout the period. Every time he's on the ice, it's like there's a beacon highlighting him, drawing their attention.

He takes hit after hit, giving it back tenfold, but by the

middle of the first period, we're run ragged. The only good news is that they're leaving me and Jenkins pretty much alone, but Mitchell is our best goal scorer for a reason, and almost all our plays revolve around his slapshot. Every time we pass him the puck, he gets pummeled.

"What the fuck is going on out there?" McKittrick asks, clapping him on the shoulder when we hit the bench for a line change.

"Hell if I know," Mitchell says, reaching for a bottle and guzzling the electrolyte drink. "This is fucking brutal."

"You've got this," Coach Turner cuts in. "Show those assholes exactly why they should have kept you, and what they're missing out on."

"Yes, Coach," Mitchell says with a sardonic smile.

But when we shift back onto the ice, he's immediately hit from behind, even though the puck is nowhere near him. He collapses to the ice—and doesn't get up. Sprawled where the ice meets the boards, he's in a vulnerable position, and I see red.

What the fuck are they doing?

Of course, the ref doesn't call the penalty. What good are they? Sure, there are twelve players and four officials on the ice, so they can't see *everything*, but such a blatant display of targeting should be obvious. On the bench, Coach is hollering, and Logan's using both hands to hold back Jenkins, who's spitting mad.

Our fans are livid, too, booing and throwing things onto the ice. Play is stopped while the ice crew comes to clean up, and I skate over to Mitchell, who's being evaluated by Amelia and Derek.

"Dude, you're bleeding," I blurt.

He touches his mouth, where a streak of blood is forming. "Bit my fucking lip when I fell. Assholes."

"You good?"

His attention turns to Derek, who frowns before reluctantly shaking his head. "I'll clear you, but we have to stitch your lip. You can't go out there spilling blood everywhere."

Mitchell's eyes darken, frustration on his face. "No, that's their job."

He has to sit out a shift while he gets cleaned up, so Coach sends Reynolds out with Jenkins and me, and although we land two shots on goal, nothing goes in. The physicality of their game means we have to up our play, but no matter what we do, we're held back by their excellent goaltender. It feels impossible. Insurmountable.

But then—Larsson sneaks the puck over the goaltender's right shoulder, and Easton levels a New Orleans defender with a massive hit, and it finally, *finally* feels like things are going the right way for the first time all game.

Line change. Jenkins, Mitchell, and I hit the ice again, and our temporary reprieve is fully over, because they're targeting him again. But it's not only Mitchell; now, they have it out for all of us, desperation clear on their faces.

We've never had beef with New Orleans, not like this. The Grizzlies take pride in playing a steady, clean game. We don't take stupid penalties. We don't want to hurt anyone. Sure, sometimes hits don't land right, or there's incidental contact that goes the wrong way. By nature, hockey is a dangerous sport.

We play the right way. We *care*.

These assholes? All they can focus on is the bloodlust. They can't see past it.

And when Mitchell skates to the left point, and Sinclair passes the puck, their goon collides with Mitchell in a massive hit that lifts our player clear off his skates. His entire body is airborne for what feels like an hour but can't possibly be more than seconds.

His helmet collides with the ice with a sickening thud that instantly makes me nauseous.

And he doesn't get up.

A whistle echoes through the silent arena. Even the rowdiest, noisiest fans have fallen quiet.

Panic laces through me. *Get up, get up, get up.* I skate closer, but the lineman holds me back.

"No, no," he mutters, his eyes focused on Mitchell.

There's a commotion to my left as Derek hurries back onto the ice, wearing grippy cleats on his shoes. He rushes to Mitchell's side, kneeling beside him and talking to him. His voice is inaudible over the rushing of blood in my ears.

Adrenaline courses through me, my vision burning red. I'm overcome with the need for retribution. Revenge. I want to rip them limb from limb until they feel every bump and bruise, every hit, every push and shove Mitchell's gone through, and do it tenfold.

The lineman's grip on my jersey tightens. "You can't go over there, kid," he says.

After what feels like an eternity, Amelia comes out with the stretcher, and they load Mitchell onto it. A sick feeling punches me in the stomach at his prone form.

This isn't good.

The refs call our attention, and although Easton wins the face-off, we're too distracted. Distraught. New Orleans scores on a breakaway, and then the period ends.

It's a subdued team that heads into the dressing room. Coach tries to give us a pep talk, but it doesn't work. We just have to get through the next twenty minutes.

Somehow, and I have no fucking clue how, we do. The score is a lopsided 7–1, those assholes reveling in our misery. But it's more than the score. It's Mitchell. In a few short weeks, he's become part of the team. He's one of us, our brother. And we look out for our own.

Coach lets us know his condition is still being evaluated, and we won't have answers at least until tomorrow. My stomach sinks. If it were a simple concussion—not that any concussion is ever simple—they would know right away. It wouldn't require overnight admission to the hospital. Something is *wrong*.

"Hey," Jenkins says as we get dressed, a downcast expression on his face. "A few of us are heading to the bar. Want to come?"

"You're celebrating this shit?" Incredulity drips from my tone.

His laugh is hollow. Bitter. "Coping. Drinking our sorrows, erasing this shitty game, whatever you want to call it."

"Nah. All I want is to get home and crash." I don't even want to see Riley, I don't want to deal with Emmy; I just want to be alone with my thoughts and misery.

"I don't blame you," he says, shaking his head. "Another time. You'll have to bring the wife out with us sometime."

"Yeah, we'll see."

With a two-finger salute, I grab my coat and head for the parking garage. I'm just—*done.*

The drive home feels like it takes forever and a year. I enter the house, stripping off my coat and suit jacket and unbuttoning my shirt as I climb the stairs. Even though I already took a shower at the arena, I need to stand under the hot spray and wash off this numb feeling.

A light shines beneath my door, and my heart skips a beat. I turn the handle and step over the threshold to find Riley sitting up in bed, wearing my T-shirt and reading a book. She's wearing the cutest fucking reading glasses, cat eye with sparkles. My heart threatens to burst right out of my chest. She's *here.* In my room, in my bed.

"Hey," she says softly. "I saw the game. It looked like it sucked."

"You watched my game?"

"Of course I did. I always do."

All this time… I had no idea. She's never mentioned it before. When I've talked about past games, she never intimated she'd seen them. Maybe she's not as indifferent to me as I thought.

Dropping my jacket and shirt, I crawl onto the bed and tackle her in a hug. Riley laughs, pushing her book aside and then wrapping her arms around me.

"What's this for?"

"I'm really glad you're here," I murmur into her neck. "I missed you."

Her body slackens against mine. "I missed you, too."

"Tonight sucked."

"I'm sorry." Her hand slides into my hair, scratching at the back of my scalp.

I lean into her, desperate for her affection. My cock gives a lazy twitch, but I'm not in the mood for sex. I want comfort— and she's freely offering it.

"Can I just hold you?" If she turns me down, I don't know what I'll do.

Riley leans forward, kissing me softly. "Anytime."

Reluctantly, I untangle my limbs from hers. I shuffle into the bathroom, brush my teeth, and drop my suit pants in the dirty clothes hamper, before returning to her—where I belong.

She sets her book and glasses on the bedside table, beside the baby monitor and a glass of water. My heart warms at the thought of her settling in. I could get used to seeing her there every night and waking up next to her every morning.

As I pull back the covers, she turns off the light, immediately sinking down onto the pillows and rolling toward me. I tug her into the circle of my arms, and her familiar scent settles my jumbled nerves.

"Hey, Riley?" I mumble into her hair.

"Hmm?"

"I'm really glad you're here."

She settles her head on my chest, her arm slung low around my waist. "Me too."

Don't leave me. I can't ask her to promise that, but the words are on the tip of my tongue anyway. Now that I know what having her in my life is like, I don't know how I'd ever survive without her.

"Get some rest," she says, snuggling closer to me. "It'll be better in the morning."

thirty-four

. . .

Riley

"I'M IN TROUBLE," I blurt, and Vanessa and Bex look at me curiously.

Emmy and Leo are playing on the floor, Cora is doing tummy time on a play mat, and the adults are drinking. Basically, business as usual for our playdates.

"What's wrong?" Audrey asks straight out.

"I… I think I have feelings for Al," I admit.

Bex laughs. "I'd hope so. He is your husband."

I shake my head, my hair falling out of my ponytail as I do. "It's not like that with us." Tugging at the tie, I worry it between my fingers. Isn't it? Things are changing so quickly, and I can't keep up.

"Except that it is," she says. "That man is so fucking gone for you."

"What are you talking about?"

"The way he looks at you… It's the way Sven looks at Van, and how Seb looks at Audrey." Bex sighs. "It's so sweet."

"He does not." I've seen the way Sven treats his wife like she hung the moon, and the way Seb dotes on Audrey. What Al and I have is nothing like their relationships. Right?

With a sigh, I admit: "I said *I love you* the other day. By accident."

Vanessa laughs. "How do you accidentally tell someone you love them?"

"Because I don't know if I do." And he was being particularly sweet. But that doesn't mean I actually *love* him. I just like him. A lot.

"You do," Bex assures me, patting my arm.

"But how do you *know*?" I've never told anyone I love them, and they've certainly never said it back to me. I was too young when my mom died, none of my foster parents ever formed a bond that way, and even Carter never said those three words to me.

"Because you constantly prioritize his happiness over yours. You trust him and opened up to him, even about the scary things. You see a future beyond the two years you've agreed to," Vanessa says.

"I do. I want… more. What we have now, it's real. But even though we're legally married, we're still dating. Still taking it slow." It's what I need, even if it's not necessarily what I want. But rushing into something isn't the right decision, especially with Emmy to consider.

"Every relationship progresses on its own timeline," Audrey adds. After all, she and Seb went from strangers to serious in the blink of an eye. "Do you constantly think about him? Does he make you feel safe? Do you want to support him, in sickness and in health?"

"I do," I whisper.

"Do you accept him for who he is, flaws and all?" Bex asks.

Al definitely isn't perfect. He snores, and he tosses and turns all night long, and he's always so fucking cheerful that it gets on my nerves, especially first thing in the morning. He jumps into things wholeheartedly without stopping to consider the consequences. These minor annoyances don't turn me off. If anything, they make me like him more. He's *human*.

Do I love him?

"How would I know? I've never been in love before."

"Oh, sweetie." Bex smiles at me and reaches over to refill my sangria. "You're already there. You just have to accept it."

"But it's only a legal marriage for custody. We're not... it's not like that with us."

Isn't it?

"You know, Sven and I started out in a fake relationship," Vanessa says. "Well, it was always real for him. It took me a while to come around. But once I did... He's the best thing in my life. Him and Leo."

Al likes me; he shows me every day how much I mean to him. But love is another story.

Last night, all he wanted was comfort. He needed something only I could give him. With any other guy, I'd be wondering why he didn't want sex, if he wasn't interested in me anymore.

Considering the way he woke me up with his head between my legs, then fucked me slowly, tenderly, until I came with a whimper, I know the fire burning between us isn't in danger. He doesn't have to be raring to go at all times. It doesn't mean I'm losing him. It just means he's a real person with thoughts and feelings that sometimes get a bit messy.

"What if he doesn't feel the same?"

"Girl." Audrey rolls her eyes. "Trust me, he does. The question is, what are you going to do about it?"

"I... don't know."

"Better figure it out, quick," Vanessa says. "Don't just tell him. *Show* him."

Now how do I do that?

―――――

Pozole simmers on the stove, the scent permeating throughout the house. Emmy is down for her nap, and I've showered, shaved, and put on a particularly spicy pair of undies beneath my leggings and oversized sweater.

Now all I have to do is… wait.

And wait.

And wait some more.

After pacing the house for what feels like ten thousand years, I curl up on the sofa with my Kindle. Except I must fall asleep, because the next thing I know, Al wakes me up with a kiss to my forehead.

"Hmm?" I blink a few times, focusing on his tall, broad form leaning above me, still wearing his wool coat.

"Go back to sleep," he murmurs, tucking a strand of hair behind my ear. He plucks my Kindle out of my hands and sets it on the coffee table. "Get some rest. I just wanted to say hi."

"No. I'm supposed to be seducing you."

He chokes on a laugh. "Say what now?"

Pushing up, I struggle into a sitting position, and Al perches beside me on the couch, his warm brown eyes trained on mine. When I'm settled, he leans over and kisses me softly.

"Hi," he whispers.

"Hi."

Fisting the lapel of his coat, I tug him closer, kissing him for real this time. The groan he lets out rumbles through me, making my core throb with want.

When he pulls back, his face is flushed, and I run my hand through his hair. He leans into the contact, humming happily.

"What's this about seduction?" He grins at me. "Eleven out of ten. Highly recommend."

My face heats. "I made pozole, and I—"

He stares at me. "You did what?"

"I asked Cari for your abuela's pozole rojo recipe. I don't

know that I pulled it off, but I—I'm *trying*. I was going to light candles and had all these plans…"

"I know you are. I see you." He takes my hand. "Pozole rojo is my favorite food."

"I also got you a red Jarritos from a market in Jamaica Plain. I'm not sure if you can have it during the season, but I—"

He cuts me off with his lips descending on mine. His fingers thread through my hair as he tugs me closer, pulling lightly enough at the strands that pinpricks of pleasure course through me.

"I love you," he murmurs.

Rearing back, I stare at him, my eyes wide and unblinking. Did he really just say that, or did I imagine it? I pinch the inside of my wrist, and it smarts. *Definitely not still dreaming.*

Time to face reality. I'm not scared. Okay, that's a lie. I'm still terrified of my feelings. But not of *him*.

"I love you, too."

The words feel foreign on my lips. I've never said them before, not even to Carter. But with him… they feel right.

Al gapes at me. "You're saying it for real? You're not going to change your mind?"

"I love you," I repeat, shaking my head. "Even though it terrifies me. Even though I don't have any clue what I'm doing. I love you."

He pulls me against him, wrapping his arms around me. With his face buried in my neck, it's all I can do to hold him, indulging in the feeling of his body against mine.

"I love you," he says into my skin. The press of his lips there makes me shiver.

"We have about an hour before Emmy wakes up. Are you hungry?"

"Not for food," he says with a low growl.

He stands, and before I know what's happening, he scoops me into his arms and over his shoulder. The stairs creak as Al marches up them, directly into his bedroom, and deposits me on the comforter.

Heat licks through me at the hunger in his eyes, his gaze sweeping over me, drinking me in. I reach for the hem of my sweater, but he shakes his head.

"Leave it. I'm not ready to unwrap my present yet."

"Oh? Your present?"

He kneels at the edge of the mattress, covering my body with his. "You are a fucking gift, and I will spend every day of the rest of my life proving that to you."

thirty-five

. . .

Al

I DON'T KNOW where I want to begin. Do I start with her mouth, sipping from her lips again and again? Or do I drag my hands over her tempting curves, memorizing the soft sweetness of her skin? What about feasting on her pussy, devouring her until she writhes against the sheets?

The longer I stare at her, the more she fidgets, shifting under my gaze. Paralyzed by indecision, wanting everything all at once, I go to reassure her, but I don't have the words.

"Fuck it," she mutters, before sitting up and reaching for me. She tugs me on top of her, my body blanketing hers. As she wraps her legs around my waist, my hard cock notches against her center, and every time she grinds against me through the layers of our clothes, seeking her own pleasure, I shudder.

Riley slips her hands under my shirt, mapping the expanse of my back. The sting of her nails digging into my sore muscles makes my cock throb, and I press into her, burying my face in her neck. My lashes flutter shut, and I have to take a deep, shuddering breath. She tastes sweet, the floral scent of her hair products grounding me.

Her words echo in my head. *She loves me.* This isn't temporary, this isn't convenient. It's real, and it's forever, and I get to love her for as long as she'll let me. My chest is tight, but in the best way. Relief, joy, need—they all crash together until I'm nearly vibrating out of my skin.

I cup her face, brushing my thumb across her cheek. She's so beautiful it almost physically hurts. The light makeup she's wearing emphasizes her bright blue eyes and her sweet lips, but I like her whether she's fully glammed up or fresh faced or somewhere in between. I just like *her*.

Shifting back, I reach for my T-shirt, pulling it over my head and tossing it to the floor. She moves to do the same, and I help her lift the oversized sweater over her shoulders. Shimmying beneath me, she wiggles out of her leggings, and soon those are gone, too.

The red lacy bra and panties draw my attention, my eyes pinging between her chest and the apex of her legs. Fuck, now I'm back to not knowing where to start. I want all of her, all at once.

Squirming on the bed, she reaches for me again. "We don't have a lot of time."

"We have forever."

Riley laughs. "Yes, but we have thirty minutes before Emmy wakes up, maybe forty-five if we're lucky. I'd like to make the most of it."

"Fair point." I scoot down the mattress, kissing down her chest and over her belly until I reach the waistband of her panties. Placing soft kisses where the lace meets her skin, I breathe in the smell of her musk, so fucking perfect. My hands grip her waist, desperate to touch her everywhere, but I force myself to stay in control.

Her hips lift impatiently, and I chuckle to myself as I mouth over the damp spot between her legs. My wife lets out a moan, tossing her head back against the pillows.

"Fucking touch me," she mutters.

"I am." I kiss the inside of her thigh, right where the elastic band meets her leg.

She groans, and this time, it's not from pleasure. "Okay, let me say it this way. If you don't make me come, I will—"

From between her legs, I look up at her, eyebrows arched. "You'll what? You'll stop loving me?"

Her face softens. "No. I will always love you. But I might be angry with you."

"We can't have that. Happy wife, happy life." That's what my dad and my married teammates have all advised, and it's a message I've taken to heart.

Peeling the panties off her hips, I draw them down her thighs and toss them onto the floor. There will be time to admire them later. Right now, I have a job to do.

Her legs fall open and I spread her farther, her pretty pink clit winking up at me. She lets out a soft sigh of impatience and I finally, finally, lower my head and taste her. The moment my mouth touches her skin, her hips jackknife off the bed, and I bar my arm across her lower belly to pin her in place.

Slipping first one finger, then a second, inside her tight, wet heat, I focus on pleasuring my wife, paying attention to the way she moans when I find that spot on her front wall that makes her pussy flutter around me, the sharp inhalation when I do something she likes and the way she sags onto the pillows and finally lets herself relax.

With her hands in my hair, tugging at the strands, it's all I can do not to reach down into my pants and jerk myself off. But I can wait. I can hold off. Her pleasure is more important than mine, at least right at this moment. I know she'll make sure I'm satisfied when it's my turn. She always does.

Before long, Riley's moans come quicker, louder. Even with her thighs clamped around my head like earmuffs, I can hear the sounds of her pleasure, the way she takes what I'm freely offering.

She comes on a gasp, her slick channel pulsing around my fingers, her release flooding my tongue and my beard. I lick my lips before trailing kisses along her inner thighs, over the crease of her hip, and up her belly, and then I press a soft, sweet kiss to the center of her chest, where her breasts meet.

"Hi," I whisper, suddenly shy.

The melodic laugh she lets out makes my heart sing. "Hi. Will you please fuck me now?"

"I'd love to, thanks." I wink obnoxiously and she erupts into peals of laughter. My low chuckle rumbles in my chest. I made her laugh. Me. I did that. And now I get to spend forever doing that, and I can't fucking wait to start—for real, this time.

Still giggling, she rolls over toward the nightstand while I remove my pants and briefs. We're still using condoms plus her IUD. If she decides she wants to have another kid, we can reevaluate down the line, but my main priority is making sure she feels safe and protected. I've never gone without a condom before, and just because we're married doesn't place the entirety of our birth control on her shoulders; it's both of our responsibility. Besides, Emmy's existence is proof enough that condoms aren't always foolproof.

Riley tears open the foil square and rolls the latex down my shaft, then gives me a few firm strokes. Her hand feels good, the pressure just enough to tease me, but what I really want is her.

Nudging her back against the pillows, I notch my cock at her entrance, my eyes meeting hers. The fondness in her bright blues makes my heart ache with a fondness of my own. How did I get so lucky as to find her? What would I have done if she hadn't shown up on my doorstep that day?

She tilts her hips, insistent, and I finally, *finally*, slide inside her. The red lace bra pushes her tits up, giving me the perfect view of the most perfect woman.

I fuck her steadily, giving her exactly what she likes.

Sometimes we play with toys, other times we go without. I'm open to trying pretty much anything if it means I can draw those sweet whimpers from her throat.

Like that one. Her breath hitches, and she lets out a soft, keening noise. My hand falls to her clit, strumming the sensitive bundle of nerves the way she likes until she comes on a cry, falling apart on my cock.

Leaning down, I swallow her cries. They taste as sweet as I imagined. She clings to me, pulling me down on top of her.

But I'm nowhere near being done. Not with her. Not with us.

thirty-six

• • •

Riley

AL MANEUVERS me onto my hands and knees, stroking reverently over my curves. I should feel exposed like this, vulnerable. But instead I feel adored. Seen. *Wanted.*

He slides into me with one smooth thrust, his cock hitting that place deep inside me I can never reach on my own. I feel so fucking full. His body brackets mine, his hairy chest pressed to my back, his legs on either side of mine. I'm surrounded by him, wrapped up in his embrace. And I never want him to let me go.

Some of my neediness has ebbed a little with my second orgasm, but this overwhelming feeling of *want* makes me practically dizzy. His steady pace is doing wonders for me, filling me completely, and just when I'm about to collapse into a pool of sated goo, he anchors me with his hands on my hips, his thumbs stroking over the flesh of my ass. It's a surprisingly sweet touch compared to the dirty things he murmurs under his breath while he fucks me.

Behind me, Al stiffens, letting out a strangled shout. His cock pulses inside me, emptying into the condom. I can't wait for the day we can go without, but until we're on the same page about more kids—and more importantly, the timeline—this makes the most sense.

Without him holding me up, I collapse onto the mattress, his heavy body half on top of me. He's my favorite weighted blanket, calming my anxiety day in and out. But after a moment, he rolls off me and pulls me into his arms, resting my head on his shoulder as he works to catch his breath. The scratch of his chest hair beneath my cheek tickles, anchoring me in this moment.

"I love you," he murmurs into the quiet of the room, punctuated by our ragged breathing.

My eyes well with tears—happy ones, this time. How did I get so lucky? "I love you, too."

His touch lingers on my skin long after he pulls away, a ghost of heat that won't fade. I close my eyes, trying to catch my breath, but it's not only the aftermath of his body against mine that leaves me trembling. It's us. Our connection. The three little words I never thought I'd hear from him—at least not like that, not whispered like a vow against my lips, not wrapped in raw need and aching tenderness.

I love you.

My heart stutters all over again just thinking about it. I'd said it back because holding it in any longer would've broken me. And now, everything feels different. He's not merely my husband in name, not just my partner in this complicated arrangement. He's mine. And I'm his.

The weight of that terrifies me. It thrills me. It makes me want to cling to him until we're both too exhausted to move, too breathless to speak. I never imagined marriage would feel like this—like surrender and freedom at the same time. Like he's cracked me open and filled all the hollow spaces I didn't know were empty.

And fuck, I never want to let that go.

The baby monitor squawks as Emmy cries in the next room, and with a sigh, I force myself out of bed as Al heads to the bathroom to deal with the condom. I scoop his T-shirt off the floor and pull on a pair of undies before padding down the hall to her room. She's sitting up, rubbing at her eyes.

"Hey, princess," I coo as I lift her out of the crib. "Did you have a good sleep?"

She clutches my borrowed shirt in her tiny fist, giving a forceful yank.

"I know, I smell like your daddy. He'll come see you in a minute."

It's a little uncomfortable to deal with the messy aftermath of sex while holding a baby. Thankfully, Al pokes his head in the door while I'm changing her, and Emmy's entire face lights up.

"I'll take care of her," he says. "You can clean up."

With a laugh, I hand her over. "I need pants."

He shakes his head. "Pants are optional." Ducking his head, he kisses me softly, then swats me on the ass. "I'm curious about this pozole you made. Don't take too long, or I'll get a head start without you."

"You wouldn't dare."

"Maybe. Maybe not." He winks at me, and my stomach flutters. I've just had him, but already I want him again. "You'll find out soon enough."

Brushing past him, I head to our room and take care of business. Definitely don't want a UTI. Unfortunately for him, I do put on pants—even with the heat on, it's still the middle of winter. Although I do keep his shirt.

Downstairs, he has Emmy in her exerciser while he prepares a bottle. He's talking to her in Spanish, and from his tone of voice, I'm guessing it's baby talk. I hear *princessa* and terms of endearment. Maybe I can convince him to teach me Spanish one day. I want to be part of the cool kids' club, and I want to be able to communicate with his extended family and his abuela.

Al's phone vibrates on the coffee table, and I pick it up

without thinking. A message floats across the screen, and my heart stops.

"What is it?" he asks. "What's wrong?"

My heart is in my throat. "The social worker wants us at the courthouse. Tomorrow."

thirty-seven

. . .

Al

I'VE NEVER BEEN SO nervous. Not the day I was drafted. Not my first game in the big leagues. Not even when Riley and I got married.

Today is the first day of the rest of my life. Today, the judge will decide if I get to keep my kid. If I'm a fit parent.

Luckily, Emmy doesn't realize anything important is going on. She babbles in her car seat as we drive to the courthouse, playing with her bare feet. I've learned it's best not to fight her on socks or shoes until the last possible moment. Clothes are a nonnegotiable, especially in this icy, freezing weather.

Riley's hand lands on my thigh. "It's going to be okay," she says. "They're just releasing the results of the paternity test."

"What if there's a mistake? What if she's not mine?" Panic laces through my veins. "What if they tell us she belongs to someone else? She's *mine*. Ours."

Joanne was supposed to come by to evaluate me with Emmy, but that hasn't happened. Did she already decide I'm not fit to be a father? Is our case already closed?

"She's your kid," she argues. "Even if she's not yours

biologically, which we both know she is, then you still love her all the same. Family is more than blood relatives. It's the people you choose to keep in your life."

"Fuck, I love you." My hand falls to hers on my thigh, squeezing, before I return my focus to the road. "I don't know what I'd do without you."

"Well, hopefully you never have to find out."

Glancing at her out of the corner of my eye, I ask, "What about in two years?"

The exit strategy. Our plan was to wait a year or two after custody is determined, and since that's today… the clock's ticking. Just because we're together now doesn't mean she won't want out.

"I think we can make it work for eighteen, at least until she goes to college." She pauses. "Unless you wanted another."

"Another kid?" My heart jumps in my chest, pounding like a brass band.

"I just…"

Yanking the steering wheel sharply to the right, I pull off to the side of the road and throw the car into park. I turn to face her in the cramped car, then take her hand in mine.

"Riley. Are you saying you want to have kids with me?"

"I mean, we already have Emmy. She should have siblings." She looks away, but my fingers on her chin direct her attention back to me.

"You want to have more kids?"

"She shouldn't be an only child. It's lonely being on your own. And you have siblings. She should, too."

Leaning over the console, I pull her as close as I can before I kiss her. Contentment and excitement hum happily in my veins.

"I would love to have more babies with you," I tell my wife. "We should start now."

Riley's laugh echoes throughout the SUV, keeping me warm and fuzzy inside. "Right this minute?"

The clock on the dashboard taunts me. "Well, no. We've got a custody hearing to get to. But after. We should start trying."

"How about we just practice for a little while?" She threads her fingers through mine. "We can start trying for real after her first birthday. I don't want two kids in diapers at the same time."

"I like that plan."

With one last kiss to seal the deal, I navigate the car back onto the road. In a few quick minutes, we arrive at our destination. My lawyer meets us in the lobby and ushers us to the courtroom.

Because of my status as a public figure, the hearing is supposed to be closed, but as we wheel in the stroller, a ton of people already crowd the gallery. My stomach twists into knots. I don't want to be a spectacle. I don't want drama. All I want is for my baby to be mine so nobody can take her away from me.

"Alberto!" a sharp voice calls, and I hunch my shoulders as I turn to face my doom.

My eyes widen. Riley's hand finds mine, and her firm grip grounds me.

Sitting in the gallery are my brother and sister, along with Viv and Chuck Gallagher, and—my parents?

"What are you doing here?" I ask.

"You think we'd miss this?" My father chuckles. "Come here and introduce us to our nieta."

Granddaughter.

They accept her. Just like that, they accept her as theirs—ours.

Riley steers the stroller in their direction, and I follow her like we're tied together, a puppy on a leash. I'll follow her anywhere.

"Hi, I'm—"

My mother cuts her off, tugging her into a forceful hug. "Mija. We know who you are." Still hugging her, she reaches out and swats me in the arm. "You didn't invite us to the wedding, Alberto. I had to hear about it from the puck bunny sites!"

"Sorry, Ma," I mumble.

"We'll do a big wedding in the offseason," she declares. "We'll have the entire family there. Your abuela is devastated."

"Sorry," I repeat. There isn't much I can do or say. I knew there would be repercussions; guilt trips are part of the deal. With any luck, they'll move on as soon as one of my cousins does something boneheaded.

My mother harrumphs. "Now, introduce me to my grand-daughter."

Riley unbuckles Emmy and lifts her into her arms, preparing to hand her over. But as soon as the baby sees Tony, she squeals in delight and reaches for him. He stands and strolls toward her, hefting her into his arms.

"Hi, princess," he coos, smoothing her wispy hair. "Did ya miss me?"

She shrieks with delight, kicking her little legs. My mother moves beside him, gazing down at my daughter with adoration on her face.

"Alberto, she's beautiful," she says.

"She's perfect," Dad adds.

"Yeah, she is."

The lawyer clears her throat. "We're about ready to get started."

I take Emmy back from my brother, snuggling her close. She clings to me, and I know that no matter what happens next, we'll get through this—the three of us.

Joanne enters the courtroom, and to my surprise, she gives

us a nod with a pained smile. That's the closest we're going to get to approval.

The judge takes her seat at the stand and calls the hearing to order. I do my best to pay attention, but it's not until Joanne says her piece that I can finally breathe.

"The State finds that Alberto Gonzales is the biological father, and as such, should have full physical and legal custody."

We wait with bated breath as the judge reviews the files, but in short order, she declares the matter closed, and I officially have custody of my daughter. The echo of the gavel might be the best sound I've ever heard.

Riley tugs me into a hug, squishing Emmy between us. She gives me a soft kiss, so sweet it nearly brings tears to my eyes. She breaks apart first and rests her forehead on mine, the two of us breathing the same air.

We did it. We beat this thing. The three of us are officially a family, and nobody can change that. This moment feels almost as monumental as the last time we were in the judge's chambers, when he pronounced us married. My life is irrevocably changed, and I'm so fucking glad. I can't imagine a world without Riley and Emmy in it.

I go to kiss her again, but the baby squawks, and reluctantly, we pull apart.

"I love you," my beautiful wife says, and no—*that* is the best sound.

"I love you, too."

"Come along, Alberto," my mother calls. "It's time to celebrate."

thirty-eight

. . .

Riley

THE LITTLE TOWNHOUSE is packed full. When Al's team captain texted to find out the results of the hearing, that somehow turned into the entire team descending on the place for a party. Not to mention Al's family. Two aunts and five cousins have joined us, plus Cari, Tony, Viv, and Chuck.

It was a fortuitous twist of fate that Colorado is playing in Boston tomorrow night, so although he's technically breaking curfew by hanging out with the Grizzlies rather than his team, his coach was fine with it as long as he doesn't get wasted. With the rest of the guys playing tomorrow, there's a lot less alcohol flowing than I anticipated.

Vanessa, Audrey, and Mel have all brought their kids, and Tyler's around here somewhere with his husband and Ainsley. Rachel's newborn is strapped to her husband Jake's chest in a wrap, separating only to feed.

It's a loud, crazy, chaotic group, packed into too-tight quarters, given the icy weather outside, but somehow… it's right.

When I knocked on his door a few months ago, I was prepared to do anything to keep Emmy in my life. I didn't expect that marrying Al would give me a family. And I definitely didn't plan on the extended Grizzlies family adopting me either. But I wouldn't trade it for the world.

My mother-in-law—*call me Luz*, she said—has monopolized Emmy, only sharing her with Tony, her favorite person. Being dethroned as the number one or two person in my daughter's world doesn't upset me too much; I know that when it's three o'clock in the morning, Al and I are the only ones she wants to take care of her. Besides, I love to see the extended family doting on her. It's something I never had, and I never want to take it away.

Cari steps up next to me, offering me a smile. "How are you holding up?"

"I'm good."

She side-eyes me. "Okay, but for real."

"I'm overstimulated and overwhelmed, but I'm so freaking happy that the custody issue is resolved, so I can hang out for a little while longer."

Once everyone is gone and Emmy is in bed, I'll take a long soak in Al's Jacuzzi tub and light a candle. Maybe I can even convince him to join me in the bath.

"My mother isn't driving you crazy?"

"Not at all." Luz has given me about ten thousand hugs since the hearing. She introduced me to her sisters and the cousins as her daughter. Not daughter-in-law. *Daughter.*

Anyone else might be turned off by how quickly she's drawn me into her circle, but it's been almost twenty years since I've had a mother. I didn't know how much I wanted one until she accepted me unconditionally.

Even if it means having to put on an elaborate wedding and wear a poofy white princess dress next summer.

"If she crosses a line, you have to tell her," Cari says. "She's not great with boundaries, but she's getting better. As long as you tell her what you're not okay with, she will usually listen."

"Any chance we have of getting out of this wedding?" I'm

half joking. I've never been comfortable in churches, and Al isn't exactly religious. Plus, I wouldn't have anyone there to support me; they'd all be his friends and family.

She laughs. "Yeah, not a chance in hell. You're out of luck."

Although, at the end of the day, I still get to be married to Al. So maybe I am the lucky one after all.

An arm slides around my waist, and I breathe in the cedar and firewood of his cologne, the scent as comforting as the first day we met. Maybe that was a sign it would all work out, even then.

Al kisses my temple. "Can I borrow you for a moment?"

"Everything okay?"

"Yeah. I just want to talk to you without an audience." He offers his hand, and I take it as he leads me up the stairs to our bedroom.

"What's going on?"

His hands land on my shoulders, gently guiding me to sit on the edge of the bed. Then he starts pacing.

"Is something wrong?"

Just tell me. Don't make me worry.

He skids to a stop, then turns to face me. "Riley. I love you, and I'm excited to expand our family, and I can't wait for what's to come," he drawls.

My heart threatens to beat right out of my chest. This doesn't sound like he's changed his mind. We've committed to each other, and we have our daughter together. We've agreed to try for more kids.

So why does my stomach fill with dread at the serious expression on his face?

"We're doing this all backward. I know my mother wants us to have the big wedding of her dreams—not yours and mine, *hers*—and I recognize that might not be what you want. But what *I* would like is to stand in front of our friends and family and proclaim to everyone that we're together, that we're in this, that it isn't just convenient. Even if it's something small. I want to celebrate us."

Tears spring to my eyes, and I rub at them with the back of my hand.

This isn't the end of us. It's only the beginning of our next chapter.

I can find the courage to wear the white dress and stand up in a church—for him. I'd do anything for him. For us.

He drops to one knee. "Riley, will you marry me again?"

From his pocket, he pulls out a velvet box, opening it to reveal a gorgeous ring. It's an emerald-shaped amethyst that matches the necklace he gave me, the huge stone circled by a halo of pavé diamonds.

"It should stack with your wedding band," he says, running his thumb over the ring on my hand. "They're supposed to go together."

A lump forms in my throat. "Al—"

"If you're not ready, if you don't want a big wedding, we can—"

"Yes," I blurt. "Yes. I'll marry you. Again and again and again."

I tug him to his feet, he slips the ring onto my finger, and I fling myself at him. He catches me—he always does.

Wrapping my arms around his neck, I reach up to kiss him, and the soft press of his lips to mine feels so perfect, so right, I can't imagine how I ever survived without him. I was stumbling in the dark, and he lit the way to this wonderful, perfectly imperfect life we share.

A familiar cry sounds from downstairs, followed by an echoing wail, and with a laugh, we separate.

"Come on. Let's go rescue our daughter from my evil, no good brother." He chuckles. "I think she loves him more than me."

"Never. You're her dad. You're her number one fan." I run

my thumb over the new ring on my finger. "But I'll always be yours."

Al stops on the stairs, turning to face me. "Fuck, I love you," he mutters, before he kisses me again.

Emmy's cries put a stop to anything further. We hurry down the stairs, surveying the situation. Tony is bouncing the baby, trying to soothe her. Leo is crying, too, inconsolable in Sven's arms. Cora is chewing on her fist. And Ainsley? She's trying to drink Tyler's beer.

Al strides forward, pulling our daughter into his arms. "It's okay, princess," he says. "Daddy's got you."

I swear at least four women let out an *aww*. I might be one of them.

Crossing the room, I stand beside them, my hand on Al's arm. "Does she need a change?"

Cari's eagle eye narrows on my hand. "What is that?"

"What's what?"

"The ring." She grins triumphantly. "He finally asked?"

Al looks at me sheepishly. "I suppose we should tell everyone..."

"We're getting married. Again," I announce.

Luz lets out a shriek of delight. Now I see where Emmy gets it from. "A wedding!"

"Dibs on best man," Chuck yells.

Tony laughs. "You can't call dibs. Besides, we're brothers. It should be me."

"You can fight it out later," Al says. "We literally just decided this five minutes ago, so maybe let's put a pin in the wedding talk until after the All Star break." He eyes his mother warily.

"Deal," Luz says with a nod.

When he slides his hand into mine, those familiar butterflies erupt in my belly. "You ready for this?" he murmurs.

I laugh. "Not at all. But let's do it anyway."

The grin that stretches across Al's lips could light up the

whole city. Maybe even the entire state. "I love this life we share."

"Me too."

I don't know what's in store for us. Whether we have another baby or four, whether we stay in Boston or he gets traded to another team, or even how long he'll be playing. If I'll try to find a job or continue to stay home. If we'll stay in his childhood home or if we'll move to a bigger house to fit our expanding family.

The one thing I know? As long as he's by my side, we can get through anything. Because we'll get through it together.

epilogue

. . .

Al

MY HEAD IS POUNDING, my stomach is in knots, and I have the strangest urge to hyperventilate. Why am I so nervous? We're already married.

Tony hands me a bottle of water. "Drink this," he says, leaving no room to argue.

My hand shakes as I try to unscrew the cap. The crinkle of the plastic in my fist sounds like a shotgun echoing.

"I don't know, man," Chuck says, his voice too loud in the cramped room. "I don't think water is going to cut it."

"Fine." Tony holds his hand out, and I blink as Chuck hands him a flask. My brother pours a shot of clear liquid into an empty Styrofoam cup and then pushes it into my hand. "Drink this," he repeats.

The putrid scent of tequila makes my stomach roil. "I'm not getting wasted before my wedding."

We had a few beers last night, sitting around a bonfire in the backyard, and even though I only had a few, the idea of drinking again so soon makes me want to hurl. Wait, that might be the nerves. Maybe both.

"One shot won't get you wasted," Chuck says. "If it does, I feel sorry for your tolerance levels."

Grumbling under my breath, I take the cup and down the shot in one gulp, shuddering at the taste. "Fuck."

"Why are you so nervous?" Tony asks.

I bite the inside of my cheek. "What if she changes her mind?"

He rolls his eyes. "She won't."

"But she might."

I could hardly sleep last night, holding her in my arms and dreading this. My ring on her finger isn't enough. She has to want this. Want *me*.

I think she does. After all, she agreed to go through with this. But now that it's the eleventh hour, all my doubts keep rushing in.

"Except she won't," Chuck says. "You're already married. This is just for show. A giant party with all of your friends." He glances around the tiny, barren "groom's room" that is essentially a storage closet with chairs. "Are… are we your only friends?"

"Mitchell's running late. And we didn't want a huge wedding party." Riley is slowly expanding her social circle, making friends with the other players' partners and also at the Grizzlies Foundation where she volunteers, and she's still close with Vanessa, Audrey, and Bex.

Six months ago, I never would have expected Mitchell and Bex to be in our bridal party, much less civil enough to walk down the aisle together. But now, with everything that's gone down since his injury, and with the way he's stood by my side from his first day in the dressing room, I know there's nobody else I trust more to have my back.

After Tony and Chuck, of course. The bonehead still thinks we're brothers-in-law, and I don't have the heart to correct him anymore. If he wants to be my family, I certainly don't want to push him away. He's a good guy at heart, just a little… *Chuck*.

Family is the people we choose to keep in our lives. Blood

relatives, friends who become family... We get to pick who we keep close to us. Who's important to us.

Cari is in the wedding party, too—she'll be escorting our flower girl down the aisle. Riley invited her to be the maid of honor, but someone has to make sure our little girl is safe, sound, and hopefully calm during the ceremony, and my sister volunteered for the gig.

She also insisted on wearing a flower crown on her head. Riley and I didn't care either way; as long as Emmy is there, Cari can wear a bikini and we'd be fine with it. The priest, on the other hand, might not be.

A knock raps on the door, and my dad sticks his head inside without waiting for us to answer.

"They're ready for you."

Sweat beads along my palms, and I rub them on my pants.

"It's going to be fine," Tony says. "All you have to do is walk a hundred yards without falling on your face. Can you do that?"

"Fuck off," I mutter. "I can walk just fine."

"The way you skate, sometimes I don't know."

I shove him, and he shoves me back, and then we're tussling like we're little kids again. I get him in a headlock, and he struggles against me, but his strength is no match for my sheer force of will.

"Boys," my dad snaps with a warning tone.

A third hand lands on my back, giving me a firm yank, and Chuck grins at me. "I want in on the fun, too."

"You're the worst." But I can't help grinning. "Come on. It's time to get married."

We troop out of the groom's closet and through the church to the sanctuary doors. I reach for the handle, but something stops me. The wedding coordinator looks at me with concern.

"Are you ready?" she asks.

"Last chance to back out," Tony mutters.

"Back out? Are you kidding?"

He holds up his hands. "Just offering."

My parents are waiting with my abuela, and Cari has Emmy on her hip, my girl all smiles at the sight of her favorite uncle. I drop a kiss on her forehead and she giggles, grabbing at me.

"Dada! Dada!"

My heart warms, as it always does when she calls me that. She's sixteen months, just starting to walk, and talking up a storm. Most of it is unintelligible to me, but Riley swears she can understand her. Her favorite words are mama, dada, and no.

I give my daughter a cuddle, then deposit her back into my sister's arms.

I can do this. I can marry my wife.

With one last deep exhale, I nod to the wedding coordinator and pull open the doors to the church.

The music changes smoothly into the start of the processional, and I throw my shoulders back. Focusing on slow, steady steps, I almost forget to be nervous until I'm all the way at the front of the altar next to Father Jimenez. He gives me a nod, and I turn to face the back of the sanctuary.

A hundred and fifty pairs of eyes are on me, and I give an awkward grimace. What I'd give to be in my full pads and helmet right now, my stick at the ready to ward anyone off.

But these are my friends and my family, not my rivals, and we're in a church, not a hockey rink, so I guess the tuxedo will have to do.

My parents escort Abuela down the aisle, and she gives me such a happy smile, my heart twists. This isn't important to me, but it's important to her.

I know the religious part of this makes Riley uncomfortable. She offered to convert, since she has no official religious affiliation, but the priest made sure she knew it wasn't required. It's not like I'm an avid churchgoer myself, attending only for weddings, baptisms, and funerals. Being married in the church isn't important to me. Being married to *Riley* is.

The music changes, and Tony walks Vanessa down the aisle. Her light purple dress highlights her swollen baby bump. Audrey and Chuck are next, her dress a different style but no less gorgeous. Mitchell and Bex follow behind them, her gown flattering her full figure.

And then I see Cari in a deep purple dress, my princess in her arms. Emmy still hates clothes, but we've learned she tolerates bows, so she has a giant, fluffy headband with a bow to match her sparkly purple dress. My sister sets Emmy down, handing her the basket of flowers, and she immediately dumps it onto the floor.

The church erupts into chuckles as Emmy toddles down the aisle. She gets about halfway down before she trips, and Cari scoops her up into a hug before she can start crying.

"Down!" my daughter demands, and so down she goes.

Then she's breaking free, running down the aisle.

"Dada! Dada!"

I swear my heart melts. Lifting her into my arms, I hold her close.

"Are you ready to see Mommy?" I ask her.

She nods, clapping happily.

The music swells, and the guests all rise as the sanctuary doors open once more.

My jaw drops.

Riley is a vision in a cream-colored gown, her hair pulled back and topped with a sparkling tiara. Lace covers the princess-like dress, delicate, but just as strong and resilient as she is.

In the hollow of her throat sits the amethyst necklace I bought her for our first charity gala. It feels like so long ago. The bracelet my mother wore in her wedding circles her wrist, and my abuela's diamond teardrop earrings glitter brightly.

My family adores her and has adorned her in their jewels. They fully accept her in my life as my wife and the mother of my child.

As she inches down the aisle with slow, steady steps, my heart threatens to burst out of my chest. Riley. Emmy. Happy. That's all I want. That's all I need.

"Mama!" Emmy's little voice echoes, and she lunges for her, nearly tipping out of my arms. Luckily, I've had a lot of practice.

"Settle, mija," I whisper.

With every step, my anticipation balloons more and more, until I think I'm about to float away.

But there she is—my bride, resplendent in white.

"Mama!" Emmy shrieks, and with a laugh, Riley passes her bouquet to Vanessa and takes Emmy from my arms.

Father Jimenez clears his throat. Cari is standing nearby, but I shake my head at her. I guess Emmy is going to be part of the ceremony.

After all, she's the reason we started this. She's the reason we're here.

"We are gathered here today..." Father Jimenez starts his speech.

I wish I could say I pay attention, but I can't focus. Not when Riley is standing beside me, looking as perfect as she does.

Throughout the twenty-minute ceremony, we pass Emmy back and forth between us as she gets bored, and when it comes time for our vows, I do hand her over to Cari.

Taking Riley's hands in mine, I promise to love her and cherish her, to honor her and devote myself to her. I promise these things freely. Because I love her, and I love our life, and I love everything there is to come.

I think of the sonogram tucked into my wallet. Six weeks. We weren't trying, but we weren't *not* trying, either. Our plan was to wait until after the wedding and honeymoon, but fate had other plans for us. And I couldn't be happier.

Riley. Emmy. Our future children.

She recites her vows to me, and that's what finally breaks me. Tears well in my eyes, and I think I'm being subtle in wiping them away, but then Tony taps on my shoulder with a hanky, and I allow myself to fall apart.

"I love you," she says, her eyes damp as well.

Father Jimenez clears his throat and launches into the rest of the formalities. It all goes in one ear and out the other, until:

"You may kiss your bride."

And when I pull Riley into my arms, kissing her to seal the deal, all is right in the world.

It didn't look the way I expected it to, but I've finally gotten my happily ever after.

———

Not ready to be done with Al and Riley? Check out their bonus epilogue five years down the road.

Want more of Tony and Viv? Check out Ruck Me Harder, an enemies to lovers, women's rugby and men's gymnastics, second chance romance.

afterword

Thank you for reading *Power Play*. This book is my baby and I absolutely love it to pieces.

Reviews are more important than readers realize. If you liked this book, please leave me a review!

Join my newsletter to stay in the loop! Lots of unfunny quips, unsuccessful attempts at wit, and general grouching about the writing process.

xoxo,

Allie

what's next?

Thank you for reading *Power Play*.

The story continues with *Game Misconduct*, where we learn more about why Bex Whitney hates Nick Mitchell so much in this enemies to lovers after a one night stand gone bad hockey romance.

Want more of the Neurospicy Book Club? Check out *Sportsball is for Lovers*, featuring Sadie and the super hot guy she meets on a kink app... where she learns that six degrees of separation don't always involve Kevin Bacon...

about the author

Allie is a queer and AuDHD writer with a hyper-fixation on inclusivity and representation. She loves the color purple, Michigan football, the Detroit Lions, and the Boston Bruins. When she's not absorbed by a book, she likes to spend time with her nephews.

A San Diego, CA native now residing in South Carolina, she is allergic to the cold, rain, snow, and mosquitos.

also by allie lasky

Meet the Neurospicy Book Club in The Thought of You, where grumpy Johanna finds out she's autistic… because her happy-go-lucky new roomie (and reformed playboy ex-football player) has to tell her.

———

For more Own Voices, try Spark: A Chanukah Novella, where neurodivergent Arielle and her childhood friend Asher finally connect after two decades of missed chances.

———

Want to see how it all started? Read <u>The Game Plan</u> to meet sweet cinnamon roll football player Miles and the feisty sorority girl who stole his heart.